COVENANT
A SUPERTEAM NOVEL
JAMES MAXEY

Tim,
Let's save
the world!

James
Maxey

COVENANT: A SUPERTEAM NOVEL
COPYRIGHT © 2017 BY JAMES MAXEY
ALL RIGHTS RESERVED

CREATESPACE EDITION

COVER ART BY MIKE "MEZ" PHILLIPS

FIRST EDITION

THE AUTHOR MAY BE CONTACTED VIA EMAIL:
NOBODYNOVELWRITER@YAHOO.COM

ISBN-13: 978-1548513238

ISBN-10: 1548513237

*Is it okay to dedicate a book to a fictional character?
If so, this book is for Brainiac 5, even though he'd hate it
because the science is a teeny-weeny bit inaccurate.*

Prologue
Feet on the Ground

Five years earlier

IT WAS A LITTLE after midnight when Sarah left her second floor motel room. She leaned over the balcony railing and surveyed the silent parking lot. Certain that no one was watching, she climbed over the railing and turned her face toward the moon. Unable to resist, she spread her arms and shot into the sky.

She stopped rising about a hundred yards up. This close to the ground, she was unlikely to be seen by radar. She was far above the lights of the parking lot and well out of range of the headlamps of the big trucks rumbling along I-40. In her dark jeans and brown leather jacket, she was more or less invisible in the night sky, despite the bright quarter moon that turned the nearby Arkansas River into a sinuous silver ribbon. Far to the east, Fort Smith, the only city of any size within a hundred miles, was a dull glow on the horizon.

Sarah took a deep breath. The night air was cool and clean, faintly floral. It was April in the Ozarks, with spring stirring trees and flowers into new life. Sarah pressed her lips tightly together in a grim smile, contemplating the unintended symbolism of the moment. She was starting a new life as well. And what was she doing on the first night of her new life? Exactly what she'd done the night before, and the night before that. Flying in the dark.

When she'd flown her charter plane into the tiny airport at Park Station, Oklahoma she'd used her new name for the first time. The guy who checked her in at the hangar had let his eyes linger on her face when she'd signed the paperwork in the small office. She'd managed not to panic. It had been two years since her face had been on television every day, and back then her hair had been long and blonde. Now it was short and dark, and she'd put on weight, filling out her face. Plus, after things went south in Mexico City, she'd escaped with a broken nose that never healed into quite the same shape. With the constant strain of life on the run, worry wrinkles had become permanent parts of her features. The face she saw in the mirror looked less and less like the face on the wanted posters with each passing day.

Checking into the motel had gone smoothly. She'd paid a small fortune for her new identity papers, but this had been the first time she'd used the credit card linked to her new name. She'd gone tense when she'd swiped the card, expecting something to go wrong, just waiting to hear the desk clerk say, "Hmm, that's odd." Those words never came. The clerk, a skinny old woman who reeked of cigarettes, had barely made eye contact as she'd handed Sarah her key and told her about the continental breakfast.

Sarah had eaten dinner at the Waffle House next door and got into bed around 10 p.m. She'd tossed and turned for two hours before the need to get into the sky had become too powerful to fight.

Still hanging in midair, she crossed her arms across her chest and grumbled, "Well, that didn't last long." She'd thought that her new job as a pilot might satisfy her urge to move above the earth, but it wasn't the same, separated from the wind by metal and glass. She could *fly*, driving her body at tremendous speeds, freed from gravity by simple willpower. It was the most fantastic, marvelous thing about her, and the very reason that she was utterly alone. More than alone. Hated. Hunted. Public enemy number one. People called her a terrorist. They said she was an alien.

Of course, she wasn't. She was human. If she wasn't hovering in midair, it wasn't hard for her to blend in. She could be normal, walking among other people. She craved an average, uneventful life the way some people crave celebrity or fortune. And she could have it, she knew, if she would only keep her damned feet on the ground.

Unfortunately, flight was hardwired into her mind and muscles. Not flying was like asking a perfectly healthy person never to walk again. How was this ever going to work?

She pulled out her phone. Her reception in the motel had been terrible, but up here she had plenty of signal. She googled the nearest bar and saw it was just off the next exit on the interstate, right across from the airfield. In addition to not flying, she'd also vowed to stop drinking. If she was off the ground, she might as well be off the wagon.

She flew slowly above the road, barely faster than if she'd been running. She hadn't brought her helmet, and hitting bugs in the dark at high speed was painful. She spotted the bar a few minutes later and almost changed her mind. The parking lot was full of motorcycles and pickups. There were a lot of people hanging around in the parking lot. From several hundred yards away she could hear the thudding bass of loud country music. This gave her pause. If the place was popular, that increased the odds of running into someone who might recognize her. The building itself was a Quonset hut. The place had a hand-painted sign out front that read, "The Hangar," and beside the words were two crude outlines of planes. She decided that the aviation theme was a good omen and descended in the shadows behind the building.

She stood in the darkness for several minutes, completely understanding the cartoon metaphor of an angel and a demon on each shoulder. The angel whispered to go back to the hotel, get some sleep, and get a fresh start in the morning. The demon whispered that she'd sleep better after a few beers. The angel told her that, as a young, unaccompanied woman, she was going to be harassed the second she walked through the door. The devil told her the same thing, and told her how good it would feel to have someone hunger for her, buying her drinks, and talking to her as if she were an ordinary person. A person they just wanted to sleep with, scolded the angel. Would that be so terrible? the devil replied. She hadn't had sex since her abrupt exit from Mexico City six months earlier. Normal people had sex, didn't they?

Her devil made a compelling argument. Stuffing her hands into the pockets of her jacket, she walked around the corner into the lights of the parking lot. It didn't take long for people to notice her as she moved toward the front door.

Inside, the music was loud enough to rattle her teeth. She really didn't know enough country music to even guess who the artist was. The place was dark, lit mainly by neon beer signs. There was a dance floor with about a dozen couples on it moving more or less in synch with the thumping bass. Tables made of old oil drums were scattered around the edges of the room and people gathered around them in clusters, shouting unintelligibly at each other.

She headed toward the main bar that ran along the right side of the room. As luck would have it, there were three open stools. She climbed onto the middle one. The bartender was girl with a three nose rings and a skin-tight tee-shirt adorned with a rebel flag. Sarah ordered a PBR and noted that she'd been seated for at least a minute without a man sitting next to her. Before her fall from grace, she'd been celebrated as one of the world's most beautiful women. Her bent nose and hints of a double chin hadn't lowered her currency that badly, had they?

To her relief, just as the beer was placed on the bar in front of her, she sensed someone sitting on the stool to her left. Her relief ended as a drunken male voice slurred the words, "Howdy darlin'. New in town?"

She cast a sideways glance at a pot-bellied man with thin gray hair who looked old enough to be her grandfather. "Just passing through," she said, tersely.

"I hear ya," he said. "Ain't it the truth? Folk's call me Lucky Bob. Whash your name, darlin'?"

"Sorry," she said. "I only give my name to sober people."

"Then wha' the hell you doin' in a bar?"

"That's pretty much what I'm asking myself," she confessed.

"Ain't it the truth," he muttered. "Ain't it the truth. They call me Lucky Bob. Hey, what's your name?"

She rolled her eyes and turned away, taking a long deep swallow of her beer.

"I know your name," said a second voice to her right.

"Get outta here, Carson," said Lucky Bob. "I was here first."

Sarah turned her head slightly to take a glance at Carson. To her great relief, he was decent looking, and roughly her age, maybe a little older. When he spoke, he didn't sound drunk. But what the hell did he mean that he knew her name?

He seemed to sense the question. "You're Sarah Buchanan, aren't you?"

"Um," she said.

"My brother works at the airfield. He's who assigned your hangar space."

"Oh," she said.

"I was waiting in the parking lot to give him a ride home when I saw you leave. When he came out to the car he told me your name was Sarah Buchanan. We went to school with a Sarah Buchanan."

"Ah," she said. "It's not an uncommon name."

"I'm Carson by the way. Carson Lee. Pleased to meet you."

"Okay," she said, taking a closer look at him. He had blond hair tightly cut in a military style. He looked trim and fit, a little short though, maybe 5'8", no taller than her.

"You former military?" he asked.

"Nope," she said.

"Just wondering. Lots of pilots are."

"Yeah," she said. "My dad was a pilot and he got his start in the military. He taught me how to fly way before it was legal to put me in the pilot's seat. I do charter flights. I was supposed to meet three geologists and take them back to Houston this evening. They got delayed and won't get here until tomorrow."

"You did a good job of finding the only night life in a thirty mile radius," he said.

"How about you?" she asked. "Former military? You kind of look it."

"Yeah," he said. "Army. Did a tour in Syria after the whole region went up in flames after Jerusalem."

She felt muscles in her temple twitch involuntarily. She'd been in Jerusalem when her sister had flattened the place. It was the reason she was a fugitive, though it really hadn't been her fault.

"I, uh, I hear it's pretty rough over there," she said.

He shrugged. "I guess. It's not the danger that wears you down, though. It's the craziness. The sense that absolutely nothing is going to work. You crack down hard, the tensions rise, and suddenly you're making more terrorists. You pull back, try to let off a little pressure, and suddenly every terrorist who's been in hiding thinks it's time to make a move. A few months into my tour, I was in a truck that got stuck in the sand. We sat there, spinning our wheels, wondering when someone was going to come along and start shooting at us. Spinning wheels in the sand seemed like a pretty apt metaphor of what I was doing over there."

"I'm sorry it was so hard for you," she said.

He gave a faint smile. "I don't mean to complain. We didn't get shot at that night. I made it home alive and none of my buddies were hurt too bad. Things could have been worse. It just drove me crazy that I couldn't see any way to make a difference." He motioned for the bar tender to bring him a beer. "Man, this is a whole lot of crap to lay on a total stranger. Sorry."

"Don't apologize," she said. "I've been through some rough times myself. Sometimes it's easier to talk about it with a stranger."

He nodded as he took a drink. "Look, I don't regret going over there. Honestly, it was probably the most important thing that ever happened to me. I realized that, maybe I couldn't fix the Middle East, but I could definitely make a difference in my own back yard. Right before I joined the army, a lot of money started coming into town because of fracking. Plenty of problems followed that money. I kept hearing about people

I went to school with getting caught up in drugs, either using them or selling them. So I came home and got a job as a deputy."

"Oh," she said, managing a smile despite her stomach tightening up. Just how cursed was she that on her first night out as a normal person she wound up chatting with a cop? She felt a weird silence growing, and before he might notice she said, "I bet you have some interesting stories to tell."

"I wish," he said, rolling his eyes.

"Your job that dull?"

"It's kind of a slog, most days. TV really doesn't come close to showing what a cop's day is really like. There's a lot of waiting around. When you do actually get a call, ninety percent of the time you're just asking questions of people who either don't want to talk or people who want to talk too much. And God help me if I arrest someone. I spend more time filling out paperwork than the perp's likely to spend in jail."

"No good deed goes unpunished," she said.

"Wow, I don't know what's got me in such a whining mood," he said. "Honestly, I love my job. Even on its worst day, things make sense. When I was in Syria, I never understood what it was I was fighting for. I mean, some alien woman came down from the sky and destroyed Jerusalem by pointing at it. How does that make any sense at all?"

Sarah nodded, hoping her face didn't betray the turmoil of her memories.

"Suddenly the whole Middle East explodes and bombs are going off in New York and London and I'm spending my time patrolling some ruined Roman temple to make sure that the locals don't ruin it some more. It was hard to see how what I was doing mattered. Here, everything clicks. I've seen what happens when someone drifts across a lane and plows head first into a semi. Arresting someone for a DUI feels meaningful. I bust some dude cooking meth in his garage, and I can sleep at night knowing I've kept his trash out of the hands of some kid. Over there, I felt like I was just contributing to the greater chaos. Here, I'm working for the greater good."

"So you're the hero type," she said.

"Not at all," he said. "But I like feeling that my job's worth doing."

"And that job's defending civilization," said Sarah.

"I can't tell if you're making fun of me," he said, taking another swig of beer. "Sorry if I come off as a little intense."

"It's okay," she said, smiling. "I mean, I kind of expected meaningless small talk when I came in, but I'm good with discussing the foundations of civilization if you're into it."

"Oh lord," he said with a sheepish grin. He turned his head away, then looked back, did a take like he was seeing her for the first time and said with a smile, "Hi, I'm Carson. I'm a Pisces! What's your sign?"

She laughed. "I think I'm a Gemini?"

"Awesome," he said. "The stars say we're made for each other."

"I'll take your word for it," she said.

"Don't," he said. "I have no idea what I'm talking about."

She laughed again, delighting in the sound. It had been ages since she really laughed.

"You dance?" he asked.

"I can try," she said, feeling her cheeks flush. This evening was working out stupidly well. Much better than she'd imagined.

They both got off their stools and turned to the dance floor. Standing in their way were three large, long-haired men dressed in biking leathers. The biggest of the three had a beard that hung down almost to his belt. His companion to his left also had a beard, but it was scraggly and kinked, like someone had glued pubic hair all over his cheeks. The guy on the right was clean shaven, and for some reason was wearing mirrored sunglasses despite the darkness of the bar. She couldn't guess how he saw anything.

The big guy with the long beard gave a sinister smile as he said, "Well, well, well. If it ain't Deputy Lee. Ain't looking so tough without your gun, are you?"

"Out of prison already, Lawton?" Carson asked. "Three months is really all you get for shooting a guy these days?"

"It's not like I killed him," said Lawton. "But it's still three months I'm never getting back. Three months you owe me. I figure I break your legs in a couple of places, you'll be in a cast at least three months. Should make us about even."

"Lawton, get out of my face," said Carson. "You might not be a genius, but even you have to know that if you lay a finger on me you'll be back in prison for a lot longer than three months."

"Then it's a contest," said Lawton. "See if you can get out of the hospital before I get out of the big house."

Lawton lunged, arms spread, aiming to tackle Carson. Carson ducked to get out of the way. A lifetime of training kicked in for Sarah as her feet came an inch off the floor. Not only could she fly, she could also make anything she touched while flying effectively weightless. Her hand darted out, her fingers dug into Lawton's beard, and with a grunt she curled under him and rolled his now weightless mass across her shoulders, increasing his momentum. She let go and he cleared the top of the bar, crashing into the booze and mirror beyond.

Carson, meanwhile, had come up from his dodge, planting his feet as he gave a savage uppercut to pubic hair face right beneath his chin. The big guy fell backward, flopping limp onto the dance floor.

Sunglass guy had barely moved. Sarah wasn't sure he saw what was going on. Screw him. Anyone who was a friend of Lawton probably deserved a beat down on principle. She went vertical in the air and kicked him in the chest with both boots. The second she made contact he was weightless. He launched a good ten feet across the room before crashing into a table. It was pure luck that he didn't hit anyone else in the crowded bar.

Sarah dropped to the floor before anyone noticed that her feet hadn't touched down for at least five seconds now. She glanced at Carson and said, "You sure know how to show a girl a good time!"

"How the hell did you learn to fight like that?" he asked.

She shrugged. "My dad was big on self-defense. I know a little judo."

"A little?"

"Maybe a lot," she admitted.

He smiled, then his face dropped. "Goddammit," he grumbled, rubbing the back of his neck as he stared at the fallen felons. "Do you know how much paperwork this is going to cause me? I can't even get a break on my day off."

The bartender said, "I've already called the sheriff, Carson." She studied the broken bottles and damaged mirrors, shaking her head. "Jimbo's going to have a fit when he sees this."

"Look," said Sarah, stepping close to Carson. In another minute, the place would be swarming with law enforcement. She'd been lucky that Carson hadn't recognized her, but she didn't feel like pressing her luck. "I'm supposed to be flying out first thing in the morning. I'd rather not be up all night making statements. Would you hate me if in all the confusion I mysteriously disappeared into the night?"

"Lawton's gotta be on probation," said Carson. "He'll be going back to jail for this even without your testimony. I'll let you go on one condition."

"What's that?"

"You give me your phone number."

"For, like, a statement...?"

"For, like, me calling you just to talk."

"Okay," she said.

"I mean," he said. "I don't know if you'll ever be back in town, but..."

"I said okay," she said, reaching into her jacket for a pen. "I need paper."

"Write it on the back of my hand," he said.

She took his offered hand, which was bleeding at the knuckles. Despite the damage, she noted how cleanly he cut his fingernails. Not that there was anything dainty about his hand. It was rugged, even leathery, covered with fine scars. This definitely wasn't his first fist fight.

She finished writing her number and said, "I can come back pretty much anytime. I mean... I can fly."

"Great," he said. "I'm off again next Tuesday. And there's a pizza place downtown that doesn't serve alcohol. We're slightly less likely to get into a fight there."

"You know, whatever," she said. "I'm easily amused."

"Excellent," he said, as she backed away and turned to slip through the crowd that had gathered around them. She made it outside and darted around the corner into the shadows, looking around to make sure she wasn't followed. Her heart was racing, her body tingling with adrenaline, but not from the fight.

Holy cow! She'd met someone! Someone decent and nice and normal. And he'd asked for her phone number! Maybe the stars really were in her favor.

She felt like she was walking on air. Looking down, she saw that she was. She'd have to be careful about that.

Turning her face toward the stars, she floated into the heavens, swearing that, seriously, this was the last time she'd fly under her own power. But as the wind washed her face she laughed, knowing that she'd be aloft again the following night, and the night after that. Maybe astrology wasn't complete bullshit. Gemini was supposed to be a twin, right? Two people with the same face. And maybe she could live with two faces, as normal, ordinary, grounded Sarah Buchanan by day, and by night, unseen and silent, still riding the sky.

Chapter One
A Job for a Superfreak

Today

WHEN APP POPPED into the warehouse the first thing that hit him was the smell. Usually he wasn't invited to look at crime scenes until weeks into an investigation. He'd been ready to look at a taped outline on a floor. He hadn't expected to find the victim's corpse still sprawled on the concrete, and definitely wouldn't have worn his new running shoes if he'd known the space machine was going to cut and paste him into a puddle of half-dried blood, sticky as jelly.

"You guys are lucky you don't have to smell this," he said to his online audience.

"Jesus," said the old man crouched next to the body as he jumped up, startled by App's voice. "I never heard you come in."

"Sorry," said App. He turned his head in a wide arc to let them see the scene, a large, shadowy warehouse, almost empty save for several large shipping containers. "Didn't mean to sneak up on you. The space machine doesn't make any sound. You're Detective Lindon?"

"Yeah. You must be App." The detective's face was thin, borderline gaunt, with a big, sharp nose and ears that seemed a few sizes too large for his bald head.

"Before we talk any further, do I have your permission to broadcast our conversation?"

"No," Lindon said. Then he looked at App's empty hands. "You, uh, don't have a camera anyway."

"I've been upgraded so that my visual and audio data can be transmitted in real time. Everything I see or hear gets shared with my followers online. Lucky for them, no smellovision yet."

"Christ," Lindon said, shaking his head heavily. "No. No cameras. I mean, I don't know how you turn off your eyes but..."

"No problem," said App. "Sorry folks. Gotta sign off. Live crime scene. App out!" Then, to Lindon, "I've stopped broadcasting. I was in fuzz mode, so no one saw your face or heard your unfiltered voice."

"Fuzz mode?"

"It's, uh, not a slur of cops," said App. "For legal reasons, I know to blur video and distort audio when I jump someplace new. Anyway, I'm no longer transmitting."

"How am I supposed to be sure of that?"

"You could feel my pulse. My blood pressure is spiking now that I'm disconnected from my social media feeds. You know how some people can't stop looking at their phone? My whole brain is like a smartphone now. If I'm not seeing tweets about me at every moment I start wondering if I really exist. I trend, therefore I am."

Lindon gave him a blank stare.

App grinned. "I'm joking. I'm fine." He wasn't completely joking. "Anything you say will be private."

Lindon closed his eyes and rubbed his eyelids. "I've only myself to blame. I knew what I was getting into when I called you." He opened his eyes again. "You got here faster than I expected. I mean, it's barely been two minutes since I phoned this in."

"It was a slow night. When you called about the murder I was happy that the evening wasn't going to be a complete snoozefest."

Lindon frowned.

"Not happy," said App, realizing what he'd just said. "I'm never, ever happy to be called about a murder. Rest assured, I'll treat this situation with all the gravity it deserves." He stopped talking, feeling like his attempt to project sincerity was coming across as mockery.

"Christ. Look at you. You look like you're still in high school," said Lindon. "I don't suppose it's too late to get Servant?"

"I'm twenty-eight," said App, which was technically true, and it was time-consuming to explain that he looked eighteen because he'd been frozen for an ageless decade as a cloud of disembodied data. "Don't worry. Servant's who you call if you need a dump truck tossed into low earth orbit. I'm the guy you want to call if you need a room scanned for microscopic clues."

"Whatever," said Lindon, sounding weary. "Gotta say, I never thought I'd wind up calling a goddamned superhero in on one of my cases."

"We're here to help," said App.

"I've seen your poster down at the precinct. Says to call you if we run into anything that might be the work of superfreaks."

"It really says superfreaks?" asked App. "Does Rick James know about that?"

"Nah. It's got something more politically correct. But I'm old enough to remember when we didn't have superhuman terrorists popping up every other week. People who can fly, burst into flame, run at the speed of sound… freaks. That word bother you?"

App managed faint smile. "I've been called worse."

"Enough chit chat," said Lindon. He motioned toward the corpse on the ground. "You see anything strange about this guy?"

"Spectrum mode," said App. Instantly the room flashed through a rainbow of colors that had no names as his retinas became sensitive deep into the infrared and high into the ultraviolet. His cones and rods rearranged themselves to see colors normally only visible to bees, birds, and some reptiles.

He squatted over the corpse. He didn't need more than ordinary vision to see that the cause of death was the big, cleanly cut hole punched into the center of the man's forehead. No, not punched. Burned, the edges of the hole neatly cauterized.

"I can tell you he was shot with a laser rifle," said App.

"Five years ago that would have been useful information," said Lindon. "Back then, only a handful of collectors could get their hands on a weapon like that. These days, even the street gangs carry ray guns." He smirked. "Kind of glad about it, actually. Thugs gravitate toward these fancy rifles because they look scary. But unless the perp is lugging around a fifty pound battery pack, most of these guns exhaust their power in two or three shots."

"Whoever did this sprung for the big battery pack," said App, gingerly touching the blackened flesh at the edge of the wound and peering into the hole. "This goes all the way through." App stood up. "I'm uploading pics of the wound to the forensics team at the Knowbokov Foundation. They can probably tell us the make and model of the rifle by the cauterization patterns."

"I've got a pretty good idea what kind of weapon did this," said Lindon. "Take a look over here."

They walked toward some shipping containers. Having been cut and pasted onto the scene via the space machine, App wasn't entirely certain where he was. Opening a few windows in his retinal display, he saw that he was in a tobacco warehouse in Raleigh, North Carolina. Tax records showed the property to be abandoned when the company that owned it merged with a British conglomerate four years ago.

"Dirty dealings in an abandoned warehouse," said App. "Every day my life feels more and more like a movie."

"Mine too," said Lindon, opening the door of the shipping container. "A science fiction movie."

"Wow," said App. The cargo stood revealed as a military quad-copter drone, a big one, the size of a small car. Hanging from its belly was a laser rifle that looked capable of punching a hole through a man's skull.

"This is the murder weapon?" asked App.

"No," said Lindon. "This is the drone that didn't work. Look around. There are twenty of these containers. Nineteen of them are empty. Someone walked out of here tonight with serious firepower."

"No kidding," said App. "You did the right thing calling us. We can't have something like this loose in the world."

"You're a little late to that party," said Linden. "North Carolina is home to several big military bases. Lots of lethal hardware coming in and out of the state, and lots of opportunities for less than honest men to feather their nests by diverting some of that equipment."

"Rest assured, the Covenant will put a stop to that," said App.

"I don't need you for that," said Linden. "By morning there will be about nine government agencies working the case."

"Oh," said App. "Then why, exactly, did you call me?"

"Because of the victim," said Lindon, leading App back toward the body. "An illegal arms deal goes wrong and a buyer or seller gets offed, that's not exactly a rare event. But this guy shouldn't even be here."

"He'd probably agree with you."

"I know this man," said Lindon, kneeling beside the body. "Name's Nathan Todd Leone."

"From your tone, I take it you weren't on friendly terms."

"This bastard shot me," said Lindon. "Twenty years ago. I was part of a SWAT team handling a hostage situation. Leone had a history of domestic abuse and had just gotten out of prison for beating his former girlfriend so hard he blinded her in one eye. The first thing he did when he got out of prison was to steal a gun from his brother-in-law and go hunting for his ex. He went to the restaurant where her mother worked, but she'd called out sick that day. Leone got into a shouting match with her manager, trying to get the mother's new address. When the manager didn't cooperate, Leone shot him. Running back through the restaurant, he was confronted by an armed citizen who wanted to play hero. Leone shot him, then killed nine more people before taking hostages and demanding that the cops produce his girlfriend."

"Jesus," said App. "You're sure this is him?"

"No question," said Lindon. "Look at this tattoo." He nudged the man's collar aside to display an elaborate tattoo of a dragon. Script letters under the drawing spelled DARGON'S BLOOD. "I mean, unless he had a twin with the same illiterate tattoo artist."

"And he shot you?"

"Yeah. He'd grabbed a two year old and was slinging her around like a rag doll against his chest. I snuck up behind him while my supervisor held his attention. The last bullet he fired that day was into my shoulder as I jumped him."

"You save the girl?"

Lindon nodded. "Small victory. He'd killed 11 people that day, four of them kids. Everything was captured on security footage. It was an easy conviction."

"So he escaped prison?" asked App.

"No," said Lindon. "He was the poster child for the death penalty. Never seen appeals shot down so fast. The day he died, I was there. Lethal injection. I watched him stop breathing. I saw his body wheeled to the prison morgue."

"Man," said App, scratching the back of his neck. "We've stepped out of a science fiction movie into a horror film. You think Leone was some kind of zombie?"

"I don't know what to think," said Lindon. "That's why I called you."

App looked up at the ceiling. "I suppose it's a bit much to hope that there are security cameras. Maybe we could get some clues as to why he was still alive if we could see who it was he was talking to when he got shot."

"We're not that lucky," said Lindon. "Though if we can retrieve one of the drones, we'll know more. This model records everything it sees and hears."

"Excellent," said App. "Then the one left behind must have heard something."

"Unfortunately, it didn't power on," said Lindon.

"Maybe its motor didn't turn on, but its CPU is still fired up."

"How do you know?"

"Spectrum vision," said App. "In infrared, I see the heat being vented by its computer." He walked back over to the drone. "Nathan, can you pull schematics on this drone?"

"What?" asked Lindon.

"Sorry," said App. "I'm talking to my support guy back at headquarters."

Inside his head, Nathan answered: "These are Raptor Class drones. Model Z909. They aren't in use in the field yet. They're being tested at Seymour Johnson Air Force Base about 70 miles from your present location."

"You're joking," said App. "There's really a place called Seymour Johnson?"

Nathan ignored that question. "I tried to check inventory levels, but, of course, they're classified. Also, I can't legally get my hands on the schematics."

"How about illegally?" asked App, holding up his hand so that Lindon would know he wasn't talking to him.

"Nemesis Technologies manufactures these things. Most of their tech is proprietary, but they don't waste money redesigning proven tech. Looking at their subcontractors, I'm guessing the recorders on this thing are stuff you can buy on the open market. They probably encrypt the data, but I'm betting we can get past that. Can you remove the top panel?"

"Got it," said App.

"Got what?" asked Lindon.

"I'm going to tinker around in the guts of the drone," said App. "See if I can find the recording equipment."

"I can't let you tinker with evidence," said Lindon. "I stalled calling the Air Force because I wanted you to look at Leone before they arrived, but I can't really put it off much longer. They won't be happy if they learn you've been poking around inside their top secret drone."

"It's easier to ask forgiveness than permission," said App. "Besides, you want to find out what happened as much as I do. If there is something recorded, I'll share everything I learn. You think the Air Force will give you that kind of access?"

Lindon crossed his arms, a scowl on his face. "Make it fast."

"Dense mode," said App. His enhanced vision switched off as his belt reconfigured his genetic structure. Now, his body had the GDF-8 mutation that granted him extremely dense muscles. With both hands he grabbed the drone and lifted it, carrying it out of its shipping container so he'd have access to the top panel.

He placed it gently on the floor, then stretched his back to relieve the tension. "This thing's heavier than it looks," he said to Lindon. "Three hundred pounds, maybe."

"That's all?" asked Lindon. "It's the size of my car."

"Carbon fiber's pretty light. Sticky mode."

"What?" asked Lindon.

"Sticky mode," said App. "My hands and toes reconfigure to have the same grip patterns as a gecko." He looked down at his now bare feet. "The belt also deletes my shoes so I can take advantage of this power." He latched onto the hull of the drone and scrambled to the top, crouching over the panel on top.

"You got the power to turn your fingers into wrenches?" asked Lindon.

"Hah," said App. "I do carry a pretty kickass multi-bot in my belt." He pulled out a six inch rectangle of chrome and set it on top of the hatch. The tool unfolded itself into a small robot with spidery legs. Faint green lights flickered over the hatch as the multi-bot scanned for bolts and screws. With a whir, its adaptable head configured itself into the star-bit needed to open the panel. In seconds, it had the first screw out, then scrambled across the surface toward the second. Before it reached the second screw, the whole machine shuddered.

"Uh oh," said App, over the whine of motors and turbines kicking to life. The drone suddenly leapt a yard into the air. A small red spot appeared on Lindon's forehead.

"Ghost mode!" App yelled, leaping into the air. As he fell, his body became intangible. He dropped straight through the drone. The second he was clear, he once more shouted "Dense mode!" He reached up and grabbed the laser rifle with both hands and jerked it sideways. A nanosecond later, the top of Lindon's left ear vanished as the rifle flashed. With a grunt, App swung his legs up, pressing his feet against the hull while he still held onto the rifle. With all his strength, he tore the gun free of its mounting. He fell to the concrete floor, landing hard amid a shower of sparks.

Nathan's voice sounded in his head. "Bad news. One improvement in the model z909 versus the z808? A self-destruct mode. Don't want these things falling into the wrong hands if they're crippled. You've got about ten seconds. I can pull you out with the space machine, but we don't have a nanomap of the detective to grab him safely."

"I'll shield him," said App, rising to his feet. He still had the enhanced strength in his legs. Leaping toward Lindon, he shouted, "Airbag mode!"

He hated airbag mode. The collagen in his skin was reconfigured to make it both highly elastic and extremely tough, with the tensile strength of spider silk. At the same time, his whole body filled with carbon dioxide, swelling him like a balloon. This wasn't his most dignified power.

He crashed into Lindon, flattening him beneath his still ballooning body, bracing for the *BOOM!* The drone exploded into a zillion shards of flaming shrapnel. The momentum of the larger pieces was absorbed by his yielding flesh. Smaller, needle like fragments riddled him with holes, but were robbed of energy before they could damage his internal organs. All the tiny puncture wounds felt like he'd been fighting the world's angriest porcupine. Worse, the holes let the gasses escape in a chorus of raspy, farting sounds, like a thousand balloons being deflated at once.

"Wud duh hull juh huppun?" asked Lindon, his voice muffled by the blanket of App's flesh.

"Foam mode," said App. His body changed back to something slightly less freakish. But any sense of restored dignity was stripped away as he started vomiting torrents of foam. It was a necessary evil, since the exploding drone had set the wooden rafters of the old tobacco warehouse aflame. He'd trained in foam mode extensively when he'd been chasing Sundancer, a supervillain who could burst into flame. He could spew his flame retardant foam about thirty feet, more than enough to douse the flaming rafters. In barely a minute, he had the fire under control.

He turned back to Lindon, who was clutching the ruins of his left ear.

"I've been in law enforcement thirty damn years," said Lindon. "Thought I'd seen every weird thing there was to see."

"Reset," said App, shifting back into his normal body, assuming the word normal applied to him any longer.

"How the hell did you get such a strange mix of powers?" asked Lindon.

App shrugged. "A hacked teleportation belt that reconfigures my body in useful and disgusting ways. I really can't give you much in the way of specifics."

"Classified?"

"Nah," said App. "I get to use the powers, but I don't completely understand how the belt works. There's a lot of math."

"You don't have a math mode?"

"Hmm," said App, rubbing his chin.

Lindon winced as he took his hand off his ear. He looked at his fingers. There was no blood.

"Sorry about your ear," said App.

"It could have been worse," said Lindon, nodding toward Leone's body.

"Yeah, but if I hadn't messed around with this thing it wouldn't have woken up."

Lindon shook his head. "I let you do it. Don't—" He stopped in mid-thought as the radio on his belt crackled to life. The dispatcher sounded agitated as she called out a series of codes.

"Gun battle out at the airport," said Lindon, translating. "Officer down."

The dispatcher shifted into plain English. "Witnesses report that that one of the combatants is a dragon."

"And now we're in a fantasy film," said App. "Sounds like a job for a superfreak. Best get going."

"To fight a dragon?" asked Lindon. "You got a lance mode?"

"That's an excellent set up for a dirty joke and I hate that I can't think of the punchline." Then, to Nathan, "A cut and paste to the airport, please. Find a nice open spot on the runway." Then, to Lindon, "I'll be in touch after I take care of this. Keep me in the loop if you find out anything about the perp. I'll get my guys to…" his voice trailed off. He'd been moved instantaneously through space in mid-sentence. Sparks flashed all around his feet as bullets struck the airport runway.

Chapter Two
Killing Machine

THE BULLETS HADN'T been aimed at him, they were only random shots hitting the ground after missing their targets. App squinted, his eyes adjusting from the dimly lit warehouse to the glare of runway floodlights. The warehouse had been chilly but out here in the wind it felt like he'd been teleported to the Arctic.

"Fever mode," he said. Instantly, his body temperature climbed to a level where the freezing air felt pleasant.

Loud *CHATACHATACHATA* sounds rattled the air. A hundred yards away, a plane was on fire in the middle of the runway. Three drones identical to the one he'd seen in the warehouse were buzzing around the burning plane, and a half dozen men in camo fatigues were firing wildly into the air with automatic rifles. App turned his social media streams back on. Breaking news was always legal to broadcast. "Getting ready to engage in battle!" he cried out. "Time to kick some ass!"

His bravado was tempered as bullets zinged around his feet again. App crouched, covering his head with both hands as bullets rained down. "Ghost mode!" he shouted. In his intangible form, he was safe from any stray shots. Unfortunately, since he'd not been moving in any particular direction, he had no momentum, and moving fast in ghost mode was impossible due to the lack of traction. He was too far from the action to do any good.

"Fast mode!" he shouted. His neurotransmitters shifted to alter his perception of time. The stray bullets fell from the air slow enough to see, bouncing from the tarmac like little rubber balls. He ducked and dodged through the deadly precipitation, wondering who he was going to hit once he reached the fight. Were the guys in camo thugs or actual military? And what the hell were they shooting at? They seemed to be aiming at something above the drones.

Then he saw it, a black beast with red eyes and nostrils belching steam dropping down out of the darkness, wings spread like the world's largest bat. His eyes bulged. It really was a dragon! Instantly, his social media likes started to explode.

The dragon obliged the internet viewers with some cool action shots as it snagged one drone in its jaws, caught another with its fore claws, and swatted the last from the sky with a tail that looked like it ended with a sword. The dragon slammed to the runway, smashing the drones. The self-destruct modes kicked in and the shockwave of the explosions caught App by the chest and threw him backwards. He landed hard on the tarmac as an enormous, Hollywood-style fireball rolled toward him.

"Ghost mode!" he shouted. "Ghost mode!"

He was intangible as the fire reached him. It didn't really help. His senses were muffled in ghost mode, especially his sense of touch. But though his nerves only transmitted pain at a fraction of their normal intensity, he still felt as if he were being roasted alive, as the flames slipped through the atoms of his intangible skin.

The second the flames passed, he whispered, "Reset," and fell to his knees. He was back to normal, at least physically. His brain couldn't yet let go of the certainty he'd been cooked alive. As his fear slipped away, he took a deep breath letting his heartrate slow.

He looked back toward the scene of the explosion. The dragon had survived. "Eagle eye mode," he whispered, and found his vision bumped to the absolute maximum sharpness. He could see now that the dragon was some sort of machine. It looked almost as if it were made of cast iron, which might explain why it had weathered the explosion so well. Its wings looked like black silk, though obviously such a delicate material wouldn't have survived the blast. He spotted bullet holes perforating the wing flaps, and the rear hind leg seemed to be leaking oil. Whatever this thing was, it wasn't impervious.

Now that it was done with the drones, the dragon turned its attention to the plane. It had torn off the left wing and was tearing back the canopy to the cabin with its razor sharp claws. Sparks flew around its snout as someone inside opened fire with an automatic weapon. The dragon reared up on its hind legs, drew its head back, and unleashed a jet of white hot steam. Even a hundred yards away, App could feel the heat. Agonized screams sounded from inside the plane. A few seconds later, everything was silent.

The dragon looked around, deliberately eying all the bodies on the ground. Apparently, one of them wasn't sufficiently dead, because it moved to the fallen man and drove its fore claws deep into the man's back.

App wasn't sure if there was anyone left to save, but he'd seen enough to know that this dragon needed to be taken down. "Fast mode!"

He took off running. In reality, he didn't move that much faster than normal in his fast mode, but his accelerated senses gave him a huge advantage over most opponents in hand to hand combat. Not that he planned to hit this dragon with his fists. He just needed to get into position use other powers to stop the thing.

The dragon saw him, its eyes slowly narrowing at it turned to face him. It lifted a fore claw, looking ready to strike, though with its molasses slowness App didn't feel as if he was in any danger.

"Glue mode!" he shouted as he reached the beast. Instantly, his sweat was transformed into a type of glue excreted by sea cucumbers. His own skin wouldn't stick to it, but anything else had about three seconds from exposure to a bonding force powerful enough to hold a bulldozer dangling on the end of an inch thick steel rod. He high fived the dragon's fore claw, then dove between its legs, coating the underside of the creature's tail.

"Wait!" The dragon cried out, in a distinctly female voice.

App rolled to his feet, shouting, "Spectrum mode!"

"I don't want to fight you," the dragon said, turning toward him, placing her glue covered fore claw on the ground as she moved. App could hear the sound of gears grinding against one another as the claw was instantly immobilized.

"What the...?" the dragon sounded confused. App studied the beast as it wasted precious seconds trying to free its claw. Whatever the hide was made of, it absorbed most of the visible spectrum and a fair amount of the infrared. In the ultraviolent, he could see that the creature's scales were made of some sort of heat resistant carbon composite. The head and torso were roughly the size of a large horse. The wing span was enormous, easily sixty feet from tip to tip. Though the signature was muted, he could vaguely make out the glowing outlines of a human form nestled within the torso of the beast. Maybe. The stealthy skin made it difficult to tell. If it was a human, it had to be a midget, or maybe a child, to fit into the torso with all the machinery inside. Whoever had built this thing had a steampunk aesthetic that App appreciated. Yes, it was a dangerous killing machine, but it was a carefully crafted killing machine with classic lines and lacy filigree highlights along the gears and pistons.

"Who are you?" App asked.

"Call me Steam-Dragon," said the dragon.

"Very well, Steam-Dragon," said App. "You're under arrest."

"No!" the woman's voice cried out. "You don't understand!"

"You just killed a bunch of people right before my eyes. I understand enough."

"You're one of the good guys," said Steam-Dragon. "I don't want to hurt you."

"Since you're not presently going anywhere, I don't think that's a problem."

"I'm leaving now," she said. With a loud *CLICK*, her whole left claw came free of the leg.

"Crap," said App, as the beast spread its wings. Its belly puffed out as internal bellows filled with air. He jumped toward the beast and yelled, "Sticky mode!" He latched onto the front of the dragon's torso and began to climb, hoping the creature couldn't bend its neck enough to unleash a blast of steam at him. He crawled onto the dragon's shoulders and straddled the beast's neck, grabbing the back of its skull with both hands.

"Eel mode!" he shouted. Instantly, he possessed the same shock capacity as an electric eel. It didn't do him any good. His teeth tingled as the electrons he unleased showered off the shielded surface.

"Acid mode!" he cried out as the creature flapped its wings and charged forward with a stumbling, three-legged gait. He tried to dig his fingers beneath the scales, searching for any bare metal he could find. In this mode his sweat could burn a hole through plate steel. But against these scales? He didn't think he was doing any damage at all.

Luckily, the dragon wasn't getting airborne. Maybe its crippled gait kept it from reaching launch speed, or maybe App's added weight kept it grounded. At least here on the creature's neck, he was out of reach of the beast's jaws and claws. Then the creature skidded to a sudden halt, bending its neck forward. "Sticky mode!" App cried, to avoid being thrown off. Then he heard a whistling noise slicing the air behind him and remembered the sword at the end of the long, serpentine tail.

"Ghost mode!" he shouted, the barest fraction of a second before his skull would have been split open. The creature jerked upward, and he found himself sinking trough the beast's body into the torso. It turned out to be filled with lights, hundreds of dials and gages glowing pale green. For the briefest flash, he saw a woman's face reflected in one of the larger dials, her face glistening with sweat and panic.

The dragon turned away, leaving him dangling in the air.

"Reset," he said, dropping to the pavement.

The dragon started galloping away, at a pretty decent clip for a quadruped missing a claw. App switched to his speed mode and gave chase, but the dragon still pulled away. His only flight capacity was his airhead mode, but that only let him drift around like a balloon. What the hell could he do to keep this thing from getting away?

"Nathan, you watching this on the monitors?'

"You kidding?" said Nathan. "The whole crew's watching. I want the résumé of whoever built that dragon. That thing's cool as hell."

"Cool or not, I need to cripple it. Cut and paste me about fifty feet in front of it. Ink mode!"

"Executing... now!" said Nathan.

With no sense of movement, App found himself in front of the rapidly charging dragon. He started to projectile vomit. Ink mode was another power it was impossible to use with any dignity, as his stomach was now lined with squid cells churning out several quarts of black ink per second. His dense core muscles let him spew the foul liquid a good twenty yards. Inside his head, he saw his social media feeds explode with people typing "EW!" and "GROSS!" But he'd gone with this mode because it was effective. In seconds, he'd completely coated the dragon's face with the opaque liquid. Assuming that the user inside the torso had done the obvious and put cameras in the dragon's eyes, she was now blinded.

App wiped his mouth, waiting for the creature to stumble or skid to a halt. He wasn't expecting the thing to keep charging at full speed. With the distance closing fast, he had maybe a second to get into ghost mode before he was trampled.

Unfortunately, his esophagus was still full of ink, and he choked as he tried to shout out the words. The beast barreled into him, knocking him backward. The impossibly sharp claws of the rear legs tore through his chest muscles, piercing his heart. A thousand little frowny faces popped up on his media feeds.

What happened after that he didn't know because he was dead.

Chapter Three
Half the Population of Earth

APP OPENED HIS eyes, staring up into a bright light. He wondered if he was ascending to Heaven for a fleeting second before remembering that he was at an airport. He was looking directly at a flood lamp. He sat up, his stomach tightening as he saw the blood on the ground around him.

"I died again?"

"Sorry man," said Nathan. "All your vitals flatlined. We had to do a remote reboot."

"Thanks," said App, standing up, trying not to get freaked out by the fact that all the blood around him was his blood, or at least his blood from a body he'd worn only seconds ago. This wasn't the first time he'd been killed. Depending on how you counted, it was death number ten. "I guess we've proven I'm not a cat."

"What?" asked Nathan.

"Never mind," sighed App. He didn't really want to make lame jokes about his resurrection. He didn't want to talk about it at all, or even think about it, which was difficult when all the social media feeds running through his mind's eyes were full of fans asking what had happened. There was a curious mix of shame and despair as he saw his current viewers had jumped from about fifty thousand at the start of the fight to just shy of a million. Ever since the first time he'd died while live-streaming, word spread fast any time he went into battle. His ego swelled at the thought of his popularity, and shrank again at thought that so many people liked to watch him die.

And what if this wasn't just his tenth death? What if every time his belt tore apart his atoms and put them back into a new configuration, he was dying and being reborn? He did this a few dozen times a day. What a way to live. Assuming he really was alive. He swallowed hard, as the constant nagging fear that nibbled at his mind threatened to overwhelm him. He'd been born Johnny Appleton. What if Johnny Appleton had died and stayed dead the second Rex Monday had first blasted his body into subatomic particles? What if he was only some digital artifact thinking it was a man? He didn't have the courage to toss that question out onto his feeds. As addicted as he was to the internet, he knew it wasn't the best place to go to have a serious philosophical debate.

"I don't suppose you could cut and paste me to the nearest bar, could you?" asked App. "I need to kill some brain cells."

"No drinking while you're on the job," said Nathan.

"When am I not on this job?" asked App. He knew his tone probably came across as petulant. He launched the tiny camera drone from his belt and took a quick selfie giving a thumbs up with the wreckage of the burning plane in the background. "Just a scratch!" he said to his viewers. "Alas, I need to go offline while I talk to the cops. Full story later!"

He shut down his social media feed and was alone with his thoughts for almost a full ten seconds. He'd used the cops as an excuse, but it turned out there really were about a hundred of them bearing down on him. They'd been holding positions further down the runway, taking cover during the worst of the firefight, but now a battalion of squad cars raced toward him.

He searched the sky as they approached. Nothing but clouds overhead. "Nathan, you have a fix on Steam-Dragon?"

"Negative," said Nathan. "It flew too low for radar tracking and cloud cover is hiding it from satellites."

"She," said App.

"She what?"

"Steam-Dragon isn't an it. She's a she. I caught a glimpse of a woman inside when I fell through."

"Your feed has a lot of static when you pass through objects in ghost mode. We didn't catch enough data for facial recognition. How good a look did you get?"

"Her gender's about all I can tell you. I'm pretty sure she was white, but the light inside was all green, so who knows. She had short blonde hair, I think? Again, only a fleeting glimpse."

"Okay. Narrowing the suspect down to half the population of earth is a start," said Nathan.

"You've got a lot of video of the dragon. Whatever it was made of, I feel pretty sure you can't just run down to Home Depot to pick up the parts. Building this took some crazy skills. That's gotta give you some leads, right?"

"Yeah," said Nathan. "But I'd like some physical evidence instead of just pictures. See if you can talk the cops into letting you take the claw you glued down. Maybe it has fingerprints on it. No way could someone build this without leaving behind a few clues."

The cops had reached him. App wasn't looking forward to the next few hours. The Covenant operated on US soil under an agreement with the Department of Homeland Security, but most local law enforcement weren't keen on the whole superhero thing. Of course, nothing breeds respect like success. If he'd beaten Steam-Dragon, he'd be spending part of the evening signing autographs. Since he'd gotten his ass handed to him, he suspected he'd be treated like an incompetent. Oh well.

"Oh!" he said, as the cops exited their vehicles in unison. "Nathan! I got so worked up about the dragon, I forgot all about the dead guy! Any ideas about how a dead convict wound up as a murder victim?"

"Yes," Nathan said tersely.

Unfortunately, there was no time for a follow up question, as one of the cops was now close enough to ask, "I saw that dragon tear your guts out. How the hell are you still alive?"

App grinned, trying to think of some heroic, witty, comeback. But the only thing his mind could give him was, *What if I'm not?*

"HAS APP REPORTED back yet?" asked Sarah as she came into the control room. It was early morning, a Monday. This wasn't her normal schedule; she normally worked in the evenings when Carson was on patrol, but Servant had been given a week off to take part in some church mission. He was helping that crazy preacher he followed build houses for the poor or something. Playing carpenter struck her as of a waste of talent for the mightiest man on earth, but who was she to judge?

"App's still in the field," said Katya as she studied the monitor feeds before her, slowly sipping her coffee. "First he had to talk to the local cops, then TSA agents showed up, followed by the FBI, then the AFSF, and…"

"What the hell is the AFSF?" asked Sarah.

"Air Force Security Forces. It was their drone."

"I swear the worst part of cooperating with law enforcement is all the acronyms," said Sarah.

"That's because you don't have to fill out all the paperwork," said Katya, shaking her head. "Nathan scrammed the second I came on duty. I'll be spending the bulk of my shift writing out reports for stuff that happened on his watch. He always does this."

Sarah nodded. "You're not the only person to complain. I hear it's kind of a pattern for him."

"Maybe you could speak to Mrs. Knowbokov about him?" asked Katya.

"Um," said Sarah. "We'll be covering a lot of stuff. I'll see if I can fit it in." She really didn't plan to bring it up. Honestly, if she made it through her shift without speaking to her mother at all she'd count it as a good day. She changed the subject: "How are your kids?"

"Thrilled that Christmas break has arrived," said Katya. "They're still with Tim's parents as part of a long weekend. I'll be starting my vacation Wednesday. Unless... well...."

Sarah nodded. There was no need to speak the unspeakable. The dervishes hadn't launched an attack since Labor Day, when they'd slaughtered seventy people at an amusement park in California before Servant had reached the scene. There was no intelligence suggesting another attack was imminent, but the Christmas holiday offered a lot of tempting targets—parades, packed malls, airports full of travelers. If there was another dervish attack, none of the Covenant's support staff would be getting time off.

The Covenant had formed to deal with a pair of superhuman terrorists, Pit Geek and Sundancer. The two villains were now presumed dead but shortly after they disappeared, the first dervishes had attacked. The Covenant's agreement with various law enforcement agencies was expanded to give them permission to counter that threat. With the Knowbokov Foundation's space machine, the Covenant could reach any spot on earth in the blink of an eye. Alas, this speed didn't help much if news of a dervish assault arrived even a few minutes late. The dervishes were said to attack so quickly they seemed like they were in multiple places at once. The attack on the amusement park had lasted barely two minutes, and when Servant had finally arrived only the body of a single dervish could be found, dead of a heart attack.

"I've got another thing I want you to find out from Mrs. Knowbokov," said Katya.

"Go ahead," said Sarah, sighing.

"Is your mother going to expand the team?"

Sarah eyed the techs on the other side of the room, then leaned close and said, "Ixnay on the othermay."

"Sorry," said Katya. Katya was one of a handful of Knowbokov Foundation employees who'd worked for her father and knew the truth of Sarah's identity. Most of the new hires thought Skyrider and the Thrill were different people.

"Who knows when my mother will make up her mind?" said Sarah. "I told her the three of us are spread too thin. But, I get the challenge of trying to find suitable recruits. The day the Covenant went public, she started getting resumes from so-called crime-fighters. Some are just crazy people, a lot are well-meaning wannabes, and the few legitimately super-powered people we have looked into have, shall we say, strained relationships with law enforcement. She can't bring just anyone on board."

"So why not put in a good word for Chimpion?"

"God," said Sarah, rubbing her eyes.

"What?" asked Katya. "She's really good. She aced the combat simulations and set a record time on the obstacle course on her first attempt. She's perfect for the team."

"She's a chimp!" said Sarah.

"She's smarter than most people," said Katya.

"Yes," said Sarah. "And doesn't the public just love that? Look, Pangea is still a haven for criminals and contraband. Putting a Pangean on the team is going to be a PR nightmare."

"Or PR gold," said Katya. "Chimpion is great once you get to know her. She really wants to be a role model, to show the world that not all of the elevated chimps are mad geniuses plotting to destroy mankind."

"I want to expand the team as much as you. More than you. App has, like, no life outside of the Covenant. Servant doesn't have family, and doesn't need to sleep, so he also puts in insane hours. But I have a life outside this team. You think it's not putting a strain on me, feeling like I'm not pulling my weight in either of my lives?"

"Chimpion is prepared to devote her whole life to the team."

Sarah shook her head. "I'd welcome ten team members—a dozen! Is it too much to ask that they at least be human?"

"Not everyone thinks of the existing team as fully human," said Katya. "Remember all the 'alien menace' headlines after Jerusalem?"

"I know, I know," Sarah said. She crossed her arms, feeling on the defensive. She probably sounded like a bigot. Katya wasn't seeing the big picture. "It's because I've been on the receiving end of a press crucifixion that I want to make sure the Covenant's rep stays spotless. People are already uncomfortable with the whole idea of a team of superhumans being treated like law enforcement. If we give a chimp the power to arrest humans, the press is going to eat us alive."

Katya said, "But the press is going to—"

Sarah held up her hands, cutting her off. "Look, I don't make hiring decisions anyway. If Mrs. Knowbokov decides to hire a chimp, I really have no say in the matter. Let's drop it. Is there anything I need to do to help with the case App's working?"

"You don't know?" said Katya. "I've already sent your assignment to your phone before you even came in."

"Oh," said Sarah, pulling her phone from pocket. "I felt it buzz but figured it was just App tagging me in a post." The retinal scanner unlocked the phone and she found a list of names. She scanned them, finding them familiar, though it didn't instantly strike her why they were familiar. Then, about ten names in, she knew why she knew them. The blood drained from her face. "Shit."

"Talk about bad PR," said Katya.

"What's happened?" asked Sarah, pressing a button to transfer the list into her helmet's memory.

"Nathan Todd Leone, AKA Mark Porter, was found dead last night. He'd been killed by a drone mounted laser rifle. All the evidence points to the possibility he was involved in smuggling high tech weapons."

"How is that possible?" asked Sarah. "I mean, we have all these guys under surveillance."

"We do," said Katya. "It's been over five years since they were set free and none of them have had any run ins with the law until now. After so many years of good behavior, watching their every move hasn't been a priority. It's not like we have spies on their tail 24/7."

"If they are turning back to crime... Jesus. Every one of these men was a killer. Some were rapists." Her eyes lingered on the name at the top of the list. "This guy, Allen Anderson... he ate people."

"Don't panic," said Katya. "Leone getting caught up in weapons trafficking is an entirely different class of criminality than his former history as a violent sociopath. Case workers say he lived with a girlfriend he treated respectfully, with no hint of his former abusive tendencies. They were having some financial difficulties due to medical bills, though. Maybe money problems drove him to an opportunistic crime? We're just starting to dig into this case now."

"But you want me to check out the other names on the list," said Sarah. "Make sure nothing looks amiss? You want direct interviews or something more stealthy?"

"Your call," said Katya. "There's not an operational precedent for a situation like this."

Sarah bit her lip. All this time and she was still dealing with the horrifying consequences of her father's good intentions. God, she didn't have time for this. After Carson's shift tonight, he'd be off for two days. Her time with the Covenant was already making him suspicious of where she went in her free time. Her job as a charter pilot gave her a reasonable excuse to vanish for a few days at a time, but he knew her well enough to suspect when she was lying to him. Was saving the world worth ruining her marriage?

"I guess I've got no choice," she said, standing. "I'll make contact in plain clothes. Pass myself off as a case worker trainee or something."

"Sound's good," said Katya. "Go ahead and get changed and we'll—"

Katya never finished her sentence. Every alarm on the compound started to scream. Katya spun her chair to look at her monitor. Her eyes went wide. Sarah knew the next word that would come from her mouth.

"Dervish!"

Chapter Four
Dervish

SARAH SLID ON her helmet a fraction of a second before the space machine grabbed her. She hated travelling via the machine. When her father had accidentally created the universe, he'd built reality around a limited set of mathematical equations that described the laws of physics as he'd understood them. Her father's evil twin, Rex Monday, had figured out how to manipulate those equations in such a way that it was possible to change the location of an object or person simply by changing the underlying math.

App's belt and Servant's force fields protected them from the effects of the jump, but Sarah dreaded every jump. The interspace between the two points was a place of insanity, where all the geometry of her body felt distorted. On this jump, she had the distinct impression that her hands were now jutting from the sides of her head while her arms ended in a pair of ears. Arriving at her destination didn't bring much relief. The body possesses dozens of invisible senses thrown into complete disarray by instantaneous transport. Gravitational pull changes with altitude and the composition of geologic substrata. Atmospheric pressure varies, as does the temperature and ambient light. Even the instant change in the way the air tasted and smelled left her body protesting that something had gone terribly wrong, leaving her slightly nauseated. The monitors in her suit triggered the delivery of nanoparticle anti-nausea drugs directly into her bloodstream, but it would take a few minutes for those to really kick in.

Sarah had no time for weakness. She had seconds to locate the dervish before he slaughtered innocents. She looked around. She was obviously in a shopping mall; her heads up display told her she was in Pallisades Center in West Nyack, New York. There were 400 stores here. Even though the mall had only opened a few minutes ago, tens of thousands of holiday shoppers were filling the concourses. Like most public spaces, people had to pass through metal detectors to enter. The Knowbokov Foundation provided one of the most sophisticated models of that technology. The ferric signature of an executioner's cleaver, the favored sword of the dervishes, had just been triggered. Her heads up display flashed to turn her face toward the door where the guards at the metal detector were standing in front of a tall, broad shouldered man wearing a black trench coat.

"Found him!" she said leaping into the air.

Someone shouted, "Skyrider!" The name sounded strange to her, though she'd been operating under that identity for a year. She still expected to hear people shout out, "The Thrill!" Of course, those shouts would have been shouts of fear, since the Thrill was branded an alien terrorist. Fortunately, her Skyrider costume had been designed to distract the public from making the connection between two female superheroes who could fly. Her old costume had been white silk, practically lingerie. Her new costume was dark blue body armor, with padded plates that broke up the feminine lines of her legs and torso. Not that anyone would ever mistake her for a man, but she'd said good-bye her poster girl persona. The Thrill hadn't worn a mask and wore her blonde hair long and flowing. Skyrider hid her face beneath a mirrored motorcycle helmet. The few times she did remove her helmet in public it revealed her spiky dark hair and her surgically altered face.

Finally, she no longer had the power that she'd been best known for as the Thrill. She'd voluntarily had surgery on her vocal cords to strip herself of the power to issue commands that ordinary people wanted to obey. She pondered the wisdom of giving up that power as she flew toward the man in the trench coat, shouting, "Don't move!"

The man moved, reaching into his coat as the mall cops went for their tasers. An instant later the mall cops were falling backwards, their heads tumbling away from their bodies, with arcs of bright blood hanging in the air as the dervish grinned, brandishing his fearsome cleaver.

"Crap, crap, crap," said Sarah when the heads up display in her helmet went crazy as the sensor array lost its lock on the man. Suddenly, there were three identical copies of the man charging toward her, all laughing maniacally, rapturous in violence. Thankfully, she'd was only a few feet off the ground, within easy reach of a sword, making her a tempting target. She'd rather he attack her than bystanders. Her body armor had been improved recently with a weave of diamond nanofibers, and the neck brace that her helmet locked into was reinforced with titanium. The first copy of the dervish shattered his blade against her neck. It didn't kill her, but it still felt like being kicked in the neck by a horse. She spun through the air, unable to think straight, until a second dervish grabbed her by the ankle and spun her around. They were near the elevator banks and he slammed her hard against the steel beams that ran skyward.

Her armor was nearly impossible to cut, but didn't provide much defense against a sharp blow to the ribs. She bounced off the beam certain that bones had just broken. Fortunately, she'd been fighting as a superhero since she was a teen and was trained to push past pain. The dervish still had a grasp on her ankle, which meant her powers had a grasp on him.

Her father had never understood how she could fly. He'd analyzed her to the atomic level, ruled out ionic propulsion, dark energy lensing, gravitational shielding, and magnetic levitation. Through some unknown reactionless propulsion, she could simply will her body to move through the air. Anything she held onto came along for the ride. She willed herself to rocket straight up 100 feet with the dervish in tow. She smashed through the thick plates of glass of the arched roof of the mall. The force dislodged her unwilling passenger who tumbled toward the floor laughing like a giddy hyena.

The dervishes weren't invulnerable, though they did behave as if they were completely pumped up with adrenaline and oblivious to all pain. Combine that with their preference for running amok beheading men, women, and children and they could still terrify a populace grown numb to bombings and mass shootings. Fearful as they were, they couldn't fly. Skyrider watched as the dervish flailed his arms as if convinced he might avoid the fate awaiting him. He hit hard, bouncing twice, until his limp body came to rest across the edge of a marble fountain.

"Got him!" Sarah cried. She winced as soon as she spoke. Her broken ribs were like knives beneath the skin. "I need medical attention," she whispered.

"You got one of him," said Katya. "Security footage shows six copies of him now."

"Damn it," said Sarah, folding her arms to her side and diving back down into the mall. She'd thought the multiple copies might have been an illusion, the product of impossible speed allowing a dervish to be more than one place at a time. She'd definitely killed the one she'd dropped. What were these others? Clones? Some sort of solid hologram? Whatever they were, they'd already beheaded several victims.

Sarah had no time to contemplate as she spotted one with his cleaver held high, about to attack a white-haired lady that had to be somebody's grandmother. She shot toward him with fists outstretched, accelerating as much as she could bear. Her armored gauntlets combined with her speed to knock the dervish from his feet, teeth flying from his broken jaw. In her head, she'd imagined racing past him in a perfect arc and taking down the next dervish an instant later. Unfortunately, her body didn't quite cooperate with that plan. The impact with the dervish compressed her rib cage. Black spots danced before her eyes. The next thing she knew she'd smashed through the window of an Old Navy and her vision cleared half a second before she crash landed onto a table stacked high with sweaters. It definitely wasn't the worst thing she'd ever fallen onto.

She sat up slowly, tasting blood in her mouth. The heads up display on her monitor showed her blood pressure dropping. No amount of grit and determination was going to keep her fighting more than another minute if a broken rib had severed an artery. She had to stop the remaining dervishes before she passed out.

"Help's on the way," said Katya as Sarah lifted back into the air, searching around for a weapon. She spotted the large sword the last dervish had dropped. It had tumbled through the air and landed in a potted plant, the hilt jutting up. She darted forward and snatched it free. The dervish blades were ugly weapons, like meat cleavers stretched to the point of parody, with a cutting edge two feet long and a shaft big enough to hold with both hands. Though the blade was effectively weightless once she touched it, the wing-like wedge of the blade messed with her aerodynamics. She slowed to adjust her grip. The target icons in her heads up display went red as three of the dervishes lunged toward her, apparently unhappy that she'd killed two of their brethren. She raised her blade in an attempt to parry at least one of the incoming blows.

All at once, the three dervishes went limp in mid-stride. They fell face first, sprawling on the floor in front of Sarah, their blades sliding across the mall floor. Looking down at their backs, she saw shurikens jutting from each neck precisely where their skulls joined with their spines.

"What the hell?" she muttered.

"Servant hasn't responded to the alert," said Katya. "You needed help. I made a judgment call."

Sarah had no time to ask what she meant. A chimpanzee dressed in green and yellow ninja garb dropped down from the balcony above to land with a crouch just beyond the dead dervishes. In each of her hands she carried razor-sharp shurikens. The two remaining dervishes were foaming at the mouth as they charged toward Sarah, screaming with incoherent rage. The chimp's arms sprang straight, her fingers opened, the shurikens vanished. Both onrushing dervishes dropped, their cleavers clattering loudly. A heartbeat later, pools of blood began to grow around their throats.

Just as they had in the aftermath of previous attacks, all but one of the dervishes dissolved into a pale light. Their swords crumbled to red dust.

The chimp turned her head back over her shoulder. Her face was hidden by a gold silk scarf, save for her brown eyes. "I'm Chimpion," she said. "You must be Skyrider."

Sarah could only nod in response.

"Are you all right?" asked Chimpion, her eyes showing concern.

"No," Sarah groaned, falling from the air, landing hard on the floor. She tore off her helmet just in time as she violently vomited dark red blood. Sometimes, when she threw up, it left her feeling better. This was not one of those times.

"We have a team member in need of immediate medical evacuation," said Chimpion, rushing to her side, placing a hand on her shoulder.

The mall vanished. Sarah rolled to her back in the Foundation's medical center. As darkness edged in around her vision, all she could see was the nurse's white shoes as they ran toward her.

Chapter Five
The First Step Forward

"**B**ROTHER CLINT," SISTER AMY called up to him from the base of the ladder. "Your pants are buzzing."

Clint put down his hammer and stared over the edge of the roof at Sister Amy on the ground. He'd had stranger things said to him during his lifetime, but it still took him a couple of seconds to parse the preacher's meaning. She meant that the pants he'd left in the truck were buzzing, not the pants he had on.

"Oh," he said. "It's probably my phone. It's embedded in my costume." He cringed a little as his fellow workers on the roof looked toward him. When he was with them, he enjoyed, for a little while, the illusion that he was just another man. Of course, no one else on the roof had a superhero uniform made of tiny self-assembling robots. When he'd first appeared in public he hadn't even owned a costume. His force fields would disintegrate any fabric they were in contact with for more than a few minutes. He'd been able to manipulate his fields to look like a costume, but this had left him naked on more than a few occasions when he'd been knocked out or rattled enough to lose his concentration. Fortunately, the geeks at the Knowbokov Foundation had finally designed him a costume that repaired itself as quickly as his fields degraded it, and he'd also finally learned to dampen his fields enough to be able to wear normal clothes like his overalls for several hours before they fell apart.

He looked past his fellow workers, shielding his eyes as he looked around the bright, white landscape and the jumble of buildings in various stages of construction. They were in western Texas, not far from the border with Mexico. Even though it was December and barely an hour past sunrise, the pale sand and gravel that surrounded them shimmered with heat. Of course, no matter how hot it got, he wouldn't feel any discomfort. The rest of his fellow laborers didn't have this advantage, which is why they'd started working on the houses a little before dawn.

"Is it something you need to attend to?" asked Sister Amy, drawing his attention back to the phone call.

Clint sighed. "Probably." He moved toward the ladder. He could have jumped down from the roof without harm, but again didn't want to draw attention to his differences. When he was with his church brethren, he wanted to forget his life as Servant, and be happy as plain, ordinary, Brother Clint. He looked toward the rising temple as he stepped onto the ladder. Here in a barren desert, a new city was springing to life. Jerusalem, the old one, had been destroyed eight years ago by a supervillain named Rail Blade. The old Jerusalem was now a flat circle of scoured white rock where not even a single weed could grow. Politics and war kept the city from being rebuilt.

Reverend Amy McPherson had decided to take the matter into her own hands, founding the Ministry of the New Jerusalem. If the old Jerusalem couldn't be restored, then it was up to her to build a new one. After years of fundraising, the time had come for actual construction. Clint felt pride in how quickly the place was starting to look like a real city, but a touch of shame that it wasn't even further along. If he'd used his full strength and speed, he could have finished the city by now. But he didn't want to show off, or make his brothers and sisters in Christ feel that their contributions were less important than his own.

Back on the ground, Clint wiped his hands on a towel that Sister Amy offered him. She wore a long white gown without a single speck of dirt showing despite her movement back and forth across a dusty construction site. He said, "I'll see what they're calling about, but whatever it is I'll tell them to handle it without me. There's still so much work to be done."

"There are a thousand men here who can swing a hammer," said Sister Amy. "You're the only who's bulletproof. If you're needed elsewhere, we understand."

"I know," said Clint. "But the sooner these houses are finished, the sooner the refugees can move in. I've been to the camps. Every day they go without proper housing is a sin."

Sister Amy smiled gently. "They may be lacking in material things, but the refugees are spiritually rich. There's something about hardship that brings a body closer to the Lord."

Clint returned her smile. "I feel that when I'm here, working with the others." He shook his head, his smile fading. "When I'm with the Covenant... all I'm good for is fighting."

"Fighting the forces of darkness," said Sister Amy.

"Fighting darkness with darkness," said Clint. "It's hard on the soul. The man I used to be... so angry, so quick to violence. When I'm fighting alongside the Covenant, that anger rises up again. It's hard to feel love for your fellow man while you're being shot at, even though the bullets bounce off."

"The Lord gave you your talents for a reason," said Sister Amy. "Go answer your call. What if the dervishes have attacked again?"

"If the dervishes attacked again," said Clint, "the fight's already over."

ON THIS, HE'D BEEN RIGHT. It still didn't ease his guilt when he picked up his phone and discovered that Sarah had almost been killed.

"Prepare for transport back to the island," said Katya.

"Why?" he asked.

"You knew your leave would be cancelled if the dervishes attacked again."

"Yeah. But the fight's over. The dervishes were stopped with their lowest body count yet. Sounds like the chimp proved herself worthy of being on the team. What's left for me to do at this point?"

"We need you ready if there's another attack."

"I can be just as ready here. Look, I'll keep my costume on under my overalls. I'll get your calls this time. You can cut and paste me out of Texas to a fight just as easily as you could move me off the island."

"Mrs. Knowbokov will have my head if we don't bring you back."

"All she wants is to yell at me face to face for letting Sarah get hurt."

"You know she's not going to yell at you. Yelling's not her style."

He nodded. "She never raises her voice, but somehow I walk out of every meeting with her feeling like my hair's on fire."

"I'm not pretending she'll be in a good mood," said Katya.

Clint looked around at the construction going on near the truck. Mixed among the adult volunteers were teenagers, some in their early teens, being taught the value of service, of working hard for their fellow men. When he was a young teen he'd been a supervillain, Ogre, god-king of the gangs of Detroit. He'd already killed a hundred men at their age, and nothing would have stopped him from killing hundreds more if Rail Blade hadn't trapped him inside a cube of solid iron. He'd changed his life since finding the Lord, and wanted to atone for his past by doing all the good he could as Servant.

But was Clint really a role model as Servant? When he talked to the younger members of the congregation, they didn't want to hear about how many houses he'd helped to build in New Jerusalem. They only wanted to hear about his latest battle. Some days, the only lesson he seemed to be teaching was that violence was the only solution to confronting evil. Yes, the Lord had given him great strength, just as he'd given men like Sampson great strength to fight against evil. Still, it was hard to preach peace and love when you lived a life of rage and war.

With shoulders sagging, he said, "Fine. Bring me back."

And then he was back. App was waiting, arms crossed, scowling as their eyes met.

"What?" asked Clint. "You didn't answer the call either."

"I was talking with cops all night. Just as I was finishing up they got a call about a huge accident involving a fuel tanker. There were lots of cars sitting right in the center of a lake of gasoline. The whole highway could have turned into a fireball if someone tossed a cigarette out the window. I'd just gone into foam mode when the dervish attacked. I couldn't leave until I was sure everyone was safe. What were you doing?"

"Putting shingles on a roof," said Clint.

"Sarah's hurt," said App.

"I heard. They've got her stabilized, right?"

"She shouldn't have been out there alone."

"She wasn't alone. She had the chimp."

"I do have a name, you know," said a voice directly behind Clint.

He turned and didn't see anyone. He looked down. Chimpion was only about four feet tall, standing directly in front of him, her hands on her hips. She was still wearing her green and gold ninja robes, but her face scarf and hood were pulled back to show her whole face.

"My hero name is Chimpion," she said. "But my friends call me Jane."

Clint couldn't help but smirk. "Like Tarzan's wife?"

"Who?" asked Jane.

"What do you mean, who?" asked App, coming over. "You've never heard of Tarzan?"

"No," she said. "Is he some sort of human celebrity?"

"He's a fictional character," said App. "He's been in, like, a hundred movies."

"Ah," she said. "I've never seen a movie."

"You've never seen a movie?" said App, astonished.

"Is this a common pattern for conversations around here?" Jane asked. "I make a statement and you repeat it as a question?"

"Sorry," said App. "I mean, I've never met anyone before who had never seen a movie. You don't have them on Pangea?"

"Of course we have them on Pangea," she said. "But I was born in captivity and lived in cages until I was three, treated as a test animal for an extensive pharmacopeia of dangerous experimental drugs. Worst still, I was subjected to horrible operations that replaced my nerve fibers with optical cables, supplying me with digital reflexes, and unimaginable pain that took me a long time to manage."

"Right," said App. "By Rex Monday."

"He tested his drugs on many of my kind, but I was the only subject to survive the surgical enhancements," she said. "With my strength and speed boosted to super-primate levels, Monday decided I was too dangerous to keep around. Rather than euthanize me, he sold me to an illegal fight promoter in Russia. I spent years battling daily in pits and rings for the amusement of others. When I escaped, I smuggled myself aboard the first plane I encountered with no clue where it was going. I wound up in Japan. There, a kindly monk took me under his wing, and I learned to deal with the anger and trauma of my years of captivity through meditation and the discipline of the martial arts. When I finally left Japan to serve the newly established nation of Pangea, the government decided that an ape with my abilities was too valuable an asset to waste. After the fiasco of Dr. Trog attempting to destroy mankind, it's been decided that I should serve as a new public face for our nation. A hero even humans will grow to respect. Thus, my role as Chimpion."

"Like Captain America, but with shuriken instead of a shield," said App.

"Captain who?" she asked.

"Oh, come on," said App.

She grinned. "Just giving you a hard time. I've never seen a movie, but to prepare for my role as a superhero I was assigned to read an extensive collection of comic books."

"Awesome," said App. "Which did you like more? Marvel or DC?"

Clint suspected that a moment of pop-culture bonding was about to take place and he didn't care to be in the vicinity as it happened. He distained small talk. The world had too many serious problems. Why anyone wasted God-given moments of life with a comic book, a movie, or even a novel eluded him. Fiction seemed like a sort of stealth drug, as effective at distracting its users from life's real problems as any of the junk he'd trafficked as Ogre. The Bible was the only book he owned, and the only book he'd ever read... assuming that, one day, he got around to actually reading it.

"Excuse me," said Clint, walking away. "Mrs. Knowbokov wants to see me."

He walked down the hall toward the infirmary, past a team in hazmat suits mopping up blood in the corridor. Before he reached the end of the hall, he spotted Mrs. Knowbokov standing at the window that looked in on the surgical center. She gazed through the window dispassionately, no hint of emotion on her face. As always, she was immaculately dressed in a tailored business jacket and skirt, wearing shoes that likely cost more than it took to build a new house in New Jerusalem.

He walked up and saw two large robotic arms moving over a female form mostly obscured by green surgical drapery. The robotic arms didn't end with scalpels or needles, but blunt steel tubes. With his own force field, he could sense the magnetic fields surrounding them.

"Mrs. Knowbokov," he said.

"I apologize for pulling you away from a busy day of hammering," she said without looking directly at him. Her arms were crossed over her chest. Her tone was flat, neutral.

"How's she doing?" he asked.

"Her prognosis is good," said Mrs. Knowbokov. "They've mapped out her injuries with micrographing MRI and have injected ten cc of surgical nanites into her bloodstream. Assuming her body doesn't trigger an autoimmune response, the nanites will repair the damage, simulating a month of healing in mere hours. By tomorrow, she should be fully recovered."

"That's great," said Clint.

"You sound relieved," she said.

"How could anyone not sound relieved?"

"You should have been there," said Mrs. Knowbokov, her voice still calm and emotionless.

"I can't be everywhere," said Clint. "Even if I could, who knows how things might have turned out? I'm told that Chimpion took out five dervishes in the span of a few seconds. That's better than I've ever done against them."

"This is the earliest we've ever intervened," said Mrs. Knowbokov. "The new generation of metal detectors we've been providing free of charge to at risk sites proved to be a wise investment. But we're still playing defense. I'm furious that you didn't answer your signal." She didn't sound furious as she said this. But she did sound sorrowful as she said, "I'm even more furious that I've failed so badly."

"Failed how?"

"I've poured millions into locating the mastermind of these attacks," said Mrs. Knowbokov. "I've pulled the diplomatic strings to organize a worldwide manhunt. The foundation has provided law enforcement agencies with the most advanced CSI tools they've ever had access too. What has it gotten us? We still don't have the first clue to the identity of the mastermind. We don't know what their goal is."

"You're just being politically correct," said Clint. "We both know this has to be tied to Islamic jihadists. I mean, the beheadings—"

"Mean nothing," said Mrs. Knowbokov. "Islamic terrorists aren't shy about claiming credit for their work. The silence behind these attacks—"

"—is meant to increase terror," said Clint. "And it's working. If we had a name or a face or some statement of purpose for whoever's behind this, people would have at least a sliver of hope that they could be stopped. By staying hidden, it increases despair, increases fear. It's a clash of civilizations. It won't stop until we have the courage to name our enemy and pin the blame on Islam."

"Clint, you don't know what you're talking about. You're just parroting the right wing propaganda fed to you by that preacher," said Mrs. Knowbokov. "She's a bad influence on you."

"Sister Amy's the main reason I'm not one of the bad guys anymore," said Clint. "She's the greatest influence a man could hope for. Well, her and Jesus, of course."

"You're free to believe what you wish to believe and worship with who you wish to worship," said Mrs. Knowbokov. "But your prejudices don't constitute evidence. We've already identified the dervish who attacked today. He wasn't Islamic. He wasn't religious at all. Until last week, he'd been a physical education teacher at a high school in New Jersey. Nothing about his background suggested any sort of ties to radical Islam, or to any other form of terrorism."

"So he's part of a sleeper cell. Pretending to be an ordinary American until he gets the signal."

"Perhaps. But… what explains the strange ability to split into more than one person? And where are these dervishes getting their weapons?"

"You can order just about anything off the internet," said Clint.

"Not without leaving a record," said Mrs. Knowbokov. "And the metal detector he was stopped at… it's the second one he passed through entering the mall. It's as if his sword materialized out of nothing, just as it fell apart into little more than dust."

"Maybe its magic," said Clint.

She rolled her eyes. "I don't believe in magic. There's some scientific explanation, which makes this all the more frustrating. The world was nearly toppled once by Rex Monday. If he's returned…"

"I thought he was dead?"

"He is. But I was married to a man who built a time machine. We routinely send the team around the world instantaneously by manipulating math. I've come to believe that nothing is impossible."

"Then it's not impossible for us to put a stop to this," said Clint. "We're making progress. People died today, but we both know it could have been a hundred times worse."

"It's only through acknowledging failure that we can move forward. The first step forward is to expand the team. Three heroes aren't enough for the risks we face. I let the PR challenges and the political costs delay my appointing Chimpion to the team. As of now, I'm fixing that mistake."

"She certainly proved herself."

"Yes. But even with her, the team needs to be expanded. Unfortunately, the other candidates who've applied are jokes. Which is why I'm sending you and App to find me a new recruit."

"You want us to find you another chimp?" asked Clint, regretting saying it the second he said it. Mrs. Knowbokov didn't look to be in the mood for jokes.

"No," she said, turning to look at him. "I want you to bring me a dragon."

Chapter Six
Cryptomnesia

"**YOU CLEAN UP NICE,**" said App as Clint walked into the jump room dressed in a dark suit.

"Technically I can't get dirty," said Clint. "Not even grime gets through my force field."

"You know what I mean," said App. "You look good in a suit."

"You could see me in a suit every week if you'd come to church."

"You are terrible at small talk," said App. "Didn't your parents ever teach you it's rude to talk about religion?"

"I never had parents," said Clint. "My father was a supervillain who raped my mother. My mother died in childbirth, probably because my energy fields killed her."

"Again, just terrible at small talk," said App.

"I'll take that as a compliment," said Clint.

App sighed. "Whatever." He adjusted his tie and looked at his reflection in the glass door. He hadn't worn a suit since, like, forever. It was weird to see himself looking so normal. Since joining the Covenant, he spent pretty much every waking hour in costume. This was mostly by choice. He'd died at the hands of a mad supervillain then woke up a superhero. The streaming feeds in his head were filled with people constantly telling him how awesome he was. Now that he had a taste, he couldn't begin to guess why Superman would ever pretend to be Clark Kent. Still, he liked the way he looked at the moment. He looked professional, like someone who could be taken seriously.

Katya came into the jump room and handed each of them a tablet computer. "App, I've already uploaded this into your memory, but figured it won't hurt to go over the highlights of what we've discovered."

App frowned at the notion that Katya regarded his mind as nothing more than rewritable media. Still, as Katya spoke, he was struck with an odd sense of cryptomnesia. His mind filled with memories he had no memory of remembering.

"Our dead ex-con was living under the name Mark Porter," said Katya.

"We have a lead on how he got out of prison? Especially being, you know, dead?"

"We're not focused on that at the moment," said Katya. "It's not important to your mission."

"Not important?" asked App.

Katya nodded. "Mark Porter has lived a quiet, law-abiding life for the last five years. Not even a speeding ticket. His past has nothing to do with the immediate mission."

"Care to explain exactly what our mission is?" asked Clint.

"Mark Porter earned his living as an airplane mechanic. He was good at his job. Two years ago, he met this woman." As she spoke, a photo appeared on the tablet. "Rebecca Henderson, twenty-six, a decorated veteran. She served in Syria repairing helicopters until an accident left her a double amputee. Both legs gone below the knees. She came back stateside and started working in the same repair shop as Porter. Pretty soon, the two of them had a thing going."

"They were romantically involved?" asked Clint.

Katya shrugged. "I'm not going to judge whether there was romance, but can confirm they were shacking up."

"Do people still say that?" asked App. "Shacking up?"

"I'm people," said Katya.

"Yes ma'am," said App.

"Anyway, cutting to the chase... does she look familiar to you?"

"She does now that you've put her picture into my brain."

"I mean does she look like the woman you glimpsed inside the dragon?"

App frowned. "Maybe?" He tried hard to remember what he'd seen. It was his own memory, a genuine memory, and yet it was so difficult to see clearly. Then again, maybe it wasn't his own memory. He'd died. He'd been rebooted, basically rebuilt from scratch. His memories were nothing but synaptic connections, recorded by the belt as a string of numbers, then put back together from subatomic particles. He was a copy of a copy. Was it any surprise his memories were blurry?

"You think she was piloting the dragon?" asked Clint.

"She's our top candidate," said Katya.

"Where, exactly, do you buy a robotic dragon suit?" asked App. "I mean, I'm checking Amazon as we speak and coming up zilch."

"Obviously, this isn't something you can buy," said Katya. "It was almost certainly printed with a 3-d printer capable of weaving carbon fiber composites."

"She built it?" asked Clint

"Or Porter did," said Katya.

"And he did have a dragon tattoo," said App. "Still…"

"Don't forget the steampunk," said Katya.

"What's a steampunk?" asked Clint.

"Seriously," said App. "One day you should visit this century. You might enjoy it."

"Steampunk is all about not enjoying this century," said Katya.

"Touché," said App.

"Steampunk is a sort of aesthetic," said Katya. "A style that imagines advanced technology as it might have existed in the Victorian era."

"That can't be of interest to more than three people in the whole world," said Clint.

"There are conventions where tens of thousands of people show up in period appropriate costumes," said App. "Or period inappropriate, I guess, since no one in the real Victorian era was carrying a plasma rifle."

"Rebecca and Mark went to a half dozen conventions a year," said Katya, flipping through a gallery on the tablet, showing App photos he recognized though it was the first time he'd ever seen them.

"Cute couple," said App. He noticed Rebecca was standing in all the photos. "I though you said she lost her legs?"

"She did," said Katya. "So Mark built her new ones."

Now App could see her carbon fiber lower legs in crystal detail in his mind's eye.

"Building new legs has to take some serious engineering skills," said Clint, looking at the same photo on the tablet.

"Doesn't it?" asked Katya. "That's why we're sending the two of you to talk to her."

"Why the civvies?" asked App. "Why not go in costume and apprehend her?"

"The men who were killed at the airport turned out to be known members of the Johannesburg Syndicate. They're international arms smugglers. If you ever wonder where all the rebel armies that pop up in the third world are getting their guns, it's these creeps."

"So the dragon was fighting bad guys," said Clint. "Maybe she's some kind of fledgling superhero?"

"We'll know more after you talk to her," said Katya. "Mrs. Knowbokov is intrigued by the possibility that there's a technologically proficient vigilante out there who might be looking for an opportunity to fight crime on a higher level."

"Forgive me for being dubious of her good intentions," said App. "She did choose to kill me instead of surrendering."

"Let he who is without sin cast the first stone," said Clint.

"I think it's going to take something a lot harder than a stone to take her down if she doesn't cooperate," said App.

"Which is why Servant's going with you," said Katya.

"Because he's no good at talking, and I'm no good at fighting dragons," said App.

"I would say this has been a successful mission briefing," said Katya.

"I know all I need to know," said Clint. "Let's go. The sooner we're done, the sooner I can get back to Texas."

As Katya left the jump room, App said to Servant, "You're still working on that New Jerusalem crap? You ever think you might be wasting your talents as a carpenter?"

"Jesus was a carpenter," said Clint.

They waited for a few seconds as the atmosphere in the jump room grew chilly, dry, and smoky. Technically, the space machine could grab them from any place and put them down anywhere. The advantage to using the jump room was that the room was manipulated to match the atmospheric conditions of the target site, reducing the vertigo that some people experienced upon transposition.

App blinked and discovered that they'd already arrived. They were standing in what looked like a junk yard. All around them was old farm equipment, hundreds of rusting bikes, and numerous huge gears the size of manhole covers pulled from God knows what sort of heavy machinery. In the center of the field of junk was a small mobile home, sitting next to a metal garage three times the size. Smoke rose from a black pipe in the mobile home's roof, the chimney of a wood stove, App guessed.

"Should we knock?" App asked.

"I don't see why we've bothered wearing suits if the plan was to bust down her door," said Clint.

They walked across the yard, with App keeping his eyes open for a dog. It looked like the sort of yard that would host a Rottweiler. They made it to the door without anything growling at them. The door had a charming sign on it with a hand holding a gun and the text, "Protected by Smith and Wesson."

"I've a hunch she's a Republican," said App. "You should speak her language."

"What makes you think I'm a Republican?" asked Clint.

"All the religion talk?"

"I honestly don't get bogged down in politics," said Clint. "Once you catch a glimpse of God's larger plan, the day to day squabbles just seem petty."

"We aren't ever going to have a conversation that doesn't come back to God, are we?"

Clint smiled as he pressed the doorbell. The doorbell didn't ring.

"They repaired airplanes but couldn't fix their doorbell?" asked App.

"They have a picture of a gun on their door," said Clint, knocking. "Maybe they didn't want company."

They waited for five seconds, then ten.

"She had a late night," said App. "Avenging a lover and killing an internationally beloved superhero. She's probably asleep."

Clint knocked again, harder. "You have x-ray vision, right?"

App shook his head. "You're confusing me with Superman. I can see in expanded spectrums, but there's not enough background x-rays in nature to let me see through stuff. If it was night, infrared would let me see if anyone was inside but daylight more or less blots out that power. Luckily, my eyes aren't what we need here." He frowned. "Though the suit's not really going to put her at ease if she does open the door." He shrugged, then said, "Bat mode."

Instantly, his ears were about eighteen inches tall. He knocked again and turned his head from side to side as the sound echoed through the interior. His brain built a reasonably clear picture of what lay on the other side of the door, though there were a few big voids, probably from padded furniture not reflecting any sound waves.

"I don't see any movement," he said, whispering. "Hear any, I mean."

"Maybe she didn't come home," said Clint. "If she's smart enough to build a dragon, she's gotta be smart enough to get out of town."

App snapped his fingers, then winced. That wasn't a great sound to hear when his aural nerves occupied so much of his brain. "Bloodhound mode," he said.

His ears vanished. His nose tripled in size, with enormous nostrils, and his whole head felt off balance from his enlarged sinuses.

"Did you catch her scent last night?" asked Clint.

"No," said App, removing his tie pin, revealing the small, sharp spike on the back of it. He placed it against his thumb and jammed hard, clenching his jaw. He pulled the pin out of his thumb and watched the bead of red blood well up.

"When she flew away, her claws were covered in my blood," said App. He sniffed the wind, and turned toward the big garage. "She's in there. At least, the dragon is."

"We would have searched there even if you hadn't hurt yourself."

"Yeah, but now we know she's here. Or at least, it's here. We should be prepared."

"Prepared for what?" asked Clint. Because he'd been dumb enough to provide the cue, at that moment the whole garage exploded.

Chapter Seven
I Warned You

APP FOUND IT troubling that he'd become such an expert at getting blown up. If the blast was from a high powered explosive like C4 or Semtex, he never felt a thing. The supersonic shock would pulverize his brain tissues before any pain registered. Plain old dynamite, though, that could really hurt, with the shockwave hitting hard enough to rupture eardrums and organs, but not always hard enough to shut down his brain. The worst type of explosion, though, had to be fuel mixtures, stuff like gasoline or propane tanks going off. The concussive force might stun you, but it wouldn't spare you from the hell flames licking at your flesh.

This was a fuel explosion. He knew it before the shockwave even reached him, as molecules of gasoline filled his still enhanced nose. He felt the punch of the shockwave a nanosecond later, the furnace blast of heat, and saw the flames rolling toward him too fast for him to shout out a command that might spare him from the coming pain.

Large hands grabbed him by the arms and jerked him from his feet. He was spun around as Servant hugged him close, turning his back to the blast. The air was still hot as a furnace but as the flames rolled past he found himself unharmed. A few seconds later smoking bits of red hot shrapnel clattered on the ground around them as what was left of the garage rained from the sky.

"Did she just kill himself?" asked App, peeking around Servant's torso.

"What makes you think she wasn't trying to kill us?" asked Servant.

App shook his head. "If she'd intended to kill us, she would have waited until we actually reached the garage."

"If she reads the papers, she has to know an explosion can't hurt me and you can be rebooted."

"Which is why it had to be suicide," said App, raising a hand to shield his face from the heat of the burning remains of the garage.

"Or escape," said Servant, looking toward the sky. "She can fly, right?"

"Yeah," said App. "But in broad daylight, we'd see her. Although… spectrum mode!"

He studied the thick vortex of oily black smoke whirling into the sky. In infrared and ultraviolet, the full complexities of the swirling air stood revealed. High up the column, he saw a familiar shape, using the smoke to hide her ascent.

"Found her!" said App, pointing. "Though without Skyrider, I don't know what good it's going to do us. She's already out of range of your jumps, and climbing."

"Jumping's not the only option," said Servant.

"You think you can throw me?" asked App.

"It's our best option for taking her alive. I could knock her out of the sky by throwing one of these big pieces of scrap metal at her, but I doubt she'd survive the fall."

"Do it," said App.

Servant did it. The g-force of the sudden acceleration left App feeling faint, but the rush of cool air swiftly pulled him back to alertness. "Sticky mode," he shouted as he raced into the swirling smoke. He couldn't see a thing, but heard the clacking of gears and the whoosh of the dragon's wings. He stretched his arms out blindly toward the sound.

His fingers brushed against something smooth and hard. He stuck instantly, jerked forward by the dragon's movement. The next thing he knew, he was free of the smoke. He discovered his fingers had latched onto the sword-like tip of the dragon's tail, making good, firm, contact with the broad side of the blade. He eyed the razor sharp edge and felt lucky he hadn't grabbed it. Sticky fingers don't do much good once they've been sliced off.

His weight at the very tip of the tail had thrown off the dragon's aerodynamics. The creature was spiraling downwards, beating its wings furiously. It swung its tail from side to side, but this did as much to shift the dragon's body from side to side as it did to toss App around.

The struggle caused the dragon to bank sharply. For a second, App was pretty certain they were heading for a crash landing, until the broad wings once more caught air and their flight leveled out.

"Let go!" the dragon bellowed.

"Not until you land!" App shouted.

"Let go or I'll kill us both!" the dragon cried. "I'm not going to spend the rest of my life in prison!"

"We're not here to take you to prison," shouted App. "We're here to offer you a job!"

"I warned you," the dragon said, folding her wings back and diving straight toward the ground.

"Don't do this!" shouted App.

"I've nothing left to live for!" the dragon wailed.

They were too close to the ground for further discussion. Two seconds before impact App said, "Airhead mode!" Instantly, the skin on the top of his head became elastic, filling with hydrogen, leaving him drifting in the air to watch Steam-Dragon meet her untimely end.

Freed of his weight, the dragon proved far more acrobatic than App would have guessed, as she arched her body and spread her wings to turn her downward momentum into forward thrust, avoiding fatal impact with mere inches to spare.

The dragon started to arc back up toward the sky, but was still barely ten feet off the ground when a white blur streaked across App's field of vision. He knew this white blur well. It was Servant, having shed his civilian suit for his combat attire, moving faster than a bullet, jumping up to grab Steam-Dragon by the tail.

Servant shifted back to normal speed as he dropped to the ground, the dragon's tail still in hand. He planted his feet wide and dug parallel trenches in the field as the dragon lost all momentum. Steam-Dragon landed on her feet and spun around snarling, opening her jaws and blasting Servant directly in the face with a gout of superheated steam.

App had drifted close to the ground, so he called out, "Reset!" As he dropped, the steam cleared, showing Servant completely unharmed.

"We're from the government," said Servant said with the ghost of a grin. "We're here to help."

Steam-Dragon thrust her jaws forward and snapped them shut around his face. The sound of gears stripping filled the air. Bright blue sparks shot out of vents near the back of the dragon's head. The dragon drew her head back, her lower jaw dangling uselessly.

"We didn't come here to fight," said Servant.

"And I wasn't put on this earth to surrender," said the dragon, jumping forward to grab Servant's shoulders with her fore-talons and raking his belly with her hind-claws. Servant didn't even flinch as her claws ran harmlessly along his force field.

Steam-Dragon fell back, whipping her sword-tail forward, jabbing it straight against Servant's heart. The blow bounced off harmlessly.

Servant crossed his arms. "Keep hitting me as long as you'd like. I'm told it's therapeutic."

Steam-Dragon crouched, her eyes narrowing. App was surprised to see she'd bothered to build facial expressions into the machine, but, obviously, the dragon was the work of an artist as much as an engineer.

"What the fuck do you want?" the dragon asked, in a voice balanced between outrage and despair.

"We want to talk," said App, stepping forward. "We know the men you killed last night weren't exactly angels."

"They killed Mark!" said Steam-Dragon. "My life is over!"

"You've had plenty of time to kill yourself if you really believed that," said Servant.

"But you're not put on this earth to surrender," said App.

"Don't throw my fucking words back at me," said Steam-Dragon. "You don't know me."

"You're right," said App. "And you don't know us. Why don't we change that? There a coffee shop around here? Someplace quiet we could go and have a little heart to heart talk?"

"What the hell do you want to know?" she snarled. "You were there last night. You saw me kill those sons of bitches. Since you figured out where I lived, you no doubt know what Mark was up to. You know I went along with it, no matter how fucking stupid I thought he was for getting wrapped up in that bullshit. We all know I'm going to rot in prison for the rest of my fucking life."

"There's really no call for profanity," said Servant.

"We aren't here to arrest you," said App.

"Even though I'm guilty?" she asked, her voice nearly a sob. "Things I've done..."

"The Covenant couldn't exist without forgiveness," said Servant. "Tell us your story. You have my word we'll never repeat anything you say to the police."

"Aren't the Covenant just the same as the police?" she asked. "Don't you operate under some special authority from Homeland Security?"

"We're kind of police," said App. "But we're police who wear tights. We don't follow the same rules."

App braced himself as gears started whirring inside the dragon and it rose up to its full height on all fours. But instead of attacking, a hatch swung open on the underside. A moment later a young woman swung out, dangling in a harness. She matched the picture in his head, mid-twenties, brown hair, skinny build. She wore a Metallica t-shirt dark with sweat and blue jeans that ended at the knees, revealing scarred stumps. She unbuckled her harness and lowered herself to the ground, then reached back up into the dragon's torso and drew down a pair of long black cylinders. App tensed, thinking they might be some sort of rifle, but then she pressed a button and large cups popped out at one end and two arched feet opened up on the other. She placed the cups over the stumps of her legs. There were no straps to adhere them, but they stayed in place as she lifted herself into a crouch, then came forward from beneath the dragon to stand on her prosthetic legs.

"We're thirty miles from the nearest coffee shop," she said. She glanced back across the field to where her mobile home was now in flames. "I'd invite you inside, but it's kind of a mess."

"We can talk right here," said Servant.

She crossed her arms and said through chattering teeth. "Easy for you to say. I'm fucking freezing. There's a Hardee's out on 87. The coffee's crap, but at least we'd be out of the cold."

"Wherever you want to go," said App.

She nodded, then managed something approaching a grin. "Next time I go running from the law, I'll remember to grab a jacket."

App took off his suit coat and held it out to her. "You can borrow mine. This Hardee's you mentioned. It far? Cause we didn't get here in a car."

"No problem," she said. "We can take mine. If it's not on fire."

Chapter Eight
Pure of Heart

APP FELT LIKE a contortionist squeezing into the tiny back seat of Steam-Dragon's old Mustang. Not that Servant looked any more comfortable in the front seat, with his head bent forward and shoulders barely allowing the door to close. The car reeked of cigarettes and the motor practically deafened App when she cranked it up. Putting the car into gear, she said, "Mind if I smoke?"

"Yes," said Servant.

"That's too fucking bad," she said, pulling out a pack of cigarettes tucked into the driver's side sun visor. She took her hands off the wheel to light it despite the fact that they were racing down the bumpy dirt road at breakneck speed.

"You always drive this fast?" Servant asked.

She laughed, smoke pouring from her mouth. "I'm taking it slow to be polite. My daddy was a stock car racer. Never made to the big time, but he raced at just about every small track this side of the Mississippi."

"I remember that from your files," said App. "His nickname was Rebel. You got your start as a mechanic working side by side with him."

"Seems y'all know all about me," she said, reaching the end of the dirt road and peeling out onto the highway. "So y'all know my name is Becky. I'm going to feel stupid calling you App and Servant when we get to Hardees."

"My real name is Clint," said Clint. "Clint Christianson."

"My real name is Johnny Appleton," said App. "But these days everyone calls me App whether I'm in costume or not."

"Now that I know your secret identities, you planning to kill me?"

"No one's killing anyone," said App. "All we want is to talk. And for you to put out that cigarette."

"Worried you'll get cancer?"

"I'm more or less immortal," said App. "I just hate the smell. My first boyfriend smoked. I've hated the stink ever since."

"Huh," she said, eying him in the rearview mirror. "I wouldn't have guessed you were gay."

"That a problem for you?"

"Naw. It takes all kinds, I guess." She cracked her window and flicked out the still lit cigarette.

App craned his neck to watch the cigarette bounce along the highway. Behind them he saw flashing red lights as firetrucks turned down the dirt road they'd exited only seconds before. "This job has really altered my moral compass. I'm more bothered by you littering than I was by you killing those guys last night."

"Those guys had it coming," she said. "They killed Mark. I saw everything."

"You were there?" asked Clint.

"Not in person," she said. "I had a drone tailing Mark. He thought he was all slick, saying he was going to stay up late in the garage to tinker some more on the dragon. I knew he was up to something by his tone. He probably thought I was asleep when I heard the garage door open around two in the morning. I went to the window and saw him pushing his motorcycle down the driveway, getting a long way down the road before he started it so as not to wake me. I sent one of our drones to follow him."

"You just happened to have a drone handy in your bedroom?" asked App.

"Who doesn't?" she said. "Of course, mine are probably a bit fancier than most. We modified an off-the-shelf model to run on a hydrogen fuel cell. The original battery kept it in the air maybe twenty minutes. After we were done, it could fly for two days, and we'd tied the controller into a cell network. We could pilot it anywhere."

"Why would you need to build something like this?" asked Clint.

"Because we could," said Becky as they whipped into the parking lot of the Hardees, tires squealing. "Building stuff together is what made us…" Her voice trailed off. She swallowed hard. "Made us such a great couple."

"Look," said Clint. "We don't have to go in to talk if you'd rather stay out here."

"No," she said, opening her car door. "I'll… I'll hold things together if I'm in public."

"Great," said App. "Because I'll need chiropractic care if I'm in this backseat one minute longer."

Inside, Becky and App ordered coffees, while Clint got a little carton of milk.

"I don't think I've ever seen anyone over the age of 10 drink from one of those little cartons before," App said as they took seats in the back of the restaurant. At mid-morning, the place was nearly empty.

Clint shrugged. "I don't drink caffeine. Or anything with processed sugar. My body is a temple."

"You sound like a Bible-thumper," said Becky.

"I'm a man of faith, yes," said Clint.

"Oh Lord," she said, rolling her eyes. "I can tell right now you and me ain't getting along."

"You a fellow heathen?" asked App.

"More or less," said Becky. "I went to church with an old boyfriend before I joined the army, but was never, you know, born again. Then, in the army... stuff happened."

"Losing your legs?" asked Clint.

She shook her head. "Not just the legs. I mean, you get over to Syria... I wasn't supposed to see combat. I had a safe job in a green zone, far from the fighting. But every day I saw the dead and dying passing through the base on the way back stateside. A lot of guys I worked with said this is a Holy War. But if war can be holy... maybe nothing's holy. If this really is all part of God's plan, sign me up for the opposition, because God's a world class dick."

"You can't blame God for the atrocities of man," said Clint.

"Why can't I?" she asked. "You Bible thumpers give him credit for the sun rising in the morning. If he gets the praise, he also gets the blame."

"God doesn't want violence committed in his name."

"Then He could stop it, right?" she asked. "I mean, that's what makes God a god, isn't it? The power to make whatever he wants into reality by wiggling his fingers. He could turn every gun in the world into dust just by willing it."

"People would just make more guns," said Clint.

"Yeah. But maybe the world would get a few days of peace. And you know what might make real peace? If people over there had enough food. If they had medicine for their kids, and roofs over their heads. I don't know if the war is causing poverty or poverty is causing the war, but God could fix it all, couldn't he? Make the deserts green, make the rivers safe to drink again. Either he chooses not to fix the world, or he doesn't have the power to do so."

"Since you weren't in combat, how'd you get injured?" App asked, wanting to change the subject.

Becky smiled wistfully. "Sometimes, the planes that flew out of our base couldn't find targets. They'd return loaded with bombs. I was at the airstrip the day one of these planes hit the runway with its front landing gear compromised after passing through a sandstorm. There were a hundred different fail safes in place to make certain the bombs wouldn't explode in a crash, but apparently no one had thought of the hundred and first way these things might go off by accident. The crash left a crater two hundred yards across. Thirty people died. I'm lucky, I guess." She shook her head as she said this.

"So you came back stateside," said Clint. "Got a job at the airport."

She nodded. "Yeah. I could have gone on disability, but I knew that I'd kill myself, just sitting around feeling sorry. I needed to keep working. First day on the job, I met Mark. Saw the dragon tattoo on his neck. Told him I used to have one myself… on my left calf." She took a deep breath as her eyes grew distant. After taking a drink of her coffee, she said, "When he found out I was a vet, he asked me how come I didn't have a pair of those fancy computerized prosthetic legs he'd read about on the internet. That led to me ranting about the bullshit I'd had to put up with at the VA. I was a candidate for prosthetics, but the waiting list was, like, two years long."

"That's crazy," said App.

"You don't have to tell me," she said. "But apparently they give priority to soldiers injured in actual combat, and those of us who just have accidents get shoved to the back. So Mark told me I should come over to his place sometime. He said he might be able to build me some legs."

"What qualifies an airplane mechanic to build prosthetic legs?" asked Clint.

"Look, if you think the main tools of a mechanic these days are a wrench and screwdriver, you're behind the times. Every last component of a plane is wired into some kind of sensor. Mark spent as much time on a computer as he did digging around in the guts of an engine. At home, he was part of the maker community. He had all these 3-D printers and knew how to download plans to make just about anything. The technology in my new legs was patented, but some vet in Germany had taken his legs apart the week he got home and posted schematics on the dark web. A few of the computerized components couldn't be printed, but Mark convinced me that since I handled inventory at work, it would be simple to order them then 'lose' them. The inventory system was a real mess long before I got there.

Sure, we'd both have been fired if anyone found out what we were doing. But... he was promising me I could walk again."

She looked out the window as a guy on a motorcycle pulled up. She pressed her lips tightly together as she watched him dismount the bike. She looked back at Clint and said, "And I didn't just walk. I went out dancing with him. I fell in love. I mean, Jesus, how could I not fall in love?" Her eyes grew misty. "Even though... right from the start, I knew something was wrong."

"Wrong how?"

"He kept secrets. There were things he'd tell me that didn't add up. Like, every other week he seemed to get a new 3-D printer delivered, one bigger and better than the last model he'd just had to have. I'm not talking about the little desktop units that cost maybe a thousand bucks. He was getting the same models big auto makers use to fabricate parts. These things cost a fortune. Of course, airplane mechanics bring home nice paychecks. He might have been living in a trailer, but he had more money than anyone I'd ever known. He told me he sold stuff he made on the internet, and did commission work for small companies that couldn't afford their own printers, but, you know, it seemed fishy. One reason I wound up in an office job was that I was good with numbers, and his income just didn't add up to what he was spending on his hobbies. I tried not to worry about it, but then Benjamin Borghart showed up on our doorstep."

"Who?" asked App.

"Benjamin Borghart. Guy had a South African accent. Said he wanted to talk to Mark about fabricating a prototype for a new kind of wind turbine his company was building. They went off to the garage to talk in private. I had a bad feeling about Borghart. Luckily, we had, like, twenty drones sitting around the garage. A few taps of my smartphone and I could hear their whole conversation. They weren't talking about wind turbines. They were talking about guns, and talking like they'd known each other for a long time."

App had information flashing across his retinal monitors. Katya was listening to this conversation, of course, and helpfully providing additional reading material. Borghart's picture appeared in his mind's eye. An ugly bastard, squat and bald, devoid of eyebrows. He had a dozen different aliases and was a wanted man in thirty countries for trafficking arms.

Becky continued: "I confronted Mark. I've never been one to hold my tongue. He told me everything. He said, sure, he sometimes did work for people outside the law. He said that he knew that didn't sound good, but ever since he'd gotten his hands onto his first 3-D printer, it had been like something had woke up inside him. He'd been a good mechanic, but fabricating stuff had triggered whole new areas of his brain. He said he felt like an artist. He felt like a genius."

"A genius who got wrapped up with illegal arms smugglers," said Clint.

She frowned. "Like I said, he had expensive hobbies. His friends on the dark web told him there were safe, easy ways to make money by helping people smuggle stuff across borders. As a mechanic, he had access to part of planes that customs would never search. He told me he never knew what it was he was helping smuggle. He guessed most of it was drugs, some of it was cash, and occasionally he had to hide some really large cargo, which he figured were weapons."

"You were still in love with someone wrapped up in such evil work?" asked Clint.

She scowled at him. "These things were going to move across borders with or without his involvement. Why shouldn't he get a little taste?"

"That's a dangerous line of thinking," said Clint.

"You think?" she said. She sighed. "Look, I knew it was dumb. But... I was bitter. I'd lost my legs in a war that I no longer believed in, and been screwed over by the government that had sent me into harm's way. If the universe wanted to throw a little money our way, who was I to say no? But, it wasn't really about the money. The thing is, I was having fun playing with all of Mark's fancy toys. I've always had a gift for drawing. Now, anything I sketched out, we could plug into a computer and turn into something solid overnight."

"What made you decide to build a dragon?"

She shrugged. "I still can't tell you if it was my idea or his. We were at Dragoncon last year and—"

"Dragoncon?" asked Clint.

"It's in Atlanta each year," said App. "Big science fiction convention. A hundred thousand nerds show up as storm troopers and superheroes. There are people there dressed like you, Clint. How can you not know about this?"

"Probably because I'm not a nerd," said Clint.

"Hardly anyone dresses up as a Stormtrooper anymore," said Becky. "But there's a big community for steampunk. We were hanging out at a bar when we spotted one guy there with a motorized wheelchair decked out as a steam-powered mini-tank. We talked about how we'd have to up our game the next year. And, somewhere around the sixth beer, I'd sketched out a steampunk inspired dragon, and Mark was punching numbers into the scientific calculator on his smart phone figuring out how big the wings would need to be to actually get this thing to fly."

"You built it as a costume?" asked App.

She nodded.

"Then why is it so, uh, lethal?"

She shrugged. "I drew it with sharp claws and nasty teeth because, shit, it was a fucking dragon. We weren't building a giant, fluffy bunny. Mark had just got the equipment to print this ultrahard carbon fiber capable of holding a razor edge, so, there you go, deadly claws. Of course we built carbon sheathes to put over them for when we finally debuted it a convention. Safety first. And, yeah, we could have built it from a flimsier plastic, instead of composite material that's pretty much indestructible. But, you know, once we did the math on the toughness and the weight, and with money being no object… why not be bulletproof?"

"And the steam breath?" asked Clint.

"It was a steam dragon. We thought it looked cool." She shook her head, knowing that didn't explain it all. "I don't know. Mark got a little obsessed about how hot we could make the jet. He wasn't going to be satisfied until he could melt lead."

"So you didn't build this thing planning to fight criminals," said App.

"Don't be an idiot. Me? A superhero? I'm not exactly pure of heart."

"But you went after the men who killed Mark instead of calling the cops," said Clint.

"I… I watched the whole thing unfold with my drone. Mark got into an argument with Borghart about how he wouldn't help smuggle the big drones they'd stolen from the Air Force. It was one thing to move cargo small enough to hide in a suitcase. These were full sized shipping containers. It was too risky. Borghart wasn't taking no for an answer, and when Mark said he wasn't going to help, Borghart explained he'd sent two men to our place to take me hostage until Mark played along. Mark lost his temper and took a swing at Borghart, punching him right in the face. Borghart snapped his fingers and the next thing I knew Mark was dead on the floor and Borghart was telling his men it was time for plan B. They were just going to flat out steal a cargo plane and get out of the country before anyone could figure out what was going on."

"So… what about the two guys sent to kidnap you?" asked App.

"Yeah. That was kind of on my mind as well when I saw headlights coming down my driveway. I slipped out the backdoor and made a dash for the garage as I heard car doors slam in the front yard. I wound up passing through the beam of a headlight and I heard a guy shout, 'She's making a run for it!'" She closed her eyes, looking as if the memories of what came next were painful. "I… I'd really just wanted to hide. In retrospect, Mark had a gun cabinet in the living room. I should have just grabbed a shotgun and charged out the front door barrels blazing. Now that I was in the garage, I didn't have a gun. I did, however, have an invulnerable dragon suit with claws that could cut through sheet metal."

"So you suited up?" asked App.

"And killed them," she said. "Hit the first guy that came through the door with my steam breath. Scalded the flesh right off his face. His buddy came in a second later, turning pale when he saw what was left of his friend. I gutted him with my claws. It was over in, like, five seconds." She smiled, looking proud of her accomplishment, before the reality of what she was saying gripped her and her face fell. "Look, I'm never going to be able to justify what I did."

"You defended yourself," said App. "No one can blame you for that."

"They can if they knew what was in my head and in my heart. It didn't feel like defense. It felt like revenge. These fuckers were part of the organization that had just killed the man I loved. I still had my drone, now tailing Borghart and his men as they headed for the airport. So why didn't I call the cops?" She wore a chilling half smile. "I didn't want these people thrown in jail. I wanted them dead." She finished off her coffee. "I'm not saying what I did was right. When I got home and found the bodies of the first two guys I killed… I more or less knew I was finished. I'd gone past any reasonable claim of self-defense. I was going to go to jail for the rest of my life. Unless people thought I was dead."

"So you blew the place up," said App.

She nodded. "I'm just glad it was you two knocking at the house and not cops. I really didn't want to hurt anyone with the explosion."

"Where were you running too?" asked App.

"No fucking clue," she said.

"What if you didn't have to hide?" said Clint. "We want you on our team."

She rolled her eyes. "You? Want me? To be a superhero?"

"You've got the codename, the costume, and an origin story," said App.

"Since the events of last night involve top secret drones, the feds will bury this story," said Clint. "With our connections, we'll ensure you won't face any legal problems over what happened last night."

"You're crazy," she said.

"You just spent a good part of last night on a murder spree dressed as a dragon," said App. "Crazy is the first qualification for joining this team."

She shook her head, looking as if the idea were the dumbest thing she'd ever heard. But instead of no, she said, softly, "Fuck it. Why not?"

Chapter Nine
Accelerator

CHIMPION WAS UNHAPPY she wasn't sent along with Servant and App on their mission. With her keen ears, she'd listened in on their mission briefing from a distance. She understood that it wasn't a combat mission, and sending a chimp to question a human suspect might make some people uncomfortable. Still, with her experience as Pangea's top spy, a mission to gather intelligence would have been perfect for her.

She tried to assure herself that no slight was intended, but it was unreasonable for the Covenant's logistics crew to refrain from sending her on missions where she might interact with humans. She hadn't joined this team to stand around the headquarters doing nothing. Perhaps it would be useful to demonstrate the full range of her skills.

As it happened, she'd been on-site before Sarah had departed via the space machine to battle the dervishes. While waiting around the island to see if she'd be accepted as a member of the Covenant, she'd taken it upon herself to learn all she could about the workings of the team. Which was a polite way of saying she'd been lurking in the air ducts and eavesdropping on the conversation between Sarah and Katya when they'd discussed the mysterious list of names that Katya wanted Sarah to investigate. Apparently the list had been downloaded into the heads up display in Sarah's helmet, and that helmet had been tossed aside the second they arrived at the medical unit. Jane found the helmet where it had rolled into the corner and put it on. She'd been eavesdropping on Sarah long enough to know the voice commands she used to control the displays. She quickly found the file she sought. Her eyes flickered over the list of names and addresses. Seeing them once was enough—her cybernetic upgrades left her with eidetic memory.

Chimpion dug deeper into the file, wondering what was significant about these people. She pulled up a gallery of photos. The first thing she spotted was that they were all male save for a single woman whose name was followed by the word "deceased." Mark Porter, the dead man App had been called to investigate, was on the list below her, also marked deceased. African Americans and Hispanics were represented in disproportionate ratios to a random sampling of the US population, with less than a quarter of the list being white. The average age of the men was forty-seven. None were younger than thirty.

None had police records, which was odd, since most of the men looked as if they'd had rough lives. Many of them had facial scars, and several had facial tattoos. As an elevated-ape, she was keenly aware of bigotry, so she reminded herself that scars and tattoos could be found on law-abiding people as well as criminals. Still, something about their faces was menacing. She looked at their addresses and found the men were scattered around the country, mostly living in rural areas. None lived in any of the ten largest cities in the US, which indicated their placement couldn't be purely random.

Why had Sarah been assigned to investigate these men?

She took one last look at the file of the only female on the list. The woman looked familiar. She was a dead ringer for the famous televangelist Sister Amy McPherson. Which was interesting, since according to her research, Servant was a follower of McPherson, actively helping her complete her controversial New Jerusalem project. But, despite the resemblance, this was plainly a different person. The woman on the list had died in a car wreck years ago and her file had the gruesome autopsy photos to prove it.

Chimpion removed the helmet and pulled out the smartphone she'd been given when she joined the team. It took her about three minutes to remove the software that tracked her keystrokes and browsing history. She wondered if all members of the Covenant had this software or just her. Now free to go where she wished on the internet, she logged into the secret portal of the Pangean dark web. With the Pangean servers beyond the reach of any human government, people who wanted the ultimate in privacy paid handsomely to use of these networks. A great deal of criminal activity unfolded on these servers. What the criminals didn't know was that, while no human government could see what they were up to, Pangean security forces kept track of everything. It took her less than ten minutes to cross-reference the recorded addresses on Sarah's list against recorded login locations tracked by the Pangean servers. There were several matches, but one small town stood out: Hemlock, Tennessee, population 150.

Chimpion's eyes narrowed as she double-checked the anomalous numbers. Usually traffic passing through the Pangean servers linked to dark web hubs trafficking in pornography, drugs, or stolen financial information. Someone in Hemlock was using the servers a bit more creatively, hacking into computers at particle accelerators all around the world. Seven terabytes of raw research data had been downloaded in the last year. She pondered the mystery man on her list who lived in Hemlock. Neil Wayne Smith, fifty years old. He was a burly man with mismatched eyes and a crooked nose that had plainly been broken multiple times. His ears were also mangled, the telltale signs of a man who'd been in numerous fights. For the last five years, Smith had worked for the state highway department as a sanitation engineer cleaning toilets at rest stops. He had no criminal record, and his only education record was a GED earned in his twenties. Why was a high school dropout interested in particle accelerators?

She scratched the back of her neck. The network information only told her the searches were coming from his small town, not that he was the person reading up on cutting edge physics. Perhaps it was nothing but coincidence. It would have been helpful to know what Sarah had been looking for, or why she was looking.

On the other hand, Chimpion could conduct this investigation with fresh eyes and no preconceptions. This was a chance to show off her skills and earn the trust of the team.

There were controls for the space machine on a terminal in the jump room. She walked over to them and unlocked the workstation with a few keystrokes. She'd heard the technicians punch in PIN numbers for access. With her superior hearing and memory, she'd been able to memorize which keys they hit from the sounds they made. She'd also watched carefully whenever the technicians keyed in coordinates, a fairly simple process. She'd already been doused with tracking nanites that told the space machine the exact location of her body. She typed in Smith's address before anyone had noticed her hack of the system. If anyone complained about her security breach, she'd explain that she'd done it to point out the vulnerabilities in the system. This was her team now. She wanted to keep it safe.

Chimpion tapped enter and the keyboard vanished. She found herself standing behind an old barn, the roof caved in. Chimpion pulled up her hood and hid the lower part of her face with her scarf. She slipped along the side of the barn until she could peek around to orient herself with the image of the property she'd viewed on Google Earth. She spotted the old farmhouse. It was in better shape than the barn, though not by much. Her breath came out in clouds as she breathed in the chill December air. She remembered her years in Russia, fighting in makeshift arenas in old warehouses and basements, places heated only by the assembled crowds turned out to watch two creatures tear each other to pieces. In the arenas, she'd heard every cruel slur that could possibly be thrown at a chimpanzee. Pangeans were thought of as inferior by the humans. Often in combat, that proved to be a valuable advantage. Chimpion shrugged off the memories. She wasn't one to dwell on traumas. When they did arise to a level of nagging awareness, she embraced them as necessary steps on the journey toward being the chimp she was today.

She studied the yard for any clues about Neil Wayne Smith. For starters, he hadn't raked the leaves that must have fallen a month or more ago. Given the general unkempt appearance of the house, it seemed plain to her that the man who earned his living cleaning toilets had no compulsion to keep his own living space tidy.

She crept closer to the house, watching for any sign of movement. She suspected Smith lived alone. At this time of day, he was probably at work. She felt certain she'd be able to move freely within the house to investigate her target.

Dogs started barking. She pressed herself against the back of the house. It was hard to tell if the barks were coming from inside or from the front yard. It took only a few seconds to deduce that the barks were coming from outside, and that at least three dogs were now racing around the western side of the house.

She leapt up and grabbed the ledge of the second floor window and climbed to it as the dogs rounded the corner. They were the biggest dogs she'd ever seen, looking like an unholy mixture of a Doberman and a bear. They were making enough noise that people in the neighboring county probably wondered what was going on, which wasn't exactly conducive to stealth. She pulled out her blowgun. *Phht, phht, phht,* the drugged darts flew swiftly, hitting the three dogs on the first try. Given their size, it would take several seconds for the tranquilizers to take hold. Best to move ahead with her mission.

The second floor window wasn't locked, but it was warped and painted over. Stealth again went by the wayside as she banged on the frame to inch it up enough to slip inside. She found herself in a room full of cardboard boxes thick with dust. It didn't look like anyone had been into this part of the house in years.

Outside, the dogs' frantic barking took on a drunken, slurred quality. One by one, they fell silent. In the new stillness, she heard a humming from the lower floors, a steady, faint whir, like a fan running. Maybe a furnace? Unlikely. The house felt colder inside than it had outside, and heat on the lower floors would have warmed this level even if there were no vents. Perhaps it was a loud compressor motor on a refrigerator?

She opened the door to the room slowly. The air of the hallway was just as musty as the closed off room. No footprints could be seen in the dust on the floor. She spotted a staircase and moved toward it, gazing down into the lower level of the house. The whirring was louder now. Definitely not a refrigerator. She moved down the steps carefully, not making a sound, no small feat given the warped and wobbly boards. She found herself in a living room that had the same abandoned, dusty air of the upstairs space. There was a television that looked like it dated from the 1960s, the screen covered with grime. Maybe Smith didn't live here after all?

Chimpion pushed open the door to the kitchen and finally saw evidence that the place was inhabited. The kitchen was huge, taking up a third of the main floor. Smith's entire life seemed confined to this room, since there was a single mattress on the floor in the corner with a mound of wrinkled blankets. Dirty dishes filled the sink. Clothes were piled onto the kitchen table. The atmosphere of the kitchen had an unpleasant odor, a mix of rotting onions, sweaty socks, and stale urine.

She spotted mail on the counter. She leafed through the envelopes. Nothing but junk mail and a tax bill for the property.

She sat on a chair, her chin resting on her knuckles as she wondered if she was on—what was the human idiom?—a wild goose chase. Smith plainly wasn't the person stealing raw research data from particle accelerators. If she'd returned from a rogue mission with valuable intelligence, she'd have been praised for her initiative and daring. Now, she'd be a joke. A dumb animal. She squeezed her fists tightly as the old taunts echoed in her memories.

Chimpion looked around. She still heard the whirring sound. It was coming from below. The house obviously had a cellar. She knew she'd wasted enough time here already, but felt like she should at least see what was making the noise. It grew louder as she approached a narrow wooden door. She tried to open the door and found it locked. She crouched and studied the lock. Given the antique condition of the rest of the house, she expected to find a skeleton lock, but instead the door was locked with a brand new deadbolt. She pulled lock picks from her utility belt and set to work. The lock was well made, not something purchased off the shelf at Walmart, but a high security model with a half dozen internal features to thwart lock picks. Even with her superior dexterity and enhanced senses, it took her a full minute to open the lock. Behind the door, she found a staircase heading down into unexpected brightness.

She descended carefully, brow furrowing deeper as each step revealed more of the room below. The cellar wasn't some dark, musty, dirt-walled space. Instead, it was walled with white ceramic tiles, spotlessly clean. The air was nearly devoid of scents save for a vague hint of ozone. Overhead, stark florescent lights made the room painfully bright.

All around the room were computers, neatly arrayed on metal shelves and wired together with tightly bound, color coded cables. An array of monitors were mounted on the far wall, the screens filled with streams of numbers, white against a black background.

She swiftly spotted the source of the hum. In the center of the room, bolted to the floor, was a centrifuge. It was an industrial model, much bigger than the ones she'd seen in hospitals used for separating blood. On a previous spy mission, she'd caught sight of a centrifuge used to process uranium. This was similar in design though a little smaller. Was Smith working on a bomb in his basement?

Fortunately, she didn't have to identify the functions of all this equipment for her mission here to count as a success. She suspected the support team for the Covenant would be very interested in her discovery. She took out her phone and started snapping photos.

She froze as she heard footsteps on the kitchen floor above.

Chapter Ten
BAM! POW!

ONE MAJOR FLAW in Chimpion's plan became sharply evident. Since she'd used the space machine to travel here without permission, no one at the Knowbokov Foundation was standing by to retrieve her. She'd also been assured that the phone she'd used to communicate with the base would work anywhere on the planet, but that apparently didn't apply to basements in Kentucky surrounded by a few hundred computers generating electromagnetic fields. Since the stairs up to the kitchen were the only way out of the cellar, she suspected her stealth mission was about to turn into a combat mission.

Chimpion positioned herself directly beneath the steps and pulled out a shuriken. It was likely that the person had noticed the drugged dogs. She'd pulled shut the door to the cellar, but hadn't locked it, so if someone came down the steps they'd be coming down in a heightened state of awareness, looking for an intruder. Her one chance was to throw the shuriken as the person came down the steps, aiming it to land behind the furthest shelf of networked computers. The person would naturally look in that direction. In the brief instant of distraction, she could slip onto the steps behind them and silently bolt to freedom.

The footsteps above belonged to someone quite heavy, moving with a halting step. This matched Smith's physical profile. The steps moved near the door, then away, toward what she believed was the exterior door in the kitchen that led into the backyard.

The lights in the cellar dimmed for a few brief seconds. The centrifuge behind her changed in pitch, taking on a strained sound. A curious hissing noise, like loud static, sounded from above. This was followed by the deep-throated barking of large dogs.

"Get 'em!" a deep male voice cried as the door to the cellar was thrown open.

The big dogs thundered down the steps, one, two, three of them from the sound. Her nose wrinkled. From the scent, it was the exact same dogs she'd drugged. They should have been out for hours.

While she might possibly have slipped past a man, she knew she had no real chance of evading dogs. Their claws clicked and clacked as they skittered on the white tile floor at the foot of the stairs. She pulled out her dart gun. Unfortunately, she wasn't Batman. Her utility belt had a finite amount of space. She only carried four darts, and had already used three. Still, better to fight two dogs than three. She stepped out from beneath the stairs.

By now the dogs' nails had found purchase in the grout between tiles and they'd wheeled to charge her. With a puff, the closest one was darted, straight in the tip of his nose. The pain made him startle, lose his pace, and the two dogs behind him leapt over.

Chimpion took her nunchucks from her belt. The dogs seemed to hang in the air, moving in slow motion. She aimed her blows carefully, striking each dog in the back of the skull, using just enough force to stun them, not kill them. In Russia, she'd often had to fight dogs. She'd always taken care not to permanently injure them. They weren't to blame for attacking her. They were being abused and manipulated by humans, fellow victims of their cruelty, and she couldn't condemn them to death. The two dogs fell limp. The third, drugged dog, lunged for her. She knocked it aside with her nunchucks, then hit again when it recovered, though its movements were showing signs of sluggishness. Following the second blow the dog stumbled sideways, then sank down, its facial muscles sagging as the drug reached its brain.

The lights dimmed again. Once more, the centrifuge whined and there was an unidentifiable hiss in the room above. She heard more footsteps. A second large man had joined the first.

"Who's down there?" a deep voice shouted. "Come out where I can see you!"

She didn't answer.

"I have a gun!" he shouted.

She'd assumed he would.

"Should we go down?" asked the voice who was calling down the stairs.

"Not just the two of us," said the same voice.

The lights flickered again, the centrifuge spun faster. Once more, the hiss. Above, more footsteps. There were perhaps four men in the kitchen now. The only reason she couldn't be certain was that all of their footsteps sounded exactly the same, as if all four men had identical weights, gaits, and footwear.

"This is your last chance!" the voice shouted down. Only, now the voice seemed to be in stereo, as if two men with identical timbres of voice had called out the words at the exact same time.

"You go," said the same voice.

"Why should I go?" said the same voice.

"The only reason I brought you here was to go."

"You didn't bring me here. I brought you here!"

"I brought you both here," said another, identical voice. It sounded like someone arguing with himself, but her ears could pinpoint that the speakers were standing a few feet apart.

"I'll go," said the same voice.

Chimpion again hid in the space under the stairs as a large man started down the steps, followed closely by another. Reaching into her belt pouch, she placed a respirator between her lips and slipped a pair of goggles over her eyes. She took out a pepper grenade. She still hoped to get out of the house without resorting to lethal force. Even if Smith was up to something unlawful, she hadn't come here to be his executioner.

Taking a deep breath as the man's feet reached the tiles, she stepped from under the stairs and tossed her grenade. It exploded in a fiery red cloud that engulfed two men carrying shotguns. She furrowed her brow as she caught sight of their faces just before the cloud hid them. Both men were the man she recognized from the photo. It wasn't that they were siblings, or even identical twins. They had exactly the same faces, with precisely the same fight-scarred features. Their clothing was identical down to the stitching, as were the guns they carried.

She dodged back under the steps, knowing what would happen next. Sure enough, twin shotgun blasts clapped like thunder as the men fired blindly. Along the far wall, several of the networked computers were blown into fragments by the buckshot.

She leapt back out and *BAM! POW!* Two solid swings of her nunchucks dropped the men where they stood. She raced up the steps toward a third identical man standing in the door. She saw his body tense as he aimed his shotgun, but her digital reflexes allowed her to reach the top of the steps and push the barrel toward the ceiling half a second before the shot went off. She drove her head hard into his gut, knocking him backward, then rolled over his falling body into the kitchen where she found another duplicate. She leapt toward him, aiming her fist right at his chin, but wound up passing through empty air as he shimmered. The hissing noise she'd heard before was quite clear now, a sound like static mixed with light rain on a tin roof. She landed and spun around, to find that her single foe had split in two. Then these two split in two. The four turned toward her, shotguns raised.

"Chimpion!" the Smith's said, in unison.

"Drop your weapons and I won't hurt you," she said.

Two of the four Smiths shimmered and split.

"Don't!" said the two Smiths who hadn't split in perfect stereo. "You'll trip the circuit breakers!"

"She can't dodge if we all shoot at once!" said the four Smith's who'd split. As if to demonstrate, they all pulled their triggers.

They were wrong, of course. Chimpion had ample time to read their body language and by the time fire spit from the shotgun barrels she'd leapt behind the kitchen table and knocked it forward. Against actual bullets, the Formica tabletop and dirty laundry wouldn't have been much of a shield, but it was more than adequate to absorb the cloud of buckshot. She rose with shurikens in each hand and whirled to face the two Smiths who hadn't fired their shotguns, throwing the razor sharp stars with precision aim into the wrists of the trigger hands. Both men dropped their guns.

Before the guns even hit the floor, she was in motion, her nunchucks whirling, as she leapt from Smith to Smith. Five seconds later, they were all flat on their backs, groaning.

"What manner of being are you?" she asked, grabbing the nearest Smith by his shirt collar and jerking him upright.

"A man!" he shouted. "And you're an animal who needs to be put down! What right do you have to break into my home? What right did you have to hurt my dogs?"

"Your dogs will be fine," she said. "Though I'd love to know how you woke them up. They should have been drugged for hours."

"I don't have to tell you anything!" he snarled. "I don't have to tell you—" at that moment, there was a loud POP and the whirring in the basement came to a sudden halt. The static hiss sounded again, louder than before, but distorted, like it was playing backwards.

The Smith she held vanished. She spun around toward the only heartbeat she still heard in the room.

A solo Smith was sitting next to the overturned table, clutching his bleeding wrist. His eyes were red and swollen, with tears down his cheeks, as if he'd been hit by the pepper spray. Through clenched teeth, he grumbled, "I warned them they'd overload the damned breakers."

"What kind of machine are you using to do this?" she demanded.

"Why should I tell you anything?" he said, his tone balanced between defiance and despair. "I didn't do a damned thing to you. Why did you break into my house?"

"I've proof that you've been stealing data from particle accelerators."

"So?" he asked. "Most of that data would be made public in a few months anyway. I just wanted an early glimpse. They really send goddamned ninja apes out now to beat up a guy for some harmless hacking?"

"Considering that you have the power to split just like the dervishes, I'd say you're guilty of more than hacking. And that centrifuge in your basement didn't look so harmless," she said. "What are you refining? Uranium?"

He snorted. "They say Pangean's are smart. That's not a centrifuge. That's my time machine."

She stared at him, not sure of what to say. Her first impulse was that he was crazy, but what if a time machine could explain the duplicates? The same man, overlapping in time, again and again?

"How did you get smart enough to build a time machine?" she demanded, grabbing him by the collar. "For that matter, how do you know anything about physics at all? I've seen your files. You flunked out of high school. Now you're analyzing particle data in your basement?"

"I was a late bloomer." He met her stare, his spine stiffening.

"It's a bit of a leap to go from cleaning toilets to building time machines."

"I don't owe you an explanation," he said, wiping the pepper tears from his cheek with his uninjured hand. "On the other hand, fuck it. What good will it do you to know? Last year, I was watching a porno about a time traveler who goes back and bangs famous broads in history. Instead of looking at all the tits, I noticed that the time machine in the film was just a bunch of random wires and flashing lights glued to an old cedar chest and... I dunno. Seeing a time machine that plainly couldn't work somehow put a picture in my head of one that might, though not forward and backward in time, but sideways. Time is forever branching into infinite alternate universes. Some of those alternates had to be very close to ours in vibrational resonance. I could see it all worked out in my head on how I could make a machine that would let the timelines overlap in the same space for a little bit. It would be a lot easier to clean bathrooms if I had four or five of me ready to push a mop. So, I started building."

"Alternate universes? Vibrational resonance?" she found herself mystified, but not at the concepts. "How does a man with no formal education even know such terms?"

"How does a goddamned chimp know enough to stand here and ask me stupid questions?" asked Smith. "Go fuck yourself. I've said enough. You going to arrest me? Cause I'm looking forward to telling the sheriff about how you broke in to my house, vandalized my stuff, and poisoned my dogs."

"You'll be talking to someone with a lot more authority than the sheriff," she said. "What's your connection to the dervishes?"

"Nothing," he said.

"You expect me to believe it's just a coincidence they seem to be using the exact same tech as you to duplicate themselves?"

"Why not?" he said. "I put plans up on the net. Got feedback from anonymous commenters. There are dozens, maybe hundreds of people who could copy my work."

Her enhanced senses were superior to any lie detector. If Smith was attempting to deceive her, he was better at it than most humans. She pulled out handcuffs and chained his uninjured wrist. She felt certain she hadn't actually wounded him, but had instead hit one of the doubles. She definitely hadn't hit him with the pepper gas, but it lingered on his clothes, and his eyes were still watering. It was as if the injuries to the doubles transferred back to the original when the machine failed. Perhaps this mission had given her some useful intelligence after all.

Chimpion pulled out her phone. With a sigh, she noticed that a single grain of buckshot had punched into it, killing it. She eyed a dirty yellow phone next to the refrigerator.

"Aw," said the man as she picked up the phone. "Don't get your monkey germs all over the mouthpiece."

She was tempted to lick his phone but, honestly, she didn't want his germs either. He cursed loudly as she dialed, but his words didn't bother her. She was too busy wondering if she was going to be fired by the Covenant on the same day she'd been hired.

Chapter Eleven
Chimp Power

A FULL DAY PASSED before Chimpion was summoned to the conference room following her debriefing on the Smith mission. She waited patiently for an hour past the time she'd been told to show up. She suspected the wait was intended to cause her anxiety. If so, it wasn't working. She sat cross-legged on the floor, eyes closed, engaged in deep, conscious breathing. She was as relaxed as she'd ever been when the door finally opened.

Skyrider glided into the room in a standing posture, her feet not touching the floor. Her arms were crossed and her face was a stern mask. They locked eyes. They stared at each other in silence for at least a minute, perhaps two.

"What the hell were you thinking?" Sarah said at last.

"I am happy to see you've recovered so quickly," said Chimpion. "Given the seriousness of your injuries—"

"Are you trying to make me feel guilty?" Sarah snapped.

"No."

"Because it feels like it. You saved my life. I acknowledge that, and I'm grateful. But you think that gave you permission to go off on a rogue mission?"

"I've operated on my own most of my career," said Chimpion. "I wasn't aware I needed permission to investigate a lead."

"You don't know how badly you've screwed things up," said Sarah. "We sent Servant and App back to Smith's house. His basement's been stripped bare."

"It was secured by local authorities before I left," she said.

"Let's just say the local authorities haven't covered themselves in glory."

"Given how much equipment Smith possessed, it had to be moved with a van or a truck. It should be a simple matter to—"

"Don't tell me how to conduct an investigation," said Sarah. "Yes, there are a hundred different ways we might be able to retrieve his equipment. But we wouldn't need to be searching for it all if you hadn't tipped off his friends that we were aware of him."

Chimpion nodded. "Fortunately, before I departed the scene, I planted a tracker on the back of one of the computers in case it went missing. I planned to—"

She was cut short by Sarah dropping a small black object onto the table. It bounced like a ball bearing, making a rapid clicking noise as it came to a halt. "This tracker? It was sitting on top of his stove."

"Oh," said Chimpion.

"You were reckless," said Sarah.

"I took a risk aware of the possibility of failure. I weighed it against the possibility of success."

"What, exactly, was going to constitute success for you?" asked Sarah. "You couldn't have known the significance of the names on that list."

"You're correct. I didn't. By investigating the target you'd been assigned to study, I'd hoped to impress you with my initiative and ingenuity."

"Instead, you've proven yourself to be duplicitous and secretive, going behind our backs. You've obviously been spying on us, learning how to use the space machine."

"I reported my enhanced senses and eidetic memory when I was hired. This team had to be aware that if I see or hear things even casually, I can recall them in perfect detail."

"Which makes you an excellent spy."

"I think so."

"Who sent you to spy on us?"

Chimpion shook her head. "No one. I came here to be part of your team, not to betray it."

"You think what you did yesterday constitutes being 'part of our team?'"

"Your criticism is valid. I failed. Which is why I've decided to leave the team."

"You're leaving before you give me the chance to fire you?"

"It saves us both a certain amount of awkwardness," said Chimpion.

Sarah said nothing. Once again, a long silence developed as they stared at one another.

"Like this awkward moment," said Chimpion, rising. "May I use the space machine to return to Pangea?"

"Only if you insist on quitting," said Sarah. "I didn't come here to fire you."

"You didn't?"

"You screwed up yesterday. But you also stopped a dervish attack without breaking a sweat, and saved my life while doing so. You have the potential to be a great team member, and the Covenent needs manpower."

"Chimp power," said Chimpion.

"What?"

"I can't provide manpower, only chimp power."

"You seriously want to argue about the words I'm using?"

"I'm just engaging in mock disagreement," said Chimpion. "From observing Servant and App, I assume that increases feelings of camaraderie in your species."

"Let's leave ragging on each other to the guys," said Sarah. "So, you'll stay?"

"I want this job more than I can express," said Chimpion.

"Why?" asked Sarah.

"To fulfill the mission of the Covenant, of course," said Chimpion. "During the recruitment interviews, Servant said that he believes if one has the power to do good, then one had the obligation to do good."

"Yeah," said Sarah. "That's what it says on our website. Now drop the bullshit and be honest. Why are you here?"

"Why don't you take my words at face value?"

"Unlike Servant, I'm not an idealist. I don't believe anyone is obligated to do good. I'm not even clear much of the time what good even is. From our very first missions, the Covenant has crossed a lot of ethical boundaries. We once ambushed Pit Geek and Sundancer in the parking lot of a mall, in broad daylight while the place was packed. A lot of people died because of that choice. We knew the risk. We also knew the risk of letting them escape."

"But they did escape," said Chimpion.

"Yes. I've had to live with the guilt of making that choice. You can see why I'm not going to fire you for making similar errors in judgment."

"If you're not an idealist, why do you do this?" asked Chimpion.

Sarah stepped down from the air. She grabbed a chair and slouched into it. "I became a superhero to spite my father."

"This was when you were the Thrill?"

"You know about that?"

"Is it supposed to be a secret? The Pangean intelligence forces keeps files on all super powered humans. We know your father was Nicholas Knowbokov, and that he trained you to be a superhero."

Sarah rolled her eyes. "Trained? More like coerced. I didn't want to be a superhero. When I finally gave in, I did so only to prove how dumb the idea was."

"That is the worst origin story ever," said Chimpion.

"I won't argue that."

"He's been dead a long time. Why are you still doing this?"

Sarah shrugged. "I ask myself that a lot. This isn't my whole life. I have... this will sound corny... I have a secret identity."

"App said he thought you might. He says you don't really hang around the island much when you aren't on missions."

"I have a life outside of being Skyrider," said Sarah. "I run my own business. And... I'm married." She crossed her arms over her chest. She looked reluctant to say more, but took a breath and continued. "It's the life I've wanted. A normal life. I found a man who loves me as me, not as some comic book poster girl come to life."

"What does he think about your life as Skyrider?"

"He doesn't know," said Sarah.

"He doesn't know? How can you explain—"

"All the time I'm missing? I'm a charter pilot. I can always say I got a last second call from a client. Plus he works crazy hours, so even before I went back into the crime-fighting biz, we'd sometimes go days barely seeing each other."

"So what made you come back to this life?"

Sarah sighed. "Sundancer. I thought she was dead. Hadn't heard a peep out of her for seven years. I'd fought her a couple of times as the Thrill. Ordinary cops didn't stand a chance against her. I couldn't just let her run amok. I couldn't return as the Thrill, but with a helmet and some armor I decided I might get away with being Skyrider to fight her."

"So why did you keep being Skyrider afterwards?"

"A man who means a great deal to me told me once that keeping the world running takes work. Civilization doesn't just take care of itself. It takes a lot of people bringing their talents to the table to make it hum. My particular talent happens to be that I can fly."

"And control people with your voice," said Chimpion.

"No longer," said Sarah. "I had surgery to remove that power. No regrets. It brought me nothing but grief. I don't think anyone ever hated me because I could fly. But people still curse my name because they think I could control people's minds."

"It's not just the Pangean's that believe Skyrider and the Thrill are the same person. Aren't you frightened that the Thrill's old enemies might come hunting for Skyrider?"

"I kind of hope for it. My other life, my real life, is priceless to me. You don't know how many nights I used to lie awake wondering when someone would discover my secret and tear my world apart. But Skyrider makes a nice decoy. If an old enemy wants to come hunting for me, they'll come here instead of... where I normally live."

"Where do you normally live?"

"Sorry. It's not that I don't trust you, but I've said too much already. Secret identities require some secrets," said Sarah. She shifted in her chair, leaning toward Chimpion. "Okay. I've told you my real reasons for being on the team. What about you? Why the hell would you want to be a superhero?"

Chimpion didn't answer quickly. Finally, she said, "I... have not had... an easy life."

"I know about your past," said Sarah. "You literally had to fight to survive. You were treated as a slave, hurt for people's amusement. That you've stayed sane is a testament to your toughness."

"That toughness makes it difficult for me to reveal any of my weaknesses. So, please appreciate the effort it requires to say this to you: I'm lonely."

"I understand," said Sarah.

"When I returned to Pangea, I thought my years of loneliness would come to an end, but I found no true companionship among the Pangeans. Chimps are more sensitive than humans to non-verbal cues. We pay close attention to body language, facial expressions, even to odors. The ritual of grooming helps chimps form intimate, non-sexual bonds that humans can never understand. It's something far deeper than friendship."

"I'll take your word for it."

"I was excluded from that bond. I'm part machine. My digital nerve centers make me fast and fluid, but they also distort the simplest of gestures in ways that other chimps find uncomfortable. I don't even smell like a natural chimp anymore. My biology was altered to accommodate my cybernetic implants. I'm an alien among my own kind."

"Then you saw us on the news," said Sarah.

Chimpion nodded. "Yes. A team of elevated humans, and I, an elevated chimp. I hoped, perhaps, for a bond between us that is far stronger than any I could form with a Pangean. Among you... perhaps I'll no longer feel lonely."

"I'll do all I can to make you feel welcome," said Sarah. "Well, not anything I guess. No grooming."

"Is a handshake acceptable?" asked Chimpion.

"How about a hug instead?" said Sarah.

Chimpion wrapped her arms around Sarah, knowing she'd earned her whole-hearted trust. She couldn't wait to tell her real employer that phase one of the mission had been successful. It was safe to move forward with the second phase of the plan.

Chapter Twelve
Debacle

KATRINA KNOWBOKOV LOOKED from the window of her penthouse office atop the skyscraper that housed the Knowbokov Foundation. It sat in the center of an island she owned, amid a small and growing city of people she employed. From her vantage point, she could see the airfield in the distance, crowded with planes as reporters from all around the world journeyed to the island. Beyond the airfield, the blue sea stretched to the horizon. She stared at the horizon for a long time, thinking about all that lay beyond. The whole world, seven billion people, all of them her responsibility.

Her late husband Niko had been a powerful telepath. He'd been able to look into the mind of anyone, and willing to leverage the secrets he found into financial and political power. He hadn't been motivated by greed but by altruism, a desire to end the suffering of mankind, eliminating poverty, disease, hunger, crime, ignorance, and war.

Katrina had killed him, shooting him in the back after a mysterious stranger gave her a hood that concealed her mind from Niko's thoughts. She'd believed in her heart that her husband was a man of good intentions. But those good intentions combined with his telepathy had transformed him into a monster, willing to blackmail world leaders, willing to turn his own daughters into super-soldiers in his ongoing wars, and willing, almost without a thought, to enslave Katrina. With his telepathy, he'd known her every thought. He'd known how much she'd come to hate him. He'd also known how trapped she was, how she didn't even have the relief of leaving him, since with his powers he would always still be following her mentally. His solution had been to offer her mood altering pills that would help her deal with her dark thoughts. He treated her hatred of him like a disease, not as the product of his arrogance and immorality.

She'd never faced trial for killing Niko. There was no one with the authority to arrest her. Niko had seen to it that their private island was a sovereign territory, outside the law of any nation. Killing Niko had been an act of passion, but also an act of compassion. His powers were too great for anyone to possess. He'd allowed himself to play God so long he'd come to believe he truly was God, inventing a ridiculous story of how he'd destroyed the old universe and replaced it with one created in his image. He suffered because of this, believing he'd created all evil in the world. With a single bullet, she'd put an end to his fathomless pain, and saved the world from the manipulations of a mad puppet master.

For a year, she'd mourned, torn between unspeakable guilt and indescribable relief. Her daughters were gone. Amelia had fled to Mars, Sarah had simply fled, assuming a series of false identities until she vanished somewhere in Mexico City. Katrina had been utterly alone, though hardly without company. A man with her husband's wealth commanded a legion of lawyers, accountants, and business managers looking after his assets. They came to her daily but she never paid much attention to their words. She signed the papers she was told to sign, and retreated back into her mourning. The fact that she hadn't been defrauded because of her negligence was a final gift from Niko. As a telepath, he hired only people who were completely honest.

Two days after the anniversary of Niko's death, Katrina had finally awakened to her new reality. One of the accountants, Sonya Kirkland, was discussing the merger of two of the corporations she owned, one a company that produced solar panels, another a company that produced batteries. Merging the two companies would streamline the operations of both. Two hundred jobs could be eliminated, and the savings would lower the cost of the batteries, boosting sales. Katrina had been born in Soviet Russia, fleeing the country with her parents when she was twelve. Her parents had been enthusiastic capitalists in their new American homeland, growing wealthy in real estate in only a few short years. Katrina had enjoyed the luxury that came with their wealth, but sometimes struggled to reconcile it with the lessons she'd learned in school in her childhood. When Sonya mentioned the elimination of two hundred jobs as a benefit of the merger, she found the notion unsettling. Sonya's manner was utterly professional. She spoke of eliminating the jobs in the same tone she used when discussing restructuring the debt of the two companies. Both were just numbers to Sonya, but only one of the numbers moved Katrina to wake to her responsibilities to make a wise choice. For context, she'd asked how many people worked for the companies owned by her husband.

"Owned by you," Sonya had corrected her, gently.

"Yes," she said. "How many people work for me?"

Sonya cleared her throat. "I... don't have a firm number. My portfolio is your renewable energy holdings, but of course you have major holdings in fossil fuels as well, plus other raw materials like iron. You're a major shareholder in most car companies, several airlines, and... then of course, there's your media empire. The drug companies. And the banks. Oh, and insurance." She picked up a pen and tapped it against a pad, before jotting down numbers. "There are the hospitals you run around the world. Your agricultural holdings. The software corporations..." She furiously scribbled numbers as she spoke in absentminded tones. Her pen stopped for a minute, then she said, with growing enthusiasm, "Telecoms! Oh, and your defense contracts. And, of course, there are people who work directly for the Knowbokov Foundation."

Sonya fell silent, looking as if she were searching for more numbers. Then, without speaking, she pulled out a calculator and started adding things up.

"I'm making a lot of assumptions," she said, apologetically. "I mean, we can do an actual audit if you want an accurate number. I doubt I'm too far off, though. Walmart is normally considered the largest private employer, and their workforce is about two and a half million. Your assets dwarf Walmart, though not many people are aware of that. Mr. Knowbokov structured his ownership of various companies to be, um, opaque. I would say at a minimum you employ twenty million people."

Katrina's mouth slowly opened.

"You look surprised at that number," said Sonya.

Katrina struggled to regain her composure. "My father... before he died, he made a fortune in real estate. He once told me he employed fifty people. The number impressed me. It seemed like a giant responsibility, to have the fate of so many people resting on his decisions. Twenty million?"

"At least," said Sonya. "Possibly twice that many."

Katrina sat silently, unable to truly fathom the number.

"Mrs. Knowbokov, you're the richest woman in the world," Sonya said. "Scratch that. You're quite likely the richest person who's ever lived on this planet, period. You remember how your husband could snap his fingers and the leaders from a dozen nations would drop everything and fly to the island? You're an economic giant."

"Oh," Katrina said, softly. Sonya studied her face and Katrina had no clue what she found there. Her ability to feel and think had been pinned beneath the heel of a monstrous fact.

Her husband, the puppet master, had turned the entire world into his puppet theater. She'd been left holding the strings.

Sonya looked puzzled as Katrina's face settled into a quiet calm. From her numb grief, she awoke into sharp and awesome responsibility. Her wealth gave her the power to make the world a better place. She would do so without the ethical quandaries created by her husband's telepathy. She'd had sufficient willpower to kill the man she'd once loved. Could remaking the world require more will than that? Nothing had been wrong with Niko's dream of ridding the world of poverty, of pollution, of pain. Now, it was her task to see that dream fulfilled. She vowed to do so as a woman, as a mother, as a sane, reasonable, humble person, and not become a monster. Her first decision was to allow the merger. Paying the displaced employees a full year's salary and health benefits while they found new jobs eased her conscience to some degree.

These thoughts were front and center in Katrina's mind as she turned from the window and walked to her private elevator. Stepping from the car in the subbasement, she was met by her closest aides. They accompanied her to a private room with one way mirrors that overlooked the newly refurbished press room. The Covenant was about to hold a press conference. She wouldn't participate, of course. She'd never been comfortable in the spotlight. She took great care that her name seldom appeared in the press. Perhaps fifty people in the world knew that she was the person who had founded and funded the Covenant, and applied the political leverage to get her team legally sanctioned by the US government.

Her husband had also valued his secrecy, despite refusing to allow anyone else their own. She sometimes worried that she was more like him than she wanted to admit. Her husband had turned his own daughters into warriors, and now she had persuaded Sarah to return from her exile and become leader of the Covenant. But who else could she have trusted in that role? Clint seemed sincere in his religious conversion. She had no doubt he strove mightily to be a good man. Still, he had spent his youth as a notorious supervillain, and even now his mission briefings revealed a man who sometimes seemed a bit too quick to lose his temper. App, while intelligent and charming, lacked a certain… gravitas. She found him too easily distracted by frivolous trivia.

Sarah had been her only option. This wasn't simply the prejudice of a mother. Indeed, her motherly instincts were to keep Sarah removed from the entire enterprise. However, the CEO within her, the calculating puppet master, knew talent when she saw it. Her daughter had what it took to lead, and she trusted her.

Now it was time to put that trust to the test. The ballroom was packed with reporters. The stage was decked out in red, white and blue, looking like a politician was about to announce a run for president more than a setting for the formal introduction of the Covenant. The team wasn't secret, having revealed itself to the world during the hunt for Sundancer. Still, while there had been press opportunities over the last few months, this was the first time the full team would be present for an actual press conference.

In a carefully choreographed reveal, the lights in the pressroom were darkened for one, two, three seconds. As the lights came on again, the Covenant stood on the stage. Though stand wasn't the precise verb for Sarah. As Skyrider, she was hanging in mid-air in front of her colleagues. Spreading her arms, she slowly descended to take her place in front of the podium. She removed her mirrored helmet. Since Sarah was still concerned about concealing her identity, and wearing an obvious mask wouldn't engender trust, Sarah had been fitted with seamless prosthetics to alter the lines of her cheeks, and made use of a nanoparticle dye that allowed her to change her hair color to black with the press of a button in her glove. The voice modulators she'd used when first returning to action had been fine-tuned so that no one would suspect her voice was altered. Her contacts at the Department of Homeland Security had pressured her to let Servant be the team spokesman, but his few previous times speaking to the press had proven him to be less than comfortable in that role. This was Sarah's debut as the new spokesperson.

"Thank you all for coming today. For viewers at home, thank you for watching. My name is Skyrider. Behind me stands the Covenant. You've been seeing us in the news lately, not always in the most positive light. As you're all aware, the world is facing new dangers. We're here to face those dangers, while taking all possible steps to not become dangers ourselves. We thought it was time to let you know who we are and why we're fighting to keep you safe. Let's jump right into introductions."

One by one the members of the Covenant stepped forward. Servant, born with a mutation that causes his body to generate powerful force fields. App: A social media superstar with the ability to download a hundred different powers on demand. Steam-Dragon: A military veteran turned inventor who fights crime with 3-d printed armor. Chimpion, the hero of Pangea, defender of all species.

Skyrider stepped back to the podium after Chimpion took her bow.

"Eight years ago, in a terrible tragedy, a battle between enhanced humans destroyed the city of Jerusalem, causing the deaths of hundreds, the displacement of millions, and robbing the world of priceless cultural treasures. Those of us on this stage played no role in that tragedy. We lived quietly among our neighbors, friends, and family, hiding our abilities, content to live ordinary lives. But last year, when the superhuman terrorists Pit Geek and Sundancer went on a rampage, Servant, App, and myself approached the government with an offer to help. We've remained active since, and many of you are no doubt aware of how Chimpion and I recently fought a dervish in New York. The world faces threats from individuals with dangerous abilities. We have the power to stop them. That power means we have a duty to act. Unlike the previous superhumans who claimed to fight for good, Rail Blade and the Thrill, we're acting in full cooperation with lawful authorities."

Katrina Knowbokov watched the conference unfold from her mirrored room. Her daughter handled the presentation well, despite her insistence on wearing her mask. Sarah had always been the rebellious daughter, and still was making choices Katrina found mystifying. But, as the formal public spokesperson for the Covenant, she was flawless. She and App were the perfect media team. App's social media charm made him a celebrity, which was all that was needed to win over a sizable segment of the public. Sarah's task wasn't to be popular. It was to be serious, to face the scrutiny of a skeptical press. Finally, the time came for questions.

"How can we take your stated mission of fighting terrorism seriously when you've included a Pangean on the team?" a reporter from Fox News asked. "Pangea openly embraced Sundancer and Pit Geek, the most dangerous terrorists the world has yet known."

Sarah batted the objection aside easily. "An independent commission has established that the government of Pangea had no knowledge that Sundancer and Pit Geek had been brought to their country by a criminal syndicate. Pangea is a young nation, going through many growing pains. Unfortunately, the press is always ready to report of the misdeeds of individual Pangeans, while overlooking the vast majority of peaceful Pangeans who long for better relations with the rest of the world."

A reporter from CNN asked, "In the wave of recent dervish attacks, members of the Covenant have responded after people are already dead. Thirteen people died in the most recent attack. How do you think they would respond to your claim that you have the power to stop these attacks?"

Sarah looked appropriately grim. "Every one of those deaths haunts all members of this team. We're taking every available measure to locate the source of the dervishes. In the meantime, the Knowbokov Foundation continues to provide public spaces with the latest technology to alert us to these threats the second they happen. With each attack our response time has gotten faster."

The CNN reporter followed up: "By use of your so-called space machine."

"Correct."

"A technology you refuse to share with law enforcement or the military."

"It's still a risky technology in the early stages of development," said Sarah.

"A technology that could save lives in the hands of law enforcement," said the reporter. "No matter how quickly you respond, there are only five of you. There are thousands of officers who could be on the scene if you shared this technology."

Katrina Knowbokov's jaw felt tight. This again. Every conversation she had with any world leader kept coming back to the space machine. The governments of the world lusted for the technology, but also feared it. Widespread implementation would utterly disrupt the world economy. Worse, Rex Monday had proven the technology could be weaponized. Sarah needed to change the subject.

Sarah moved on from the CNN reporter, but now the press pool had a fever. Why wasn't the Covenant doing more? Why not share all their advanced technology? They claimed to be under the authority of the United States government, so why was their base on an island outside US jurisdiction? As the questions grew more hostile, Katrina surveyed the rest of the team. Steam-dragon, of course, was inscrutable behind her mechanical persona. Chimpion appeared unperturbed. App, however, looked anxious. Servant's neck muscles kept growing sharper in relief as the hostile questioning stirred up his anger. Fortunately,

Sarah kept her calm through all of it, and finally said, "You've brought up a lot of excellent issues and I hope we've been able to address them to your satisfaction. Right now, though I'm afraid we've no more time. Our press office will be glad to answer additional questions submitted in writing. Thank you all for coming."

As she stepped from the podium, all the reporters shouted after her, tossing out questions they hadn't gotten to ask. Their voices were a jumble, but one question seemed to break through:

"Servant! What's your relationship to Sister Amy McPherson and her New Jerusalem boondoggle?"

Servant whirled back to the podium, his face red. The edges of the metal podium bent as he grabbed it and leaned into the mic. "What is wrong with you people? We aren't the bad guys here."

"Why should we believe you're the good guys?" someone shouted. "Care to respond to the allegations that you used to be the supervillain known as Ogre?"

"I won't dignify that with a response," said Servant. "You're like a pack of hungry dogs, looking to tear into someone. Why aren't you hunting down the dervishes? See if they bother answering your questions."

"So your moral standard is simply to be better than the dervishes?" someone else called out.

Servant trembled, opened his mouth to speak, then closed it. He took a deep breath. "We all know what part of this press conference you're going to be leading with tonight," he said. "So as long as you plan to broadcast my words, broadcast these: To whoever is behind the dervishes, you're a coward. Attacking shopping malls? Amusement parks? This is your holy war, killing unarmed women and children? You want war? Fight a warrior. You know where the Covenant's headquarters is. Let's see you attack this place. Think of the propaganda battle you'd win if you caused even one death. But you won't attack us, because you're cowards. With every day that you refuse to face us the whole world will know."

Without another word, Servant spun and disappeared in a white blur.

Katrina Knowbokov pressed her hand against the glass of the booth to steady herself. What a debacle.

Chapter Thirteen
Intentionally Cryptic

"WHAT THE FUCK was that?" Sarah screamed at Servant the second they left the stage.

"Watch your language," said Servant.

"Oh, you're going to hear much worse than that before I'm done with you. That press conference was meant to make the world trust us. How does you acting like a madman— "

"It's Sister Amy," said App. "That's what set you off, isn't it?"

"No. They were hostile the whole time. They were determined to crucify us when they came into the room."

"But it wasn't until they mentioned New Jerusalem that you snapped," said Sarah. "Look, it's never been great PR that you're worshiping a woman some people think is a cult leader."

"You're embarrassing yourself," said Servant. "Christianity isn't a cult. My association with Sister Amy is probably the best PR this team has."

"Oh lord," said App. "Look, I try to live and let live, but how on earth can you not see that she's a fraud? She's raking in millions with this New Jerusalem scam."

"That money is feeding refugees," said Clint. "I've been there, working the bread lines. That money pays for buildings, which I know, since I'm helping build them. If you ever left your social media bubble and went out into real world maybe you'd know what you're talking about."

"Guys," said Steam-Dragon, "Maybe y'all should take a deep breath."

"This might not have been a complete disaster," said Chimpion. "Lashing out at the press isn't exactly an unpopular position."

"Forget the fucking press," said Sarah.

"Language," said Clint.

Sarah poked her finger into the middle of Servant's chest. "You issued a direct challenge for the goddamned dervishes to attack us in our headquarters."

"We should have done this weeks ago," said Clint.

Sarah threw her hands into the air. "We couldn't do what we do without the support of the Knowbokov Foundation. These are the last people in the world you should be drawing a target around! How do you think they are going to feel hearing that you're using them as bait?"

"You'd prefer to trade the lives of strangers for the lives of the people we work with?" asked Clint.

"I'd rather not have anyone being attacked."

"Good," said Clint. "I agree. I'm sick of playing defense. We don't know who's behind these attacks. We don't know how the dervishes stay under the radar of law enforcement, how they get armed, or how they get their inhuman strength and speed. We're always fighting them in situations where we have to kill them in order to defend innocents. We need to take one alive if we ever hope to get answers. Fighting them on our home turf is our best hope of doing this."

"You really think they'd be dumb enough to take the bait?" asked Steam-Dragon.

"I mean… whoever is behind this has to be pretty suspicious about you practically inviting them to attack," said App.

"It would be high risk to attack us," said Chimpion, "but also high reward. Now that Servant has issued his challenge, if they attack us on our turf and kill even a single person, they'll prove there really is no defense against them."

"How can we even know that's something they want to prove?" asked Sarah. "We don't know their motives."

"We know their motives," said Clint. "Islamic terrorism. Holy war."

"The dervishes haven't been Muslims," Sarah said, exasperated.

"Why waste Muslim lives when they can brainwash infidels?" asked Clint.

"It doesn't matter what their ultimate motivation is," said Chimpion. "They're terrorists. No matter their underlying mission, the goal of every attack is to spread fear."

"Then it's up to us to be whatever the exact opposite of a terrorist is," said App. "They spread fear, we spread hope. We're hopists."

Steam-Dragon gave a low chuckle. "If you're right, then damaging us is a double win for them. Great idea, Servant."

"I can't tell if that's sarcasm," said App.

"I honestly don't know," said Steam-Dragon. "I mean, if they do attack and kill people, I think Clint will go down as one of the dumbest motherfuckers ever to breathe. But if we actually captured one before they hurt anyone… I dunno. Maybe he's a genius."

"He's not a genius," said Sarah. "Look, I get your frustration. Not being able to track down the dervishes is driving me crazy. I'm even open to the idea that we might somehow be able to make a target they can't resist and try to trap them. But what could possibly possess you to do this on live TV without running it past anyone?"

"I did run it past someone," said Clint. "I talked with Sister Amy about it a few weeks ago. I mean, not the part about losing my temper in a press conference, but about how I might make myself a target. As a superhero who's publicly a Christian, attacking me has to be a great temptation. Sister Amy said she couldn't tell me what to do, but said I should trust what the Lord puts in my heart."

"Then you should have told them to attack New Jerusalem," Sarah said, crossing her arms across her chest. "You had no right to put every member of the staff here in danger."

"Everyone who works here is part of the Covenant, even if they sit behind desks instead of going out in the field," said Clint. "They voluntarily signed on to fight on the side of good. They have to know that makes them a target of evil. The innocent people in a mall or a park or a bus station, and the carpenters and workers at New Jerusalem, they've done nothing to make themselves a target. To me, the choice seems clear."

Steam-Dragon sat on her haunches. "He's starting to make sense. I hope they do attack. Servant's right. We can totally kick their ass."

"Don't be cocky," said Sarah. "I've got more experience fighting supervillains than any of you and the dervishes nearly killed me. You don't think they learn from past mistakes? You don't think our enemies can adapt, switch tactics, and take us by surprise?"

"Maybe you're scared because they did whip you," said Steam-Dragon.

"You're out of line, Steam-Dragon," said App. "Sarah's courage isn't up for debate. On the other hand, Clint's little speech isn't really a topic of debate, either. He said what he said."

Chimpion nodded. "It's too late to worry about whether or not it was a good idea. It's time to start planning how to respond if they do attack."

"Actually, we've been planning that for a while," said Sarah.

"What do you mean?" asked Clint.

"The Knowobokov Foundation isn't putting all this anti-dervish tech out into the world without implementing it over the whole island. We have ferro-sensitive fields feeding us data for a two mile radius around the building. They couldn't sneak a sword into the perimeter if they tried."

"Not a steel one," said Steam-Dragon. She flexed her claws. "You can, however, print a razor sharp edge hard as diamond using carbon composites."

"True," said Sarah. "But you guys work here. You've got to have noticed all the cameras."

"I've even spotted the hidden ones," said Chimpion.

"These aren't cameras you can buy off the shelf. They see way beyond the visual spectrum, and are backed up with cutting edge software. It's a pretty good bet the dervishes have an elevated heart rate and body temperature when they launch into their attacks. Our cameras will trigger an alarm if they detect a sudden spike in metabolic activity."

"No matter how advanced they are, all cameras have blind spots," said Chimpion. "For my morning warmups I like to travel from the basement to the roof without using the stairs or the elevators. I've got my time down to three minutes, nine seconds. Not a single camera has spotted me."

"I need to talk to the prisoner," said Servant.

"Smith?" said Sarah. "He's off limits."

"Why? You've gotten no information from him," said Servant. He cracked his knuckles. "Give me five minutes and he'll tell us everything we want to know."

"You don't think we've got people a bit more skilled at interrogation than you are?" asked Sarah. "Smith's a dead end. He genuinely doesn't know how the dervishes got their hands on his tech."

"Any answers yet on how a janitor suddenly got smart enough to build a time machine?" asked Chimpion.

"Hmm," said Steam-Dragon, before Sarah could answer. "Maybe there was some kind of smart virus going around. I mean, don't get me wrong, Mark was smart the day I met him, but around the time we started building my suit he, like, jumped to mad scientist genius. It was exciting, but also kind of scary."

"And I still want to know why he was a perfect match for a man who died on death row over a decade ago," said App.

"What?" asked Becky.

App looked sheepish. "Sorry. That might have been something I should have mentioned to you earlier. Or, maybe it's something I shouldn't have mentioned at all."

Chimpion looked at Sarah. "Speaking of things that shouldn't be mentioned, you told me not to tell about the list. I've held my tongue, but no longer."

"List?" asked App.

"When Becky's partner was killed, Sarah was given a list of names to investigate. There was some connection between Mark and Smith."

Sarah's lips pressed tightly together.

"What's the connection?" asked App.

"You know something about Mark?" said Steam-Dragon.

"Why didn't you tell us?" asked App.

"I don't have any firm information," said Sarah. "There's no point in spreading rumors and speculation."

"Then only share facts," said Chimpion. "You have a list of names. We know at least two of them have turned into technological geniuses in less than a year. What's significant about the people on the list? What connects them?"

"I'm not at liberty to say," said Sarah.

"You gave me a speech about the importance of being a team player," said Chimpion. "Now it's your turn to be part of the team."

Sarah shook her head. "Look. What I know… it's crazy. I don't mean it sounds crazy. I mean it's just flat out beyond anything that passes for sensible, believable, actionable information."

"You do know that you're saying this in the presence of a dragon, a talking chimp, Christian Superman and a guy who downloads superpowers off the internet, right?" asked App.

"Yes," said Sarah. "And I also know that every word we're saying is being streamed to the Knowbokov Foundation thanks to App. The information is classified. I tell you, and, boom, I'm in jail."

"We all have security clearances," said Servant.

"She doesn't," Sarah said, looking at Steam-Dragon.

"It's just because the paperwork isn't finished," said Steam-Dragon.

App said, "Privacy mode."

Sarah looked at him.

"I don't stream everything I do to the servers," said App. "Back when the lab techs first put me back together, Mrs. Knowbokov approached me about being part of her team of superheroes. I was disoriented from having missed a whole decade of my life, and more than a little disturbed to find out that the belt was recording everything I saw or heard or felt. One of the things I demanded in exchange for joining the team was privacy when I needed it."

"But our conversation was being recorded until you put yourself in privacy mode?" asked Steam-Dragon. "That's kind of creepy. I didn't know I had to watch what I said around you. You need a warning label, man."

"If we do truly have a moment of privacy," said Chimpion, "It's time to be a team player, Skyrider. What do you know?"

"You don't think it's going to look suspicious that we were talking about how I couldn't talk just seconds before App turned on his privacy mode?" said Sarah.

"It's definitely going to be suspicious," said App. "So even if we all start talking about the weather, our handlers are going to suspect you spilled the beans, though of course we'll all back you up and say you didn't. Why not go ahead and tell us?"

Sarah sighed. She looked at Servant. "You know who I really am, don't you? I got this vibe from you that you figured it out the first day we met."

Clint nodded. "I did fight you and your sister a few times before Rail Blade took me down. You've plainly had some work done on your face, but I still recognize your body language. And the way Mrs. Knowbokov fawns over you, especially when you were injured… I don't feel like she works hard to keep your secret."

"Are the two of you being intentionally cryptic?" asked Steam-Dragon.

"I haven't always been Skyrider," said Sarah. "I used to be… the Thrill."

"That mind control bitch?" said Steam-Dragon. "The terrorist who helped destroy Jerusalem? The fucking alien?"

"I never controlled anyone's mind," said Sarah. "I was witness to the destruction of Jerusalem, but I certainly didn't cause it or condone it. And I'm as human as you."

"I don't consider that something to brag about," said Chimpion.

"I mean, I was a little girl when all this happened," said Steam-Dragon. "But I remember all the news stories. I remember people talking. And later, when I was serving in the Middle East, everyone said all the trouble over there started when you and your sister destroyed Jerusalem."

"How ignorant of history can you be?" asked Sarah. "The problems in that area are a lot older than either of us. But I don't need to explain myself to you. I'm not to blame for the city's destruction. I could tell you the whole story, but it's long, and it's not really what you want to talk about."

"I lost my legs fighting in a war they say you started," said Steam-Dragon. "So maybe I do want to talk about this, yeah."

"Fine. Another time. Right now, you want information on Mark. You want to know what connected him to the mad scientist in Kentucky. You want to know why his name was on my list."

"All this is true," said Steam-Dragon.

"So here's the truth," said Sarah. "My name is Sarah Knowbokov. My mother is Katrina Knowbokov, the woman who funds this team. And my father… my father was Nicholas Knowbokov, and he's the reason for that list of names. I'll tell you why, but you aren't going to believe me."

Chapter Fourteen
Genius Psychopaths

"MY FATHER WAS a telepath," said Sarah.

"Dr. Know," said Servant. "Rex Monday was obsessed with destroying him when he tried to recruit me."

"You met Rex Monday?" asked Sarah. "Why didn't I know this?"

Servant shrugged. "I didn't see how it was even remotely relevant. It was a long time ago, a different life. I was twelve years old and already a major player in the Detroit underworld. Rex Monday turned up one day. Told me he was my true father, that all his children had superpowers, and that he wanted me to join him to fight some sort of revolution."

"Your dad was a supervillain, Servant?" asked Steam-Dragon.

"I was a supervillain also," said Servant. "People called me Ogre back then."

"I remember a TV movie about Ogre," said Steam-Dragon. "Wasn't Ogre killed by Rail Blade?"

"Not killed. Something worse," said Servant. "She trapped me in a giant solid iron cube. My protective fields kept me from being crushed, and fed me just enough energy to keep me alive."

"Your fields give you energy?" asked Chimpion. "Not the other way around?"

Servant scratched the back of his head. "I'm probably not explaining it right. The eggheads around here have tried to break it down for me. I couldn't eat enough calories in a lifetime to generate a force field strong enough to protect me from a bomb blast. Apparently, my cells tap into something called vacuum energy. This energy is everywhere in the universe, and can keep me alive without food, water, or rest."

"Are you immortal?" asked Steam-Dragon.

"We're all immortal," said Servant. "We just won't be spending eternity in these bodies."

"Great," said App, shaking his head. "You've given him a chance to preach."

"You'd welcome the sermon if you'd been through what I've been through," said Servant.

"How did you escape the iron cube?" asked Chimpion. "I've seen pictures of it. It's huge."

Servant nodded. "Rail Blade retrieved me after a few years so her father could dissect me. They had no idea I was still alive. For that matter, I had no idea I was still alive."

"What do you mean?" asked Chimpion.

"The whole time I was trapped inside the cube, I didn't know what had happened. I couldn't move. Couldn't breathe, or see or hear anything. There were no smells. The only thing I felt was heat and pressure. I genuinely believed I'd died. I thought I was spending an eternity in Hell for my sins."

"Wow," said Servant. "No wonder you found religion."

"Yes," said Servant. "And religion found me. Since Rail Blade didn't expect me to be alive, she was unprepared for me lashing out blindly, knocking her out. She had pulled me out into a sewer, so I still couldn't see a thing, but on mindless, animal instinct I started walking. It had to be the hand of God moving me that night. I staggered from the sewers, dazed, blinded by the faintest light, deafened by the rustling of wind through grass. The three years of isolation had crushed my will, shattered my mind. Blind and dumb, I stumbled on a sidewalk. While I was on my knees, a hand touched my shoulder, and the first voice I'd heard in three years asked if I was okay. I looked up and there was an old black woman standing before me. She had a Bible in her hand. It turned out to be a Sunday evening, and she was on her way home from church. She took me to her home and fed and bathed and clothed me. Her kindness was unlike anything I'd ever experienced. When Rail Blade finally tracked me down a few hours later, I surrendered to her peacefully. I'd seen hell, and told myself I'd do whatever I needed to do not to go back ever again."

"But you weren't in hell," said Steam-Dragon. "It wasn't God that put you in that cube. It's like me waking up in a hospital and finding my legs were gone. It feels like hell. It feels like the punishment of God. But if you stop and think it through, there was no God, just dumb luck and dumber politicians that got us wrapped up in a war that couldn't be won. I think some philosopher said hell is other people. That seems about right to me."

"There has to be a hell," said Servant. "Whether it's a lake of fire or simply a cold, silent void, I don't care to discover. Without hell, there could be no ultimate justice. Some men are beyond the reach of human law. Adolf Hitler died without ever facing trial for his actions. But what human punishment could possibly suffice to punish his crimes? His execution wouldn't have balanced the scales. Without Hell, we'd be living in a universe with no underlying justice."

"That's a great argument coming from a guy who just confessed to being a supervillain," said Steam-Dragon. "Ogre killed a lot of people. You never faced your day in court. And now, what, you'll avoid hell because you've made nice with God? You can murder people, peddle dope, and God gives you a free pass?"

"There is no free pass," said Servant. "But there is grace. Who I was isn't as important to God as who I am. That's why it's called being born again. Ogre won't get into heaven. Servant will."

"How did this turn into theology hour?" said App. "We're completely off topic. What's up with that list of names, Sarah?"

"Right," she said. "Like I said, my father was a telepath. But maybe a better word to describe his powers is omnipath. He could read anyone's mind anywhere, at any time. He claimed it took enormous effort just to hear his own thoughts, and not be overwhelmed by the constant roar of the collective minds of the entire world. This is one reason he dedicated his life to making the world a safer place, doing all he could to eliminate hunger, disease, criminality, and war."

"Well he sure did a great job of that," said Steam-Dragon.

"Yes," said Sarah. "He did."

"I was being sarcastic," said Steam-Dragon.

"That wasn't lost on me," said Sarah. "But what if my father got closer to his goals than I was willing to give him credit for when he was alive? By any objective measure, there are fewer wars today than at any time in the past. The death toll in the World Wars numbered in the tens of millions. Today, a fraction of that total die in the various global conflicts. The same is true of hunger. There are millions of people underfed, but nothing like the mass starvation of earlier centuries. In most advanced nations, your odds of dying from a contagious disease is relatively low, even with drug resistant bacteria."

"So, what, your father gets the credit for these things?" asked Steam-Dragon.

Sarah shook her head. "I mean, obviously, the roots of this progress, like the discovery of vaccines and antibiotics, have their origins before my father was even born. Still, my father devoted a great deal of his time, money, and influence to help make the world a place of greater safety and fairness. Which brings us to the list. The people on this list helped my father think through the world's problems."

"Really?" asked Steam-Dragon. "So Mark was, like, an advisor to your father?"

Sarah shook her head. "Mark was a murderer. So was Smith. Both were executed via lethal injection. The same was true with all the other names on this list."

"What do you mean, executed?" said Steam-Dragon. "Mark was alive. And maybe he cut some legal corners at the end of his life, but he definitely wasn't a murderer."

"Mark wasn't a murderer, no," said Sarah. "But the man he used to be was. He had a long history of violence against the women in his life that culminated with him killing a lot of people in a fit of rage."

"You don't know what you're talking about," said Steam-Dragon.

"Even if you do," said App, "I don't see how a guy like that was going to help your father. Especially since, like you said, he was dead."

"Here's where things slip into crazy," said Sarah.

"You've sounded so sane up until now," said Steam-Dragon.

"My father had, shall we say, unofficial agreements with several wardens. If the prisoner put to death had no family, my father would take possession of the body. He'd also arrange that the lethal injection wasn't quite 100% lethal. By any ordinary test, the inmate was a corpse. But enough of a spark of life was left that my father could revive the bodies."

"Why the hell would he do that?" asked Steam-Dragon.

"My father had a lot on his mind," said Sarah. "So he... uh... he borrowed some extra minds."

"Borrowed?" asked App.

Sarah took a slow breath before diving into the truly weird part. "Dad put the prisoners into these big, life-sustaining tubes of goo. Then he would use his telepathy to take over their minds, wiping away all traces of their old personality, devoting each prisoner's brain to thinking through problems. He just... just had too many thoughts to keep them all in one... one head." She shook her head. "Christ, even I can't quite believe it. But, I swear, it's true."

"And Mark was one of these prisoners?" said Steam-Dragon.

Sarah nodded.

"But... he wasn't abusive. He was a good person! Gentle and sweet and—"

"He did have a hobby of building battle armor with razor sharp claws," said App.

"If these people were all murderers, what were they doing out on the streets?" asked Chimpion. "Why weren't they back in prison?"

"You did hear the part where I said they'd all been executed, right? Legally, these people were dead. On a purely technical sense, after my father died there was no legal framework to return these people to prison. There's also the complicating factor that what my father was doing to these people wasn't exactly legal. The wardens who cooperated with him were operating outside the law. Some of them had been blackmailed by my father. Some bribed. Others persuaded by reason. Others were… persuaded by me."

"With your mind control," said Steam-Dragon.

Sarah nodded. "It wasn't really mind control, but, whatever. Before I had my vocal chords surgically altered to rid myself of the power, my voice emitted a subsonic frequency that stimulated the pleasure centers in people's brains. Agreeing with me gave people a sense of extreme euphoria. A thrill, as it were."

"You had your voice surgically altered?" asked App.

"I didn't want the power anymore," said Sarah. "My power didn't affect everyone. My sister and father were immune. So were a lot of the villains we fought, thanks to some technological assistance from Rex Monday. But ordinary people… even my own mother… I could and did manipulate without a second thought. When I was younger, I enjoyed the power I had over other people. I mean, I don't think I was cruel. I didn't cause people to do terrible things like jump off buildings. But, you know, I'd, occasionally have people, uh, I guess I had them… lend me stuff."

"You'd rob them by asking for stuff when they couldn't say no," Steam-Dragon translated.

"You could put it that way," Sarah said, crossing her arms. "It's not like I didn't feel guilty afterward. But the temptation was always there. But the worst thing about my powers was… anyone I talked to wound up liking me."

"What a terrible cross to bear," said Steam-Dragon.

"It was," said Sarah.

"From now on, when I'm being sarcastic I'm going to raise my hand," said Steam-Dragon.

"But it was terrible. Can you imagine going through your life without a single genuine friend? Without any hope of actual love, since anyone you met was attracted to you not for who you were, but because your voice was some sort of sonic opium?"

"It can't be as terrible as having someone who does love you then finding out that person was some sort of zombie psychopath," said Steam-Dragon.

"But when we turned the prisoners loose, they weren't psychopaths," said Sarah. "If Mark seemed like a decent, loving man, it's because he was. After my father died and we released the prisoners from the goo tubes, they all had profound amnesia. None of them had any memories at all of who they once had been. To make their brains more compatible with his own, my father had removed their capacity for aggression. He'd wiped away any and all traumatic memories or unhealthy desires. With most of these criminals, that meant he'd wiped away their entire personalities. They were all taken to a special hospital that deals with traumatic brain injuries. None of them ever showed any signs of remembering their old lives. They all accepted that they'd been involved in accidents that had given them amnesia, and didn't fight when we assigned them new identities and careers following careful assessments of their intelligence and aptitudes. None of them were geniuses, but some of them, including Mark, were suitable for highly skilled, technical labor. It wasn't too hard to place them in jobs in the real world. Social workers kept close tabs on them, and all of them had regular meetings with psychiatrists and doctors. For years, the prisoners have lived quiet, unremarkable, law-abiding lives."

"And now two of them turned into mad scientists in a matter of months," said Chimpion. "I think it's well past time we paid a visit to the other names on the list."

"The Knowbokov Foundation is way ahead of you," said Sarah. "The second you got back with your report, Chimpion, we contacted the FBI and requested they check in with the rest of the names on the list. At least, the ones who were still alive. One of the prisoners died a few years back in a car accident. Which, uh, I should probably mention, has sort of a tangential relationship to you, Clint."

"How so?"

"You know that the pastor you follow, Amy McPherson, isn't the first famous preacher in her family."

Servant nodded. "You're talking about Delilah McPherson."

"Where have I heard that name?" asked Steam-Dragon.

"You would have been only a child when Delilah McPherson was in the news," said Sarah. "She had a big ministry down in Florida and was a pretty famous author writing books about how if you gave your money to God, he'd give it back and make you rich."

"But that's not why you would have heard of her," said App. "You'd have heard of her because she used to get her older parishioners to make out their wills to her, then, because she wasn't the patient type, she'd hasten them along to their graves. By the time they finally caught her, she'd poisoned thirty-two people."

"Delilah's failings were what led Sister Amy to launch her own ministry," said Servant. "But what does this have to do with the list of names?"

"Delilah was one of the death row prisoners my father revived. She died in a car wreck after her release, though. It really doesn't have anything to do with our current situation, but as long as I'm telling you everything, I want to tell you everything."

"Great," said App. "But what happened when the FBI went looking for our zombies?"

"Long story short and terrifying, all the other names on the list have vanished. At pretty much the same moment Chimpion arrested Smith, everyone else on the list ditched their jobs and families. Witnesses say that they stopped talking in mid-sentence, turned glassy eyed, and walked away."

"When were you going to tell us about this?" said Chimpion.

"When my mother told me I could," said Sarah.

"Seriously?" asked Steam-Dragon. "You're a grown woman and you still need your mother's permission?"

"Think of it as payback," said Sarah. "From as soon as I could talk, I could make my mother obey my every command. Imagine having this sort of power during your teen years. If I could live my life over again, I'd do all I could to spare her from the trauma I put her through. Now that I'm back in her life, I'm not blind to the new dynamic between us. She enjoys manipulating me. She has power over me and she's not afraid to use it."

"What power does she have?" asked Chimpion.

"Aside from mountains of money and armies of super-scientists?" said App.

"She knows who I really am," said Sarah.

"So do we now," said App. "You're Sarah Knowbokov. You just told us."

Sarah shook her head. "Servant's not the only one who was born again. After I went into hiding following the destruction of Jerusalem, I drifted around a few years, using my powers to live comfortably. Finally the guilt and self-loathing became so great that I decided to have surgery on my vocal cords. It worked. My ability to control others was gone. In the aftermath, I took a new identity. I have an entire life outside the Covenant. It's... astonishingly banal. I move about in small town anonymity. I've got friends, loved ones, a community. Most importantly, I have a husband. He doesn't have a clue who I used to be. Then, the day Sundancer and Pit Geek robbed that bank in Richmond, I got a phone call from my mother. With her resources, she'd known where I was for a long time. She told me that the Knowbokov Foundation had already recruited two superhumans to hunt for Sundancer, but she wanted me to lead the team. I hung up the phone. Ten seconds later I got a text letting me know that if she could find me, someone worse might figure out my secret as well."

"Especially if she told them," said Steam-Dragon.

"She's never made that threat," said Sarah. "She says she just meant she didn't know how much of Rex Monday's old network was still active. If Sundancer and Pit Geek were back, hunting down their old enemies might be on the top of their list. Still, even though she never tells me she'll tell other people, she mentions my vulnerabilities every time I tell her I'm done with the team."

"We'll have to discuss your relationship with your mother another time," said Servant. "If there's an army of mad scientists out there with murderous pasts, our priority has to be finding them."

"Which can't be too difficult," said App. "The fact that they all vanished at the same time means they had to be in communication with each other. We can get our contacts at the NSA to look at phone records and emails and—"

"We've already done that," said Sarah. "There's no evidence at all that these individuals were ever in contact with each other through any traditional methods."

"Let me take a look at the list," said App.

"It's not like I have a copy on me," said Sarah.

"I saw the list," said Chimpion. "I have names, addresses, dates of birth and, in the case of Delilah McPherson, her date of death." She pulled out her phone. "I've already had my contacts in Pangea researching the names."

"I don't see how they can know more about them than we already know," said Sarah.

Chimpion said, "Human law enforcement plainly didn't catch onto the fact that Mark was buying industrial strength 3d printers, or notice anything odd about Smith ordering all the high tech gear he needed to build a time machine. These purchase were made with supposedly untraceable cryptocurrency. A lot of this takes place on Pangean servers, and the metadata we record can be analyzed for information invisible in any single transaction, but detectable in the bulk data. All of the names on the list started making these encrypted transactions in the last year. In another day or two, we should know what they were buying."

"A day or two might be too late," said Servant. "We can't just sit around doing nothing. We need to get out to the neighborhoods where these people lived and start interviewing people ourselves."

"Going out into residential neighborhoods after you've begged dervishes to attack us could cause panic. Our missing psychopaths have to have left some sort of trail. Sooner or later we'll get an actual lead. For now I want all of you to head to the gym to run combat training scenarios. Let's stay sharp for when something does happen."

"My staying sharp doesn't really have much to do with a gym," said Steam-Dragon. "My suit does all the heavy lifting."

"Your mind is the true power behind the suit," said Chimpion. "I've watched the video records of your fights with App. You're not using your suit to its full potential. There is much I can teach you about the art of combat."

"Whatever," said Steam-Dragon.

Sarah left the others and headed to the command hub to let Nathan and Katya know about the connection they'd discovered with the beheadings. She walked into the room and found them both waiting for her.

Nathan grinned as he said, "Servant certainly made that interesting."

"Why does this amuse you?" asked Sarah.

Nathan shrugged. "The internet's already filled with parodies. Some of them are funny as hell."

"It happened ten minutes ago!"

"More like fifteen. That's, like, a whole year in meme time," said Nathan.

"App cut his mics," said Katya. "What did you tell them?"

"Not much. Just, you know, everything."

"Your mother is going to kill you," said Katya.

"That would be easier than what she'll actually do," said Sarah. "Screw it, I'm glad I spilled the beans. We shouldn't have been keeping this information from the rest of the team. Chimpion's already got her contacts working on leads we didn't have before. And Becky, especially, deserved to know the truth."

"How did she take it?" asked Katya.

"Who the hell knows?" asked Sarah. "I mean, her face is hidden while she's in the suit. She protested at first, but I think she accepted the truth. How she feels about it is anyone's guess. I don't think she's the type who's quick to share her real feelings."

"For what it's worth," said Nathan turning away from her toward his computer, "I think you did the right thing. Now take a look at this video of Serv—" He stopped speaking.

"What about the video?" asked Sarah.

"Die!" Nathan shouted as he leapt to his feet, drawing his arms back above his head. His fingers shimmered as an executioner's sword materialized from thin air. With a high-pitched laugh, he brought the blade down toward Sarah's unprotected head.

Chapter Fifteen
Evasive Action

NATHAN SWUNG THE executioner's sword with a two handed grip. Sarah wasn't wearing her helmet, but she was wearing her body armor, and sheer instinct brought her arms up in time to bear the brunt. The blow knocked her from her feet, almost always a good thing in her case, since she was much faster off the ground than on it.

"Katya!" she cried as she rose toward the ceiling. "Run!"

Katya didn't run. Instead, she laughed maniacally as she lunged toward Sarah and swung a blade of her own. Now in the air, Sarah spun to have her thigh bear the brunt of the blade. The swords looked wickedly sharp, but the diamond nanothreads of her outfit couldn't be cut by any known metal and the non-Newtonian fluid lining of her suit absorbed some of the kinetic energy, reducing the impact of a blow that would have severed her leg to one that merely felt like she was being whacked with a crowbar.

"Damn it, damn it, damn it!" she shouted as she rocketed toward the hallway. At high speed she had no room for error as she threaded through the doorway and executed a perfect ninety degree turn. As always, her body went where her mind willed it in utter disregard for all laws of physics.

She couldn't stop to look back, but felt confident that Nathan and Katya were in hot pursuit, which suited her fine.

"Servant!" she shouted. "Main hall! Nathan and Katya have turned into dervishes!"

There was a white blur at the end of the hall that came into focus as Servant formed a one man barricade in front of the door, bending out of the way at the last second to let Sarah flash through into the safety of the next room.

"Don't hurt them!" she yelled, spinning around to see how close behind they were. Pretty close, it turned out. Nathan wasn't particularly athletic, but he was moving with insane speed, and there were now five of him. Katya ran marathons for a hobby so she was even closer, as were her four doppelgangers.

The Nathans and Katyas cackled like hyenas on methamphetamines as they chopped at Servant's neck.

"I'll take those," said Servant, snatching the blades away.

"Sarah!" Chimpion suddenly shouted over the coms. "App's down! The whole freaking med team just changed into dervishes!"

"Don't hurt them!" shouted Sarah.

"They're doing their best to hurt us!" Chimpion shouted back. "They chopped off App's head!"

"He'll walk it off," said Sarah. "Immobilize your opponents, but don't do any permanent damage, and definitely don't kill them!"

Steam-Dragon's voice came over the com. "I don't have a lot of non-lethal options in my toolkit."

"Then stand there and get hit!" said Sarah. "Chimpion, take evasive action."

"Way ahead of you," said Chimpion. "I can keep out of reach until they burn out."

"Crap," said Sarah. "Staying alive isn't good enough. We've got to keep them from having heart attacks!"

"Any ideas how to do that?" Servant asked. He kept snatching away the blades and breaking them, but new blades kept appearing in their hands.

"Can't your force fields manipulate time? Slow them down!"

"They alter my time inside the field. I can't project it onto other people."

"I just took all but one here with a sleep gas grenade," said Chimpion.

"And I've got my jaws clamped around the torso of the last one," said Steam-Dragon. "He's fighting like crazy. He's going to tear himself apart."

"The ones I knocked out are stirring," said Chimpion. "They seem to be fighting off the gas."

"Crap, crap, crap," said Sarah, finding her helmet where she'd left back in the control room. She pulled on the helmet and fixed her gaze on the clock in the heads up display. Dervishes usually burned out in under five minutes. At least a minute was already gone. How the hell was she supposed to stop the burn out when they didn't know what was causing this? Even if they could save the crew, how could they fight a foe that could possess anyone at any time?

She took a deep breath. Think. First, since she hadn't started believing in magic, Nathan and the others weren't possessed. She knew a thing or two about making people do things against their will. Since her father had been able to take over people's minds, perhaps a telepath was to blame. As for the magically appearing and disappearing swords, her own sister had been a ferrokinetic with the ability to pull raw iron atoms out of the quantum froth that undergirded reality.

If they were dealing with a telepath, how could she shield the brains of the dervishes? Physical objects had never been a barrier for her father. Distance, on the other hand, had provided some limitations. The further his powers stretched, the more people his power touched, and the harder it became for him to filter signal from noise.

"Are the dervishes still contained?" she asked, as her mind raced. If she started grabbing them, how far away could she get them in the minutes they had left?

"I don't know that mine is going to survive his injuries," said Steam-Dragon.

"I've had to hamstring one of my opponents," said Chimpion. "I'm counting on the medical nanites that saved you to save him, assuming they don't all die of heart attacks. Their frenzy seems to be growing!"

Sarah snapped her fingers. "Nanites!"

"You think they can cure them?" asked Servant.

"Nope," said Sarah, zooming to the armory. "But nanites can help us get these people to the other side of the planet."

She flew to a supply cabinet and jerked on the door. The whole cabinet moved. "Goddammit, it's locked!"

"What's locked?" asked Servant.

"The cabinet where they keep the nanites they inject us with so that the space machine can track our locations."

"I can get in," App's voice said over the coms.

"I thought you were dead!" said Chimpion.

"Yeah," said App. "Been that kind of day."

Sarah said, "Hurry up and get into the—"

"I'm already here," App said as he drifted through the wall beside her in his ghost mode. He turned his feet toward the ground and said, "Acid mode."

Sarah stepped back as his dripping hands grasped the sides of the cabinet. He tore off chunks of metal like they were tissue paper, and in second had exposed the trays full of syringes within. He stepped away and said, "Reset."

Sarah lunged forward, sticking her hand into the jagged hole he'd made, grabbing a fistful of syringes. She handed them to App and said, "Get these into the dervishes! Go!"

"Where are we sending them?" asked App.

"Go!" she said. She didn't have any seconds to spare to explain her plan. She flew back to the command hub and landed in the chair where Nathan had been sitting when all this started. He was still logged in. She wasn't an expert in using the space machine, but she'd sat through a few training sessions. While she didn't have the skill to program a new destination, she remembered how to pull up a list of saved coordinates. When they'd fought Pit Geek and Sundancer, their final battle had taken place on Midway Atoll. That wasn't the exact opposite side of the globe, but it wasn't off by much. If they were up against a telepath, there would be a world full of minds preventing his control.

The computers were state of the art, but time crawled as she waited for past destinations to load. Then she had to scroll through mission dates, seconds ticking as she scanned the list of dates and times. On the day they'd gone to Midway they'd hit nearly 100 other destinations while trying to stop explosive clones of Sundancer. "Come on, come on," she whispered as she clicked on the different GPS coordinates, bringing up maps showing what they corresponded to. Why couldn't they sort these things by names people actually used? Who the hell memorized the GPS coordinates of places they'd been?

"Yes!" she cried as a map revealed a tiny triangle of an island in the middle of an ocean. She was certain this was Midway, since the western end was a plain of smooth black glass, a remnant of Sundancer losing control of her powers.

By now, App would have had at least a minute to inject the dervishes with the tracking nanites. "Damn it!" she said, exasperated. "How the hell do I load a new target form into the system?"

"Control F8 brings up the load menu," said Chimpion, startling Sarah since she was standing right behind her.

"How did you—"

"I've got all my dervishes tied up now," said Chimpion, nudging Sarah aside. "Here, let me do it."

Sarah gave up her seat and Chimpion's long, nimble fingers flew over the keys. In seconds, she'd loaded the dervish nanite maps into the system. She selected them, then pasted them onto the map of Midway. A few more keystrokes, and she sent the rest of the team after them, then with one last keystroke sent herself.

Sarah arrived to find the dervish victims laying naked on the black glass, gasping and groaning, their doppelgangers vanished. Chimpion apparently hadn't fine-tuned the grab to also bring along their clothes, or, she noted, their swords.

"Katya," she said, flying to her side. She dropped to her side and grabbed her by the arms. "Katya, are you okay?"

"Why did you do that to me?" Katya said, her voice sobbing. "Why? Why?"

"We had to cut and paste you out of the range of whoever was controlling you."

"Whoever...? It was you! You made me attack!"

"What the hell are you talking about?" Sarah asked, wondering if Katya had gone mad.

"It was your voice. Your voice inside my head. It told me to do terrible things. But... it made me so happy! So happy to kill for you! I couldn't control myself!"

"I never told you to kill anyone!" Sarah protested.

"It was your voice!" said Katya. "You're old voice! You told me to attack, and I felt such pleasure I couldn't control myself!"

App was helping Nathan to his feet. "She's right," Nathan said, his voice trembling. His body looked emaciated, bathed in sweat, his face haggard. "I also heard a woman's voice. Didn't sound like you, exactly. And it told me to attack you. So it couldn't be you. Could it?"

"It's not me," said Sarah.

"You forget that I've been on the receiving end of your powers, years ago," said Katya, still looking at Sarah with suspicion. "The experience was so similar. I could feel my whole mind instantly flood with endorphins and adrenaline. I felt as if I was unstoppable. I felt... thrilled."

"There something else you need to tell us, Skyrider?" asked Steam-Dragon. "Some evil twin we need to know about?"

"It was my dad who had the evil twin. I've honestly got no idea..." she didn't finish the sentence. Suddenly, everything was plain. "Oh my god. To make a dervish, all you need is to recreate my father's telepathy, my sister's ability to pull iron blades from thin air, and my voice."

"So you are involved in this?" asked Steam-Dragon.

"Of course not," said Sarah. "But my father had analyzed my powers. He knew how my voice activated the pleasure centers of the brain.

He'd written out complicated formulas explaining my sister's ability to create iron from seemingly thin air. While he never told me he'd analyzed his own powers, it's impossible to believe he didn't. What if the secrets of his telepathy are stored somewhere in the Knowbokov Foundation databases? What if someone has hacked in and learned to simulate our powers?"

"None of you had the kind of accelerated metabolisms displayed by the dervishes," said Servant. "None of you could split into multiple bodies."

"We already know that you can use a time machine to create multiple selves. Dad once built a time machine. As for the manic speed and strength, when I was the Thrill if I'd told someone to run as far and fast as they can until their heart burst, they would have done so with a smile on their face."

"Then it all makes sense," said Steam-Dragon. "Apparently the villain behind all this is your father's ghost."

"That's stupid," said Sarah.

"Don't believe in ghosts?" asked Steam-Dragon.

"Actually, I used to date one," said Sarah. "No, the idea is stupid because, while my father had his failings, he wasn't a terrorist. On his worst day, he'd never dream of creating something like a dervish."

"But he put part of his mind into the brains of murderers who could dream of such things," said Servant.

"Fuck," said Sarah, grabbing her forehead as it if were about to split in two. "You're right! Somehow, the prisoners have gotten Dad's memories, and maybe his powers, then reverted back to their murderous ways." She glanced at Servant, who stared at her sternly. "This would be a bad time to preach to me about my fucking language."

"If there really are over a dozen serial killers with your father's genius lurking out there, I may be tempted to use a few bad words myself," said Servant.

Chapter Sixteen
Wild Goose

"**WHAT THE HELL** just happened?" asked Simpson, one of the technicians still at the base, his voice crackling over the radio.

"Katya, Nathan, Lacy, Ty, and Frank were all converted into dervishes," Sarah answered. "We moved them to the other side of the planet to get them out of range of whoever was controlling them."

"Did it work?" asked Simpson.

"Yes, but all five need medical attention, especially Ty. But if we cut and paste them back home, I'm worried they'll turn into dervishes again."

"At least they won't have their swords," said Simpson. "They were left behind when you snatched them. Their, um, clothes too."

"They can pull new swords out of thin air," said Sarah.

"Transport me back with Ty," said Servant. "He got chewed up pretty badly by Steam-Dragon and is going into shock. I'll be able to hold him if he does change back into dervish mode. If he doesn't change, we can bring the others back one by one."

"Good plan," said Sarah. "Simpson, make it so."

It was made so. The team was given updates as Ty returned, showing no signs of reversion. Two minutes later, he was in the medical unit, receiving a transfusion of medical nanites.

"I think it's safe to bring back another one," said Servant. "Let's do Lacy."

"You heard him, Simpson," said Sarah. "Bring her back, and App to watch over her."

The process was repeated, until finally Sarah and Katya were left alone. Katya's eyes looked haunted.

"It really wasn't me," said Sarah.

"I know," said Katya. "I'm just rattled. It wasn't... it wasn't like I was being controlled. It was like I was being given permission. Like this violent monster was hiding in me the whole time just waiting to be invited to jump out. I... I was laughing. As I was attacking you, I... I... oh God. What if it happens again?"

"I won't happen again," said Sarah. "I promise, we're going to stop this."

"What if you can't?" asked Katya. "What if... what if somehow, you're causing it?"

"Katya, we've known each other a long time—"

"Yes," said Katya. "And I remember how you used to abuse your powers. I remember how undisciplined you were. What if... what if there's some part of you that's inherited your father's telepathy? What if you're subconsciously controlling others?"

"There's nothing in my subconscious that would make me turn other people into terrorists. I'm a good person. You know this."

Katya nodded. "Your sister was a good person. Then, Jerusalem."

Simpson's voice came through the coms. "Ready to come back?"

"More than I can say," said Sarah.

"Simpson!" Sarah said the second they were pasted into back into headquarters. "You said we'd captured the dervish swords. Where are they?"

"Ah," said Simpson. "About that..."

"What?" she asked.

"Watch this," he said, pulling out his tablet and tapping it a few times. "Here's the camera inside the evidence locker. We tossed the swords inside to keep them safe until we could analyze them."

"Good," she said. "I know they won't have fingerprints or any of the typical forensic evidence we'd look for, but—."

"Watch," he said, pointing toward the screen.

Sarah blinked. The swords had been replaced by a pile of brown dust.

"Son of a bitch," she said.

"Instantaneous oxidation, just like all the previous swords. Still, we do have some data we didn't have before. There was a definite electromagnetic pulse when the swords materialized, and a corresponding one when they vanished. It's identical to the magnetic signatures we have on file for when Rail Blade would create and dismiss her blades."

"So we've been overlooking an obvious suspect," said Chimpion, immediately behind Sarah.

Sarah looked down at her. "You really need to stop sneaking up on me."

"She's like a short, hairy Batman," said App as he approached, with Servant and Steam-Dragon close behind.

"Spit it out, Chimpion," said Sarah. "You obviously have a theory about who's responsible."

"Your sister. Killing people with blades is her MO."

"Random mass murder isn't her thing," said Sarah.

"She destroyed an entire city!" said Steam-Dragon.

"She evacuated people before she did so," said Sarah.

"And killed a lot of them from strokes and heart attacks when she grabbed them by their blood," said Chimpion.

"Look, my sister isn't a problem anymore," said Sarah.

"Is she dead?" asked Servant. "After Jerusalem, she issued a threat to destroy more cities, then no one knows what happened to her."

"She's not dead. At least, I don't think she is. I haven't had any contact with her in years."

"So a known mass murderer with at least one of the necessary powers to pull of this attack is still alive and in hiding," said Steam-Dragon. "Why hasn't she been a suspect before now?"

"Because it's a dumb theory," said Sarah.

App scratched the back of his neck. "Why, exactly, is it dumb?"

"Amelia was never mean or cruel. She only used lethal force when absolutely necessary to save innocent lives."

"Until Jerusalem," said Servant.

"Look, I was there. It was… it was a bad day for everyone. There was all out war that day. Amelia—Rail Blade—used her powers to destroy all the guns and knives people were fighting with, and they just picked up cobblestones and kept fighting. Then this kid committed suicide trying to kill us and… Amelia snapped. Anyone would have."

"Only when ordinary people snap, they can't flatten cities with their minds," said Steam-Dragon.

"Let's grant that she was a person with good intentions," said Chimpion. "The trauma of being responsible for so many deaths would have changed her. If you haven't spoken to her in years, how do you know her insanity hasn't progressed?"

"Even if she's bat shit crazy now, she couldn't be behind this. She didn't have my voice powers, or Dad's telepathy."

"But she had firsthand knowledge of these powers," said Chimpion. "She probably had access to your father's computers with the data explaining how your powers worked."

Sarah shook her head. "It's not her."

"You know her best," said Servant. "But what could it hurt to ask her a few questions?"

"Good luck with that," said Sarah.

"We won't need luck," said Chimpion. "I'll put the Pangean research team on the case. I'm betting we'll know where she is by morning."

"Oh, I know where she is," said Sarah.

"Then tell us," said Chimpion.

"She lives in a really remote location," said Sarah.

"Why is that a problem?" said App. "With the space machine, we can go anywhere on earth."

Sarah gave a slight smile.

"Oh my god, she's on Mars," said App.

"What?" asked Servant. "How did you jump to that conclusion?"

"I can't be the only one here that follows the news," said App. "The Mars enigma? The magnetic field?"

"Ooooh," said Steam-Dragon. "That does make sense."

"Care to enlighten us?" asked Servant.

"Seriously, you haven't heard about the Mars enigma?" said App. "The satellites we've got in orbit around Mars have been sending back photos of things that look a lot like structures, big faces, pyramids, domes, large tubes. Conspiracy buffs have whole websites devoted to proving that Mars once hosted a civilization whose remains you can literally see from space. Of course, NASA always comes along and explains how the objects match up with comparable natural formations on Earth. They also explain sharp angles and straight lines in the original photo data as digital artifacts. Of course, the more NASA explains away the structures, the more people think there's a cover up."

"Put me in the cover up camp," said Steam-Dragon.

"I'm not as convinced," said App. "I mean, some people are building whole histories of an ancient Martian civilization based on blurry photos. That said, there's a site in the Valles Marineris that sure as hell looks like a big glass dome, and it only shows up in photos starting seven years ago. Earlier photos don't show it, though, of course, earlier satellites had a lot less resolution, and scientists point out that dust storms bury and uncover rock formations all the time."

"I've studied those photos," said Steam-Dragon. "The dome definitely looks manmade. Martian made. Whatever."

"And then there's the magnetic field. That's what's really known as the Mars Enigma," said App. "When we first sent probes there, Mars essentially had no magnetosphere. Then, boom, seven years ago, satellites started detecting magnetic fluctuations, faint at first, but getting stronger. Now it's almost powerful enough to shield the planet from the solar wind, which means, if it persists, Mars could one day hold onto a dense atmosphere again. Scientist have no idea where the magnetic field is coming from, but what if—"

"It's Amelia," said Sarah. "You're right. She's on Mars. She's probably living in that dome."

"What the hell is she doing on Mars?" said Steam-Dragon.

"Hiding, obviously," said Sarah.

"So she can escape justice?" said Chimpion.

"So she can protect the rest of the world from herself," said Sarah. "Look, I haven't spoken to Amelia since the incident in Jerusalem. But, I know her. She knew she wielded dangerous powers and took great care to stay in control. In Jerusalem, she lost that control. Despite all her power, she was still a person. She had bad days. Unlike most people, her bad days could flatten cities. So she left. She didn't go to Mars to escape justice. She imprisoned herself on another planet to protect us."

"It's not a prison if she went there voluntarily," said Servant, gruffly. "She committed the greatest war crime in history. It wasn't up to her to decide what her punishment should be."

"Excuse me?"

"She wiped Jerusalem off the map. This was a sacred city. What could possibly be a worst crime?"

"Oh, I dunno, the holocaust?" said Sarah, putting her hands on her hips. "The killing fields of Cambodia? The firebombing of Dresden? Stalin starving his own people? Amelia tore up a bunch of old buildings. Let's keep things in perspective."

"Old buildings? The Church of the Holy Sepulcher housed the tomb of Jesus. It's wiped out. The Wailing Wall was the most sacred site of the Jews… gone forever. While I'm no cheerleader for Islam, the Dome of the Rock was sacred to Muslims, and a priceless cultural treasure regardless of who was in control of the city."

"The fact that all these 'priceless' places were crammed up right on top of one another came at a pretty high price. That part of the world has been fighting over religion since the Stone Age. Amelia didn't create the mess over there. We were there to try to solve it."

"You did a great job. The world's certainly all peaceful now that Jerusalem's gone," said Steam-Dragon, holding up a fore claw.

"Could you try for five minutes not to be an asshole?" asked Sarah. "Look, I'm not trying to defend my sister—"

"Kind of sounds like you are," said Steam-Dragon.

"—but Amelia wasn't evil, isn't evil, could never be evil. She was the best person I've ever known."

App said, "But if she's crazy—"

"She was sane enough to get herself off the planet," said Sarah.

"Because even she thought she was dangerous," said Servant. "If she thought she could turn evil, why would you doubt it?"

"Don't talk to me about turning evil," said Sarah. "I fought you when you were a goddamned supervillain. You want to compare Amelia's body count to the lives lost in your gang wars?"

"No," said Servant. "But I take some small comfort that the people I killed weren't innocent. I was at war with other crime-bosses and thugs, the worst of the worst."

"How about the children dying from the drugs you were pushing?" said Sarah.

"Whoa," said App, holding up his hands. "Everybody take a deep breath. We're not going to accomplish anything fighting among ourselves."

"We're also not going to accomplish anything if Sarah won't help us find her sister," said Chimpion.

"Uh, I think we've agreed she's already found," said Steam-Dragon. "I mean, you can see her dome on Mars from space. Can't the space-machine take us there?"

"If so, Sarah shouldn't come with us," said Chimpion.

"I'm still leader of this team," said Sarah.

"Because your mother writes our paychecks," said Steam-Dragon. "I didn't vote for you."

"You're only on this team because my mother thought you'd accomplish more good working for us than rotting in prison," said Sarah.

"I agree with Chimpion," said Servant. "You shouldn't go to Mars. You're plainly compromised in your judgment."

"And you aren't?" asked Sarah. "You spent a long time thinking you were in Hell because of what Rail Blade did to you. I hardly expect you'll be objective regarding her innocence."

"Then Servant stays behind as well," said Chimpion. "App, Steam-Dragon, and I pay Amelia a visit. Maybe she isn't connected with these attacks, but it would be negligent not to pursue this lead."

"It would be negligent not to go to freakin' Mars," said App, smiling. "I mean, we're superheroes! We need least one outer space mission on our résumés."

"No one's going to Mars!" Sarah said, exasperated.

"We should put it to a vote," said Steam-Dragon.

"This isn't a democracy," said Sarah. "Look, we're facing a real threat. The dervishes hit us where we live. As team leader, I need to direct our resources where they'll do some good, not send the team off on a wild goose chase."

"If wild geese were killing people, chasing them would be logical," said Chimpion. "People who can manifest swords from thin air are killing people. It's logical to—"

"This discussion is over," said Sarah, turning her back to the others. "We're getting nowhere."

"Where would you like us to get?" asked Steam-Dragon. "If it's all about allocating resources, where do we go to stop these dervishes? Or is your plan to have us hang out in the gym training until they attack again?"

Sarah didn't answer as she pushed open the door at the end of the hall.

"That's what I thought," Steam-Dragon called after her. She chuckled, shaking her head. "She's probably going to go tattle on us to her mama."

Chapter Seventeen
Old Novels

SARAH DRIFTED INTO the jump room, her helmet dangling in her grasp. She looked down at its blank surface, staring at her own blank expression reflected within. Before joining the Covenant, living her other life, she'd gone days, even weeks, without thinking about Jerusalem. And Amelia. Poor, sweet, murderous, and terrifying Amelia. Sarah had grown up with someone she thought she knew and understood, only to bear witness that the sister she thought she knew was, in fact a god, wielding power over life and death. She still couldn't process the contradictions. Her sister was a hero. Her sister was a monster. Her sister was beyond all understanding. Part of her felt like she needed to go back and convince the team not to pursue Amelia. No. Screw it. She had problems in her real life. This superteam crap wasn't something she wanted to deal with anymore, at least not at the moment. Maybe not ever. In a weary voice she said, "Destination alpha, Simpson."

She waited five seconds, ten. The walls around her didn't change.

"Forget about the environmental adjustments. Just move me."

"Uh," said Simpson over the intercom, "No can do."

"Why not?"

"Mrs. Knowbokov gave orders that we're not to transport you until you speak with her."

Sarah gritted her teeth. The second she'd stormed away from her argument with the others her phone had started buzzing. Barely two minutes had gone by and she had two voice mails and three texts. They had to be from her mother.

"Just cut and paste me," Sarah said. "Tell her I threatened you. I'll take the heat."

"You know our conversations are recorded, right?" said Simpson.

"Right. So an imaginary threat won't cut it. How about this? If you don't move me in the next five seconds I'm going to fly into the control room and start punching people. I'm in no mood for a lecture, but I am in the mood for hitting people."

"Really, Sarah, you're a little old for temper tantrums," said a woman's voice directly behind Sarah.

Sarah's shoulders sagged. Without looking behind her, she said, "Hello, mother."

"Please step to the floor," said her mother. "And look at me when you speak."

Sarah's feet were only about three inches off the floor. She spun around in the air like she was on a slow moving turntable, facing her mother.

Katrina Knowbokov seldom smiled, but at the moment she looked positively dour. She looked ready to scream and curse, which would have been a welcome change for Sarah. Her mother normally conveyed anger by letting her voice grow toneless, almost robotic.

"I heard about your confrontation with the others," said Katrina. "You didn't handle it well."

"I won't pretend I did," said Sarah. "You can't expect me to be happy that my teammates want to hunt down Amelia."

"I know that confronting Amelia may be an emotional challenge," said Katrina. "But you're a Knowbokov. Your father and I raised you to show a bit more fortitude."

Sarah rolled her eyes. "Dad taught me a lot of things that turned out to be bullshit. And all I learned from you..." Sarah couldn't complete the sentence. Not because she hadn't learned something from her mother, but because the lesson she'd learned was too terrible to say out loud. By giving in to the temptation to use her powers over others on her own mother, Sarah had learned, long before Amelia fell from grace, that she, too, had the soul of a monster.

"Are you going to finish that thought?" her mother asked after a brief pause.

"No," said Sarah. "I don't want to argue. I'm tired. I just want to go home."

"This island is your home," said her mother. "Now that the dervishes have attacked our home, you can't waste time in your make-believe hobby life."

"I said I didn't want an argument. Why are you trying to start one?"

"Because I want you to grow up," said Katrina. "Whether you like it or not, you have a duty to defend others. I've had to twist your arm to get you to do what should be only natural for you, and lead this team. Instead you cling to the illusion that this isn't your true home, and your true responsibility. That other life you live... it's no different than the dollhouse you owned as a little girl. You enjoy the fantasy that it's real, but you must know in your soul that it's all built upon a lie."

"Mother, this whole team is built upon lies. My other life is the only place where I feel honest."

"Truly? So you've finally told your husband your history? Finally talked to him with your feet off the ground, as you insist on doing now?"

Sarah's jaw tightened as she answered the questions with silence.

"That's what I thought," said Katrina. "Now that we've established what's real in your life and what isn't, I want to discuss the parameters of your mission to see your sister."

"There is no mission," said Sarah. "What's wrong with you?"

"What is right with me is that I can judge evidence without allowing my emotions to get in the way. We witnessed firsthand the dervishes using ferrokinesis. It would be negligent not to follow that lead wherever it may take us."

"Maybe it's time you used your emotions in making decisions," said Sarah. "A mission to see Amelia is a complete waste of time. She's not turned into some sort of long distance, puppet master terrorist. Despite her slip up in Jerusalem, she was a good person. You know this."

"Do I?" asked her mother. Then, she looked as if she thought better of her remark, took a slow breath, and said, "You're right. She was a good person. But good people can do horrible things. Your father was a good man, with good goals. You know where this led him."

"Okay," said Sarah. "Let's look at this rationally. No emotion, just think this through. Amelia's lived peacefully on Mars for years. Why would she start attacking us now? If she did want to attack… why bother with these dervishes? Amelia can flatten entire cities just by thinking hard. She could manipulate the earth's core to trigger earthquakes and volcanoes and probably put an end to all life on Earth if she pushed herself. If she had gone bad, we'd already be dead."

"You're assuming she's acting rationally," said Katrina. "What if she's lost her mind? What if she's being manipulated somehow?"

"Who could possibly manipulate her?"

"Your father could," said Katrina.

"You, of all people, can't seriously believe in ghosts."

"Why not? You took a ghost for a lover once."

"Who says 'took a lover' anymore? You read too many old novels."

"You, my dear, haven't read enough of them," said Katrina. "Richard is now on Mars with your sister. We know he was capable of murder. Who can say he's not involved in all of this?"

"I can say," said Sarah. "People don't change so fundamentally. Neither Richard nor Amelia were terrorists. Period. Why are we even arguing this?"

"Then we'll forego arguments," said Katrina. "I'm the final authority on assigning the Covenant missions. You'll go to Mars and speak with Amelia because I'm ordering you to do so."

"No," said Sarah. "I quit."

"You can't quit," said Katrina.

"I honestly think I can," said Sarah. "I'm not a slave. I've been ambivalent about being a superhero ever since you called me back."

"You can't seriously abandon your duty to protect the world from these dervishes."

"If it wasn't dervishes threatening the world, it would be something else," said Sarah. "There's always going to be some nut out there waiting to create havoc. I agreed to stop Sundancer and Pit Geek because it felt like unfinished business. I never planned to stick around after that."

"Sarah, you have a responsibility to—"

"Responsibility?" Sarah shook her head. "You said my other life was like a doll house. Don't you see that you're the one who's playing? You're dressing up people in costumes and sending them out to fight like they're your personal collection of action figures. Have fun with your game, but I'm done playing."

"This is no game. With your leadership, the Covenant could be the ultimate force of good in the world."

"You sound like dad," said Sarah. "We aren't the ultimate force for good. You know who is? Ordinary people. They've been tackling problems a lot worse than dervishes for a very long time. Father wanted to end disease, crime, and war? Long before he came along, men created hospitals, courts, and diplomatic institutions like the UN."

"You're forgetting that I am one of those ordinary people you so revere," said Katrina. "All those accomplishments of ordinary people didn't happen by accident. Someone saw a problem and had the ingenuity and will to solve it. I saw a problem when Pit Geek and Sundancer came out of hiding. I implemented a solution. It worked."

"If the Covenant had never formed, nothing would have changed. Sundancer was killed by her own powers, and Pit Geek committed suicide. We just happened to be standing nearby when they defeated themselves."

"The ultimate problem, though, wasn't these two supervillains," said Katrina. "The true problem was your father and his broken universe. He altered the laws of physics to make superhumans possible. I don't have the power to alter the laws of physics. I can only work to negate the horrifying consequences of his actions."

"Wow," said Sarah. "So that's where this is coming from? The Covenant is just a weird way you're getting back at dad."

"You're being absurd," said Katrina. "How can you hope to lead this team if you can't see the true good they can accomplish?"

"You know that's my argument, right?" said Sarah. "Why am I bothering with any of this? I don't want this. I've never wanted this."

"I know." Her mother shook her head slowly. "I'm to blame, ultimately. I spent too much of your childhood withdrawn into the cocoon of my own thoughts, afraid of your father. Afraid of my own children. I failed you. I suppose it should come as no surprise that you've become so... self-involved."

Sarah shrugged. "That sounds like an excellent topic the next time you see your therapist. Now, if you'll excuse me, I'm going home."

"You're not going anywhere until I give Simpson permission to use the space machine," said Katrina. "I can't let you leave until—"

"Mother," said Sarah, rising higher in the air. "I don't need the space machine. I can outrace fighter jets. I'll be home before nightfall. I won't be back."

"So that's it," said Katrina. "You're going to run away from your problems?"

"I'm actually running toward my problems," said Sarah. "I've got a life I need to get back on track. Good luck with the Covenant. I know you mean well. Maybe you'll save the world after all. But you'll have to do it without me."

She spun away and headed for the main hall before her mother had the bright idea of sealing the exits. She could and would fight her way out of here if needed. Fortunately, the doors all opened as she approached. In under a minute, she was outside.

Sarah pulled on her helmet and spoke her destination. A map appeared with a flight path traced in green. She looked up into the blue sky, spotting the slender pale arc of the daylight moon. Without looking back, she rocketed toward heaven faster than the speed of sound, leaving thunder in her wake.

Chapter Eighteen
The Parable of the Talents

KATRINA KNOWBOKOV PASSED the remainder of the team still gathered together in the hall. She couldn't hear what they were talking about as she approached, but from their low tones and furtive glances in her direction, she suspected they were engaged in gossip about Sarah.

Without bothering to break her stride as she passed, she said, "See Simpson for your space suits. You're heading to Mars."

"Alright!" said App, raising his hand toward Servant for a high five. When Servant left him hanging, Steam Dragon reached out with a fore claw curled into a fist.

"I can't really high five without injuring you," she said. "Fist bump?"

He bumped her, then said, "Until this moment, I didn't know we had space suits."

"OF COURSE WE have space suits," said Simpson, leading the team into the equipment room. "Mrs. Knowbokov insists we plan for every contingency."

Simpson put his hand onto a pad next to a steel door at the back of the room. The door opened to reveal an even larger warehouse beyond the door, a room App had never seen. He let out a whistle as his eyes went wide.

"This looks like James Bond's garage," said App, craning his neck to take in all the various bits of gear scattered around the room. "Holy cow! Are those hover bikes?"

"They don't really work," said Chimpion.

"How do you know?" asked App.

"Yeah," said Simpson. "How do you know? These prototypes are classified."

"I took one out for a test drive," said Chimpion. "Learned the hard way that the battery pack overheats after only two miles. I had to lug the bike all the way back from the other side of the island."

"How the hell did you get in here?" asked Simpson. "For that matter, how the hell did you get the bike outside without triggering a thousand alarms?"

Chimpion shrugged. "If I told you ninja magic, would you believe me?"

"I'd believe you," said App. "This is a day when all kinds of magic is happening. I can't believe the whole team's going to Mars!"

"Well, not the whole team," said Simpson. "I, uh, I assume you know Sarah's not going?"

"We kind of got that impression when she stormed out, yeah," said Steam-Dragon.

"Give her a few more minutes to calm down and she'll come around," said App. "I mean, Mars! Who says no to Mars?"

"Sarah," said Simpson. He scratched the back of his head and said, "Um, I'm not sure if I should tell you this, but I think she's quit the team."

"No way," said App.

"Good riddance," said Steam-Dragon. "Was it just me, or did she strike anyone else as snooty?"

"I had no problems with her personally," asked Chimpion. "But I found her blind defense of her sister disturbing. The fact that the dervishes claim to hear her voice is even more troublesome. What if she has a more sinister reason for wanting to prevent us from investigating her sister?"

"What are you saying?" asked App.

"What if, somehow, she's involved?"

"That's crazy," said App.

"I don't know, man," said Steam-Dragon. "I mean… she's been lying about her real identity to all of us."

"Sarah's a good person," said Servant. "But anyone could tell she wasn't happy on the team. I was surprised she didn't quit immediately after we defeated Sundancer and Pit Geek."

As they spoke, Simpson led them toward a bank of large metal containers, looking a little bit like oversized stainless steel refrigerators. He opened the door to one of them, revealing a space suit. "This one's for App. The next locker has Chimpion's. Servant doesn't really need a suit. Unfortunately, we haven't had time yet to make one for Steam-Dragon."

"It really wouldn't be too tough to modify my armor to hold a pressurized atmosphere," said Steam-Dragon. "I think I can have it ready pretty quickly if y'all have a good 3-d printer."

"We've got everything you need," said Simpson. "I'll assign our maker crew to help you out. App and Chimpion, we should have you try on the suits and let the techs make adjustments. Servant, even if you don't need a suit to survive on Mars, we'll need to upgrade the phone circuitry in your costume so you can all talk to one another on Mars. Your current gear synchs with satellites that will obviously be out of range."

"Don't bother," said Servant. "I'm not going."

"What?" asked App. "Dude, you have to come."

"I don't think I should," said Servant.

"Because you're worried you might be biased against Rail Blade?" asked App.

He shook his head. "No. I'm more worried she'll be biased against me. I look different now, but with her sensitivity to electromagnetic fields she'll recognize my force field. I don't want to put the rest of you in jeopardy if she decides to attack me."

"If she attacks us, I'd really like you at my side," said App.

"You'll be fine without me," said Servant. "Besides, one of us should stay on call in case there's another dervish attack."

"It's too soon," said App. "There's always weeks between attacks."

"I wonder why?" asked Steam-Dragon. "I mean, if you can turn anyone into a suicide swordsmen from a distance, why wait between attacks? And, another question, why did our attacker only make five dervishes? Why not a whole army?"

"We've been discussing that in our strategy briefings," said Simpson. "There's obviously some sort of cost to creating these suicide swordsman or we'd simply be overrun with them. Judging from the radioactive isotopes with found in Smith's cellar, he apparently needed some sort of small fission reactor to power his time machine. Dr. Knowbokov's own time machine used an experimental fusion reactor to power jumps further in time. We're currently looking for patterns of someone drawing massive power from existing grids, or of someone purchasing all the resources they'd need to build their own power plant."

"We still shouldn't have the whole team off world at once," said Servant. "Sister Amy always tells me to trust what's in my heart. I don't feel like I'm meant to go to Mars."

"We are very different people," said App. "Since I was a kid, I've dreamed of going to outer space. The most frustrating thing about losing a decade of my life as a disembodied cloud was getting put back together and finding out we still didn't have a Mars colony. I can't believe I didn't think of using the space machine to get there before now."

"This is going to be a risky jump," said Simpson. "Getting you there is no big deal, but we normally rely on the nanite maps of your body in order to get you back. Even if we boost your transmitters, there's still an eighteen minute signal lag due to the distance. After you send a return signal, you're going to have to stand completely still for a long time until we can grab you. Move more than a few inches and we might miss part of you. We'd hate to leave any limbs on Mars."

"Please don't," said Steam-Dragon. "I don't have many left to spare."

By now, the technicians Simpson had summoned to help modify Steam-Dragon's suit had arrived. Chimpion joined them, listening intently, asking questions about the suit's construction.

With no one watching them, App led Servant away from the others and asked, "What's the real story?"

"Real story?"

"About you not going to Mars. Seriously, man, you can't just claim it's not in your heart and expect me to buy it."

"Believe what you wish," said Servant.

"Are you really that afraid of Rail Blade?"

"Of course," he said. "You should be as well. If she wants you dead, you will wind up dead."

"I can't believe you're backing down because you're scared."

"My fear of Rail Blade is perfectly rational. But that's not why I'm staying here. I'd be willing to go to Mars and fight her if I thought it was a necessary mission."

"So you agree with Sarah? You don't think Rail Blade's involved?"

Servant shrugged. "Figuring out mysteries isn't my strong suit. But something about going to Mars feels... wrong."

"Wrong how?"

"I've vowed use my powers to make the world a better place," said Servant. "This world. Our world. Detouring to Mars feels like I'd be betraying that vow."

"Even if there's a threat to Earth on Mars?"

"Rail Blade's powerful, but I hardly think she could be coordinating these attacks from Mars," said Servant. "If she is involved, my hunch is you're going to get to Mars and find her dome empty."

"That would still be good information," said App.

"Information we could get by sending a drone," said Servant. "Whether anyone will say it or not, this isn't about getting intelligence. This is about confronting Rail Blade. She's a bear in her den. For some reason you're all eager to poke her with a stick."

"I'm not looking for a fight," said App. "But a trip to Mars is definitely on my superhero bucket list."

"I hope everything goes well. But look at it this way. If we all left the planet, and the dervishes attacked here again, you could get stranded. It's safer if I stay behind."

"That is a good argument. A lot better than the one about your gut. I still feel like something's bothering you that you're not talking about."

"I would hope it's something bothering you as well," said Servant. "Are we even a team without Sarah?"

"Uh, yeah," said App. "I mean, don't get me wrong. I liked Sarah. But she was always standoffish. I could never really talk to her. I always got the feeling she wanted to be someplace else."

"That's why I felt a bond with her," said Servant. "I also wish I was someplace else. I keep thinking about all the good I could be doing if I weren't part of this team."

"What else could you do? Have you looked in the mirror lately? With your build, your career choices were either a pro-wrestler or a superhero."

Servant smirked. "Sister Amy would agree with you. You're familiar with the parable of the talents?"

"Not so much," said App.

"A master gives his three servants talents, which is a type of money in the Bible. One of the servants buries his talents to keep them safe; the others invest them and double their money. The master is pleased with the two who doubled his money, but casts out the one who didn't make use of his talent. My superpowers are God's investment in me. I have a duty to make it pay interest."

"Which you're doing by being a superhero."

"I tell myself that. But I feel... separated from people. Wearing my uniform and showing off my powers makes it seem as if I'm bragging. I don't want to be seen as someone better than the people I serve."

"You do call yourself Servant," said App. "That's a pretty humble appellation."

"I hide my true face," said Servant. "My public identity is a lie."

"You'd be slapped in jail if you showed your Ogre face," said App. "Also, dude, you'd give children nightmares. Who needs that? You're not living a lie. You're protecting God's investment in you. What good would your talents do if you were behind bars?"

"I know it," said Servant. "But I don't always feel it."

"Don't fight destiny. You were meant to be a superhero. Are you coming to Mars or not?"

"Not," said Servant. "If you'll excuse me, I'm needed in Texas."

"Texas? You're heading back to New Jerusalem? I thought you were going to stay here and guard the place."

"I can come back with the tap of a button. Tomorrow's Sunday," said Servant. "I'd hate to miss church. You should come with me some time. It might change your life."

"I can make the same argument about Mars," said App.

Chapter Nineteen
Home

SERVANT STEPPED FROM the jump room onto the flat, sun-bleached high plains of west Texas. It was late afternoon. All around him were construction vehicles, cranes, bulldozers, cement trucks. A veritable city of RVs had gathered here to house the workers. The air was thick with fumes from all the motors and churning generators.

Though it had been only a few days since he'd last visited, he felt as if he were stepping into a place he'd never been before. New Jerusalem had grown a great deal in his absence. Since the day the old Jerusalem had been destroyed, a small band of faithful Christians had been working hard to make certain the city was rebuilt, in accordance to Biblical prophecy. Sister Amy, with her charisma and wisdom, had emerged as the leader of the movement. The necessity of building the city was never in question. There were events that had to unfold before Jesus returned, and many of these events were prophesied to take place in Jerusalem.

At first, the rebuilders had intended for New Jerusalem to be rebuilt where it had stood. There were thousands of property owning survivors from the city. It was assumed that their legal claims to the land would be recognized. Unfortunately, when Rail Blade had ground the city to dust, she'd also ground up every last shred of paper within several miles of ground zero. It had been difficult enough to prove who owned what building in such an ancient city when there had been records and actual structures linked to them. With no records and no structures, there was no court in the world up to the task of determining who owned the land within the white zone.

Then one night Sister Amy had a dream. In this dream, she saw a new Jerusalem rising from a white plain, and a new temple of Solomon, which would be consecrated with the blood of a red calf without flaw or blemish. She'd woke with images of the landscape fixed in her mind, and rented a bus and traveled across Texas until she found the land in her vision.

Servant strode toward the new temple. The structure glinted white in the sunlight. The city was being built from white stone similar in color and texture to the original stone of Jerusalem. The once tan desert soil was now a glinting diamond bed of white dust.

The temple looked like a stark stone structure from ancient times, a distant age of blood sacrifice and prophet-kings. At the same time it looked fresh, a new temple for a new age, the physical embodiment of the Lord's covenant with mankind. Ancient or young, it looked timeless, not so much a thing built by man as a thing that had grown from the earth, a place that had always stood and always would stand. It looked, beneath the pale white sky, like heaven come to earth.

Sister Amy walked down the broad front steps of the temple, her arms spread wide, her smile halving her face. "Brother Clint! So good to have you back!"

"It's good to be back, Sister," said Servant. "I wish I hadn't been taken away with the temple so close to completion. There's so much I could do here."

"Anything you can do here can be done by other," said Sister Amy. "The world has an abundance of carpenters and bricklayers. It has very few men who can match the speed and ferocity of these terrible dervishes."

"I know," said Servant. "But I still want to be of service."

"You will be of great service, I assure you," said Sister Amy, embracing him. "I dare say that the entire success of this project depends upon you, my brother."

"How so?" he said, as she stepped back from him.

"The Covenant, they trust you, even though they know your past?"

"Yes. No one in the Covenant has had an easy past." His voice grew soft. "They… they keep secrets, just as I keep secrets. I wonder, sometimes, if we shouldn't just confess our pasts to the world. Repent of what we've done, and move forward."

"Perhaps one day," said Sister Amy. "For now, I think it's more important that you do what good you can without the distraction of a scandal. It's good that you have a shared bond with your teammates. How about the technicians? Do you have a good relationship with them?"

"A good working relationship, I suppose. I'm somewhat of the odd man out among the team at the Knowbokov Foundation. There are a handful of believers, but most of the people I work with are agnostic or outright atheists. My proposal for a moment of prayer to start all meetings didn't go over well. Still, for the most part, religion isn't discussed at work, despite my best attempts to bring up the subject. I think the team respects me for what I can do, at least."

"Excellent," said Sister Amy. "Though they don't know it yet, they are going to help us complete our ultimate goal."

"Finishing the temple?" asked Servant. "Why would they be of any help at all?"

"Not finishing the temple," said Sister Amy. "Moving it. Nothing can stand in the way of prophecy. The Lord provides a path for all who seek it. We're going to build the temple here, where it's safe to work. When the time comes to consecrate it, well, according to the Bible, the temple must be in Jerusalem."

"Which is why we've built New Jerusalem," said Servant.

Sister Amy shook her head. "You think God can't tell the difference between Israel and Texas? When the time comes, we'll do this right. And the key to the whole thing is the space machine. With your help, we'll instantaneously move the whole temple into its proper place. You'll help us with that, won't you Brother Clint?"

He stared at her. "I... I'll... I really feel like this is something I need to think about."

"Think about it, yes," she said. "And feel about it! Search your heart. You'll know what's right."

"You tell me that again and again," he said, smiling weakly. "I don't know. Maybe other people listen to their heart and hear a way forward. I listen to my heart, and, sometimes, I'm listening only to silence."

"Everything happens for a reason, Brother Clint," said Sister Amy. "Your powers, your membership with the Covenant. Even your three years in a private hell, which gave you the scare you needed to stop fighting God's will and start following it."

"I want to believe that," he said.

"Then do," she said. "It's not something you need to decide immediately. The genetically engineered red calf born without flaw or blemish won't be arriving for a little while yet."

"Good," he said. "There's a lot on my mind. I... I may not be able to stay here long. Skyrider... she's left the team. And my other teammates, they... well, they'll be travelling. I'm not sure when they'll be back. I could be called away at any second."

"If so, we'll understand, like always," said Sister Amy. "We're proud of your service, Brother Clint. Hopefully, things will stay quiet until the rest of your team gets back from Mars. Now, come with me. I want to give you a tour of the progress we've made while you've been gone."

Clint followed her, his mind in turmoil, though he kept his face blank and said nothing. Why hadn't she told him about her plan to move the temple before now? And, more troubling... how did she know the rest of the team was on Mars?

AFTER SARAH REACHED the mainland, she flew low to avoid triggering defense radars that might have targeted her as a threat. She dropped her speed to around four hundred miles per hour, still a dangerous velocity when she was barely two hundred feet above the ground. Her path was mostly over rural areas, so she didn't have to worry about avoiding tall buildings, and she was safely above the tree line. Her biggest worry at this height was colliding with birds and bugs. Her helmet had built in radar that scanned her flight path out several miles and highlighted any flying creatures bigger than a mosquito. Even with her flight suit, running into a bird at four hundred miles an hour carried a lot more of a punch than a dervish's sword.

Often when she flew, she reached a state of peace, her mind literally lost in the clouds. As night fell, she couldn't stop thinking about all the things she should have said and done. She had no regrets about quitting, other than the constant regret that she'd ever joined the Covenant in the first place. Of course, this regret was founded in a deeper, darker, more long-lasting regret, that she'd ever been so foolish as to believe she could live a normal life. Was her mother right? Was her life with Carson based on a lie she was telling him, not to mention herself?

As the waves of second guesses and might-have-beens became a cacophony inside her skull, she filled her lungs to capacity and screamed, then filled her lungs and screamed again, rage, frustration and pain tearing from her throat and torn away by the wind, the wordless, haunting cry of a wild and wounded animal.

With her primal emotions released, her words returned and she shouted, "I didn't want this!"

She clenched her jaw tightly. Her throat burned, feeling raw. She'd covered two thousand miles since leaving. The sun was well below the horizon when the smattering of lights of her town came into view. In her dark uniform she was effectively invisible in the night sky, silent as a gliding owl. She slowed her speed to match the flow of cars along the interstate before veering off over the woods. Side streets passed beneath her until she reached a neighborhood of older ranch style homes surrounded by trees. Despite her stealth, dogs howled as she flew behind a row of houses, gliding over backyards in the darkness.

Sarah spread her arms and lowered her legs to land in her own backyard.

The lights were on in the living room and kitchen. Carson's truck was in the driveway. She frowned. She hadn't expected him to be home from work yet. She'd flown off without any of her civilian clothes. She'd planned to slip in through the back door unseen by neighbors. Worse, her car was in the driveway. She hadn't moved it because she'd been certain she'd be back much earlier and would have been if her mother had let her use the space machine. If Carson had been home long, he had to be wondering where she was.

She had no money on her, nor any credit cards. It wasn't like she could go into a store in her hometown dressed as Skyrider to buy new clothes anyway.

She took a deep breath. She could figure this out. Sneaking into the house while he was home was too risky. The house she'd shared with Carson could have fit comfortably into the ballroom of her childhood home. It was a three bedroom, two bathroom ranch built in the 70s, 1500 square feet, almost too much room for a childless couple. Not that they'd planned to be childless. Carson had wanted to have children, she'd wanted to have children, and then... and then she'd gotten cold feet. What if her children inherited superpowers?

Carson didn't know about her powers. He had no clue she'd once been world famous as the Thrill, and, at the time they met, she didn't even feel like she was keeping a secret from him. Sarah Knowbokov was dead. She was Sarah Buchanan, and some days felt like she'd been Sarah Buchanan all her life. (The fact that her old name was Sarah and her new name was Sarah had made the transitions between lives a bit easier, in retrospect. She'd purchased her new identity when she's still had her old powers, using them to manipulate a hacker who made a good living from identity theft to get her new papers. When he'd given her papers saying her new name was Sarah Buchanan, she'd been angry that he'd wasted her time. But as she looked over the papers, she saw that the real Sarah Buchanan was a decent match for her age and height. The real Sarah Buchanan had been a homeless teenager who'd gotten involved with an underworld boyfriend and learned a little too much for her safety. Homeless Sarah had no close relatives, just a couple of cousins living in California. She'd been legally missing for six years when Sarah stepped into her life.)

Sarah hid behind a large tree at the edge of her yard and took off her helmet. She took her personal cell phone from the pouch on her belt. Carson had called her and texted her. She hadn't heard it or felt it while she was plowing through the air. She'd been in such a hurry to get away from her mother she'd forgotten to patch the phone into her helmet display.

She dialed him back.

"Sarah?" he answered. "Where the hell are you?"

"Getting groceries," she said. "I thought I'd stop in and pick up a few things."

"Who drove you? Your car's still in the driveway."

"No one drove me. I walked."

"It's 20 degrees outside!"

"They have these new things called coats," said Sarah, trying to sound playful. "They also have these things called credit cards, and, stupid me, I forgot my purse. Since I see from your text that you're home, could you pop down to the store and get me?"

"Why didn't you answer my calls? Why didn't you reply to my texts?"

"My phone was on silent and I didn't feel it vibrating in my coat pocket. I wasn't expecting you to be home already, so I didn't look at my messages until I was at the store."

He didn't say anything for a couple of seconds. Then, "Okay. I'll be there in five minutes."

She put her helmet back on because, he was right, it was freaking cold. From the yard, she listened as he left the house. The second she heard his motor start, her feet were off the ground and she zipped to the backdoor, her key already in hand. She undressed in midair as she flew into the bedroom. She tossed her helmet onto the top shelf in the closet and jammed it behind some boxes, then finished peeling off her flight suit, cursing at how many buckles the damn thing had. She jammed everything into the bottom of the laundry hamper. Carson did laundry, like, three times a year, max.

She grabbed jeans and a sweater, and took a pair of boots and held them in her teeth as she flew down the hall pulling on her pants. She spit out the boots at the front closet and pulled on her sweater, then jammed her feet into the boots. She flung open the closet door and grabbed coat, gloves, and a scarf. She was out the back door maybe sixty seconds after she'd first entered the house, then, *WHOOSH*, up she shot into the sky. She couldn't fly at top speed since her civilian clothes couldn't take the stress, but she did have the advantage of being able to fly in a straight line to the store while Carson had to make a couple of left turns at stop signs. She arrived at the store in two minutes, frowning at how brightly lit the entire parking lot was. She prayed that no one was looking up, since her scarf was bright white. She landed behind the store near the dumpster then walked quickly around to the front. Her short flight had one nice side effect: She was legitimately freezing. Her cheeks felt red and stiff. She certainly looked as if she'd walked two miles to the store on a winter evening.

She waited next to row of Christmas trees for sale and watched for Carson. The second he pulled into the parking lot, she jogged toward his truck, and pulled open the passenger door before he even had the vehicle in park.

"Let's get home!" she said.

"I thought you needed something from the store!"

"It's nothing that can't wait until tomorrow," she said. "I'm freezing. Let's just get back to the house so I can get some hot chocolate inside me, stat."

He looked at her, at first studying her face as if he was trying to figure out if she was joking. Then his brow narrowed and she realized he was looking at her coat.

"What?" she asked.

"I... I thought I saw that coat in the closet when I grabbed my coat."

"Well, obviously you didn't," she said, rolling her eyes.

"I guess I didn't," he said.

"What are you doing home so early?" she said.

"Jimbo was off last Friday, so he volunteered to stay late to make up his hours."

"I wish you'd called me," she said.

"I did call you!"

"Right," she said. "Wish I hadn't left my phone on silent, then."

"What the hell possessed you to do this?" he asked.

"Come to the store?" she asked.

"In the dark, in the cold."

She shrugged. "I needed some fresh air."

"Just needed to get out of the house, huh?"

"Sure."

"You spend a lot of time out of the house," he said, sullenly.

She frowned. "So?"

"Nothing," he said, and put the truck into gear. They didn't say another word to each other on the drive home. She resented his silence, but not as much as she resented her own. What could she say to him? Tell him more lies? Tell him the truth? Carson wasn't an idiot. He had to have noticed just how much time she was away since joining the Covenant. She wanted to tell him that it was over. That she would no longer vanish on short notice for hours or even days at a time with little more than a quick voice mail and thin excuses. Being Sarah Buchanan Lee was going to be her full time occupation from now on.

They pulled into the driveway. Carson didn't open his car door. He stared straight ahead at the house. She waited for him to make the first move. He didn't.

"We just going to sit here?" she finally asked.

"No," he said. He swallowed hard. "I'm not coming inside."

"What? Why?"

He didn't look at her. He stared straight ahead at the house. Finally, he whispered, "Because I know what's going on."

Chapter Twenty
Truth

SARAH'S HEART RACED. What did he know? Did he know everything? If he knew... would that be wonderful, or terrible?

The silence between them extended a long time. She opened her mouth to speak.

He cut her off. "There's really nothing you need to say." He didn't sound angry. He sounded weary. "I... look. I know I..." He closed his mouth and took a deep breath through his nose. Softly, he said, "I could have done things differently. This isn't... this isn't all your fault."

"What... is it you think is your fault?" she asked.

Now his jaw clenched. "But it's not my fucking fault," he growled. "I mean, what? Just because we can't have kids, it's over? You're seeing another man?"

"What?" she was both relieved and mortified, and the word came out half as a laugh. "Another man? What are you—"

"Please don't," he said. "I can barely, just barely, take being cheated on. But I can't take being treated like an idiot. Christ, Sarah... sometimes... the excuses you make... it's like you think I'll believe anything you say."

"You... you shouldn't," she said. She leaned her head against the door window. It was cold as ice. "I... I'm not always honest with you."

"So who is it?" he said.

"It's nobody," she said. "There is no other man."

"Of course you say this immediately after telling me you're not always honest with me."

"I'm honest about everything that matters," she said. "I swear to you, I've never been unfaithful."

"Then what could you possibly be hiding from me?" he said. "I mean... those bruises you sometimes get. You said you were taking a judo class. You're not in any of the classes here."

"You're checking up on me?"

"Sarah, Bob Mills is the only guy in town who teaches judo. I ran into him and asked how you were doing. But it turns out he'd never had you in a class."

"Ah," she said. Which, in retrospect, was something she should have checked up on before using that particular lie. "Yeah. I wasn't really taking a class."

"Then why the bruises? Why the lies about where you are?"

"I don't know which bothers me more," she said. "That you think I'm having an affair, or that you think I'm having an affair with someone who beats me."

"Don't turn this around on me," he said. "I'm not the one who's lying about how he spends half his life."

"It's nowhere near half," she said.

"Fine. 40 percent. Ten! What does the number matter? You're doing something behind my back, something you'd rather lie about than be straight about. What could possibly... is it drugs?"

"Don't be stupid."

"Look, if it is drugs, there are programs—"

"How the hell could it be drugs?" she asked. "I mean, you're a deputy. You probably know every drug dealer in the county. You don't think it would get back to you if I were buying drugs?"

"Drugs weren't my first instinct," he said, sounding defensive.

"No, your first instinct was that I was a slut," she grumbled.

"What the fuck is your damage?" he exploded, banging his fist on the dashboard. "How the hell can you be angry at me?"

"Please don't shout at me," she said.

"Please tell me the goddamned truth," he screamed.

She swallowed hard, a lump in her throat. She was on the verge of tears.

"God damn," he sighed. "This is how this ends? You crying, me driving away angry, never knowing what secret you had that was so goddamned terrible you couldn't talk about it with me?"

"No," she said. "No, I don't want you to drive away. I... I want to tell you. I've wanted to tell you a long time. Since I met you. I... I came close, right before we were married. But... Carson, I love you. I love you more than anything else in the world. I can't lose you. I can't."

"You won't," he said. "You won't, if you just tell me the truth. I can handle anything. I swear... an affair, drugs... if you... if you've murdered someone."

She burst out in sobbing laughter. "Great. So now it's murder."

"Is it... is it murder?"

"Not too many," she said.

He looked pale.

"That was a joke," she said. "You used to get my jokes."

"I used to get a lot of things about you," he said. "Thought I did, at least." He squeezed the steering wheel again. "It's got to be something pretty terrible. I mean… what wouldn't you tell me? You tell me… tell me everything."

"Oh, Carson," she said, her voice catching in her throat. "I… I can't tell you. I can't tell you."

"Why?"

"I… I have to show you," she whispered.

"Show me what?"

"My… my secret," she said. "If I don't show it… you'll never believe me."

"Okay," he said. "Show me."

"Follow me," she said, opening the door.

"Where are we going?" he asked when she didn't head straight for the front door.

"The backyard," she said. "It's dark there."

"Great," he sighed, closing the truck door. "You're a vampire."

Hmm. Maybe she could convince him of… She shook her head. No. No more lies. Time for truth. She said, "Come on," and headed for the darkest corner of the yard, in the shadow of the trees.

"This where you've got the bodies buried?" he asked, following her. She could tell he was trying to make a joke. Tell also, a little bit, that he wasn't.

"I haven't killed—" she stopped. "I started to say I haven't killed anyone. But, honestly, I have."

"Oh my god," he said, stopping a few feet away from her. Then he grinned. "Okay, sorry. I know you're not some kind of crazy serial killer, so please stop joking."

"I'm not joking," she said. "And I'm not crazy, and I'm not really a murderer. I've only ever killed to defend myself or others. A dozen people, maybe. Two dozen, tops."

His grin slowly faded. "You… you're serious."

She crossed her arms. "I… I used to have a job. Like yours. Protecting people. Sometimes, things turned violent. We fought a lot of people who thought nothing at all about killing other people. We had to meet force with force, to protect the innocent."

"So, wait a minute," he said. "Are you… were you, like, in the military? Some sort of secret forces? Is that what you couldn't tell me?"

"No," she said. "I mean... not the military. The team I was part of... we didn't really have a name. And we weren't working for any government. But recently, the, uh, the team, a team, got back together. Now we do work with the government. We're called, um, the Covenant."

"The Covenant."

"I, look, I didn't like the name. Servant suggested it and my mother liked it and I didn't care enough to fight it because I thought I was going to quit in less than a week."

"Servant," said Carson, in a flat voice. "The super guy. With the white suit. That Servant."

"That's the guy."

"And... you work with him?"

"Carson," she said. "Look at my feet."

He looked down. He stared for nearly a minute. His eyes slowly rose the length of her body, stopping for several seconds just below her face. Finally, he summoned the courage to look her in the eyes. "You... you're feet... aren't touching the ground."

She nodded.

"You... you can... you can fly."

"Yes."

"How long have you..."

"Been able to fly?"

"Yes."

"Since before I could walk. Truth is, I didn't really get the hang of regular walking until I was, like, five."

He didn't say anything, just kept looking into her face.

It was time for the really hard part. "I used to be called the Thrill. I fought crime with my sister, Rail Blade."

"The... the alien who destroyed Jerusalem?"

"She wasn't an alien," she said. "I'm not an alien. I'm completely human. Totally ordinary. Except, you know, the flying stuff."

"And... and you control minds," he said softly. "The Thrill could control people's minds."

"Okay, no, she couldn't. I couldn't. I just, there was this voice thing I did and... look. It doesn't matter anymore. I had a surgery. It altered my vocal cords. I don't have that power anymore."

"Did you... when we met, did you—"

"Have that power?" she asked. "No. I came here maybe a month after I had the surgery. You were the first guy I talked to for any length of time at all after I gave up my old powers. It was… intoxicating."

"Intoxicating?"

"Because you liked me. I could tell you liked me. And it wasn't because of any mumbo jumbo weird powers I had. You like me for being me."

His couldn't look into her face. "But you weren't being you."

"No," she whispered. "And yes. I mean… I used to be someone different. But I stopped being that person. I gave up the sky and came down to earth. And you, you kept me grounded. I've never had a single regret about meeting you, except for being a coward and not telling you everything."

"If you'd told me everything," he said, "I'd have had you arrested. I mean, the Thrill is wanted by the FBI. I mean… how can you… how can you be—"

"I wasn't guilty of any of the things they say I've done," she said. "Except, you know, for some of the things." She crossed her arms. "Things I did for the greater good."

"According to what the FBI says, you used your mind control powers to defraud wealthy men. They say you could ask for anything and people would give it to you."

"Those definitely weren't my best years. But everyone I stole money from was a crook in some way," she said. "Which doesn't make what I did right. That wasn't how I wanted to live. So I gave up my powers and came to live here."

"Why here?"

"Because I met you, duh."

He looked dubious.

"I had some money. From that time in my life where I was, uh, borrowing from crooks. But I didn't want to live on ill-gotten gains forever. My father—my real father, Niko Knowbokov—owned a fleet of private planes. Even though I could fly on my own, I also learned to fly his planes when I was young. So, as long as I was faking an identity, I also arranged for a pilot's license so I could have some honest revenue. And then, on my very first job, I ran into you. You know it was love at first sight."

"Love," he said, in an almost bitter tone.

She didn't know how to answer that. Wasn't even sure it was a question.

"And now... you're a superhero?"

"I don't really use that word. But, whatever. Yeah."

"I hate them," he said. "Every cop I've ever met hates them. Every time the Covenant is in the headlines, we hate them a little more."

"We're trying to be helpful."

"You fly above us. You turn into ghosts, or are bulletproof. I mean, how the hell am I supposed to deal with this? What the fuck?"

"Keep your voice down," she said. "At least let's go in the house so the neighbors can't hear us."

"You go in the house," he said, turning away. "I'm going to the cabin."

"Please don't go," she said.

"You don't have the right to ask me to stay," he said. "You're a stranger to me. A stranger. I'm going to stay out at the lake for a few days. When I come back... please be gone."

She didn't follow him, didn't call out. What could she say? What was there to say?

She watched as his headlights pulled down the driveway. With her feet still six inches off the ground, she willed herself to float toward the back door. During her confession, she'd been chilled to the bone by the awful truth of her secrets. Now, she was just plain cold.

Inside the house, she put up her jacket. She went back to the bedroom. She heard something in the closet. She opened the door and found her helmet beeping. She'd forgotten to put it in silent mode. She pulled the helmet down and put it on. Using retinal commands, she launched her voice mail.

"Sarah, it's Richard," said the recording. The hair rose on the back of her neck. Richard Rogers. Her first lover, and the man who ditched her for her sister. She hadn't heard from him in seven years. This couldn't possibly be good news. "I... there's really no way for you to call me back, and this isn't something I want to leave on voice mail. I'm going to call again in one hour and pray you'll answer the phone. It's... look, just make sure you answer the phone. One hour. Until then, be careful."

Chapter Twenty One
God of Mars

APP STUMBLED IN the fine red-beige dust before falling to his knees. He looked about, mouth agape, at the long, rocky plain he'd landed on. Through the dust haze, he could faintly make out the distant, towering walls of the canyon.

Chimpion stood beside him in her pressure suit, showing no signs of disorientation. App's belt normally spared him from vertigo following a space machine jump, but it was fine-tuned to earthly environments, not Mars. To his right, Steam-Dragon dropped to all fours, spreading her wings to steady herself, a nearly pointless effort in an atmosphere far thinner than the air at the peak of Everest.

"Fuck," whimpered Steam-Dragon. "I think I'm going to be sick."

"The fractional gravity is likely affecting your inner ear," said Chimpion. "You'll adjust in a few minutes."

"Holy moly," said App, taking Chimpion's hand as she offered it. With her support, he rose to his feet. "We're on Mars!"

There was gurgling, retching sound through the coms.

App grimaced. "Did you throw up in your suit?"

"Oh god," moaned Steam-Dragon. "It's everywhere. There's no way to even wipe my chin! Can we go home now?"

"No," said Chimpion. "Suck it up."

"That's a terrible choice of words," said App.

"Jesus," whined Steam-Dragon. "The smell."

"You've survived worse," said App.

"Yeah," she said softly. "Yeah. I have. Okay. I'm… I'm okay. What next?"

"I've got a hunch that's what we're looking for," said Chimpion, pointing behind them.

App turned around. In the distance was a geodesic dome big enough to hold a small town. They were at least a mile away, maybe two, and this far from home, the space machine couldn't be used to take a shortcut.

"The air's too thin for me to fly," said Steam-Dragon. "Guess we'll hoof it."

"This will be easy with the gravity so low," said Chimpion, jumping in a long arc that carried her a dozen yards across the dusty, rock-strewn ground. "Come on!"

App followed. He couldn't match the length of Chimpion's leaps, but it was still a bit like jumping on a trampoline. He lacked Chimpion's agility, however, and the soil proved deceptively difficult to land on. The fine dust was like jumping into talcum powder that lay over an unseen layer of sharp and shifting rocks. Steam-Dragon didn't even try to jump, trudging along in a four legged gait, her head hanging low as she surveyed the places where she put her feet. Her dragon face didn't convey a wide range of expressions but she certainly looked sullen. From time to time, Becky's voice came over the coms, but she wasn't talking to them as she whispered, "Ew. No. Oh no. Jesus no."

Chimpion, on the other hand, had the posture and body language of a child rushing toward the tree on Christmas morning. She looked the way App had wanted to feel. When he'd been in kindergarten, his teacher had told him that one day men would live on the red planet. He'd taken it as an iron-clad promise that he'd be one of the first people on the rocket ship. Lots of children had such dreams, but in retrospect, App could see the dark appeal of life on another planet. He'd found it comforting to think that there was an entire planet where his father didn't live, where he could be free from violence and abuse.

Now that he was here, his father came to his mind with every step. The land here was barren, hostile, cold, and dimly lit, devoid of any nurturing elements whatsoever. His anticipated excitement had given way to full blown disgust. Fuck Mars. Just fuck it. Mars didn't want him around, and he didn't need Mars in any way to live a fulfilled, happy life.

"You're being oddly quiet, App," said Chimpion, standing atop a house-sized boulder.

"Just wondering why the hell this seemed like a good idea when I first heard it," he said, leaping up to join her atop the rock.

"There's nothing to worry about," said Chimpion. "We're just here to ask Rail Blade a few questions."

"To ask questions of someone modifying the magnetic field of an entire planet with her mind," said App. "What if we're doing more harm than good by coming here?"

"What can we possibly hurt?"

"Aside from us?" asked App. "How about Earth? Rail Blade didn't come all the way to Mars because she wanted company. What if she gets pissed off by our showing up on her doorstep and heads back to Earth to make sure she doesn't get any more visitors? She could rust everything on Earth made of iron. Overnight, there's no cars, no skyscrapers, no big ships or bridges or construction equipment. She could send mankind back to the Stone Age."

"If she's that big of a threat, ignoring her isn't a responsible path," said Chimpion.

"Maybe pitching out some of these objections before we got to Mars would have been helpful," said Steam-Dragon, finally catching up. "Then I wouldn't be trapped in dizzy world with my own vomit seeping into my crotch."

"It's not too late to turn back," said App.

"It's far too late to turn back," said Chimpion. "You don't think she knows we're here already?"

"Maybe she doesn't," said Steam-Dragon. "She's not omniscient."

"So you admit she's not a god," said Chimpion.

"Well, no," said App. "But—"

"She's just another human being with powers," said Chimpion. "There's no opponent on earth we'd leave alone simply because they were dangerous to confront. You, Servant, and Skyrider didn't back down from Sundancer even though she could have burned half the planet."

"Right. You're right," said App. "Though, no offense to either of you, I'd be a lot less worried if Servant was here."

"So she could beat him again?" asked Steam-Dragon. "If Rail Blade does seem hostile, I'll hit her hard and fast. I don't have any metal in my armor. I've got a shot if I take her by surprise."

App stared at her. "I don't know whether your attitude is encouraging or terrifying."

"Let's get this over with," Steam-Dragon said, moving forward. "The sooner we finish this, the sooner I can get home and take a shower."

By now, they were close enough to the dome that the dim light and dust no long obscured its details. Within the dome they could see vines climbing along the interior walls, the leaves ranging in shade from pale pea green to nearly black. Flowers of varying sizes and colors hung from them, red rosettes, pink disks, tiny yellow starbursts, and grand white trumpets that resembled doll-sized wedding gowns. Beads of moisture clung to the interiors of the windows, forming droplets that left trails as they rolled down the panes.

"Uh, guys," said Steam-Dragon, her head still pointed down. "Look at this."

They looked. In the dust leading from the dome, footprints. App wasn't exactly a skilled tracker, but he guessed the tracks belonged to a barefoot human woman and two or three shoeless children, along with a larger set of prints that looked like a man in boots. The prints overlapped each other. Whoever had walked here had taken this path more than once.

"No one said there'd be children here," said Steam-Dragon.

"We don't know that there are," said Chimpion. "Who knows how old these footprints might be?"

"What, you think they belong to ancient Martians?" App asked.

"Unless Rail Blade is capable of virgin birth," said Chimpion. "I mean... she came here alone, right? Nobody came with her."

"Just more questions to ask once we get inside," said Steam-Dragon. She pointed her snout along the trail of footprints. "Look where they're originating from in the wall of the dome. That look like an airlock to you?"

"Maybe," said App. "Should we go up and knock?"

"Let's not wait for an invitation into the dome," said Chimpion. "Out here, even with our pressure suits, we'll be battling the terrain as well as Rail Blade if things get messy. Inside, it's obviously warm enough to grow plants, and pressurized enough to support liquid water. We can probably survive even if our suits are compromised."

"Agreed," said Steam-Dragon. "We obviously don't want to break in through the glass. App, can you ghost your way into the airlock and see if you can find the controls?"

"What makes you think I would know how to operate an airlock even if I do find the controls?"

"How hard could it be?" asked Chimpion.

"I don't know," he said. "Ordinarily when I hit a situation requiring a new skill, I can find a You-Tube video demonstrating just about anything. Disconnected from the internet, I feel like part of my brain is missing."

"Just improvise, okay?" said Steam-Dragon. "How did you become a superhero again?"

"It's the belt that's the hero," said App. "I'm just along for the ride. But, give me a minute. I'll see what I can do."

He jumped toward the dome, entering ghost mode. He drifted through the hatch that opened to the outside, and solidified inside a steel tube with small windows along the top. The tube was tall enough to stand in comfortably. At each end was a door with a wheel attached, like something you might find on a submarine. Switching to full spectrum vision, he didn't see anything at all electronic about the doors. They seemed to be purely mechanical. He turned the wheel and found it moved smoothly. Opening the door also proved easy. The iron door probably weighed a ton, but it was carefully balanced on nearly frictionless hinges. He motioned for Steam-Dragon and Chimpion to come forward.

"It wasn't locked," he said.

"Must be a safe neighborhood," said Steam-Dragon.

They sealed the outer door behind them. As App spun the wheel to the interior door, air hissed into the room.

"Oxygen levels are breathable," said Steam-Dragon, monitoring the changing atmosphere. "Pressure's kind of low, but a hell of a lot better than what's outside."

"I wouldn't take your suit off just yet," said Chimpion.

"Not planning on it," said Steam-Dragon. "No way I'm stepping inside that dome less than fully armored."

"I'm transmitting coordinate and visual scans for the airlock back to headquarters," said App. "It might make a good target for the space machine to bring us back."

"Agreed," said Chimpion, moving forward.

They stepped into the dome, gazing upward. App had seen it was big from the outside, but from inside its scale was even more impressive, larger than any sporting arena he'd been inside. He noticed that while there were vines all over the place and neat rows of various vegetables, there were no trees. He took note of the numerous bees buzzing around among the flowers, wondering how they'd gotten to Mars. Then he did a double take, as his enhanced vision revealed electromagnetic fields around each bee. His eyes went wide.

"Those aren't bees," he said.

"They're tiny robots," said Chimpion. "They're made of metal."

"I don't think they're robots," said App, stepping toward a nearby flower for a closer look at the nearest bee. "They don't have any circuitry or motors. They're being moved entirely by electric fields, like little puppets on strings of magnetism."

"Yes," said a voice that came from all directions at once, as the bees vibrated their wings at a frequency that simulated human speech. "They move because I will them to move."

"Are we speaking with Amelia Knowbokov?" asked Chimpion.

"You've entered my home uninvited," said the omnivocal bees as they gathered around the trio of travelers. "I believe you should identify yourself first."

"My name is Johnny Appleton, but everyone calls me App," said App. "I work with your sister, Sarah. We all do. This is Chimpion and this is Steam-Dragon."

"You work with Sarah?" asked the bees. "Then... she's still alive?"

"She is," said Chimpion. "Though she recently was nearly killed by men who had the ability to pluck steel blades from thin air."

"I see," said the bees. "And you believe I'm somehow implicated in this?"

"We'd be negligent if we didn't at least ask you a few questions," said Chimpion.

"The last talking chimpanzee I encountered belonged to Rex Monday," said the bees. "You'll forgive me if I'm suspicious of why you're here."

"We chimps were enslaved by Rex Monday," said Chimpion. "We were his test subjects, not his allies. You've nothing to fear from me."

"No," said the bees. "Nothing at all. I've evolved past any danger the three of you might pose. With but a thought, I could craft blades inside your chests and carve out your still beating hearts."

"It's not going to come to that," said App. "Sarah said you weren't a bad person. If you intended to kill us, you wouldn't be talking to us. Why don't you send the bees away and come out so we can talk face to face."

"It's been a long time since I've truly had a face," said the bees.

"You mean... what?" asked Steam-Dragon. "Like all you've got is a skull?"

"With my ferrokinetic senses, I feel the blood within you Steam-Dragon. You're missing your legs."

"Yes," said Steam-Dragon.

"Mars isn't a safe environment for human flesh," said the bees, swarming together in front of the trio. "I lost my toes to frost bite shortly after I arrived, but it was a simple matter to replace them with iron prosthetics. Since my consciousness animates iron, I could even feel with them, with the same range of sensation I had with my old toes."

The bee swarm grew thicker. "But Mars wasn't done with me. I lost an arm during a cave-in while exploring a frozen aquafer. I replaced it with iron and moved on, but failed to consider the possibility that ancient Martian microbes might inhabit the ice that had crushed my arm. In a matter of days, an infection spread that my earthly immune system had no defense against. My body was nothing but nutrients to be devoured by microbes hungry for the moisture within me. Hour by hour, flesh dripped away, a foul, black goo. Hour by hour, I replaced what I'd lost, transferring my old consciousness into iron skin, iron bones, and an iron heart. Even my brain was lost, but no matter. My mind endures as magnetized bits of information within my iron form.

The bees clumped together into a form vaguely human, then definitely human, then definitely female, tall, well-muscled, shapely as a classical Venus, utterly nude, and made completely of glinting black iron.

"Amelia?" asked App.

"No more," said the iron woman. "That person is long since dead, as is any humanity she once possessed. My name is Rail Blade. I am the only god of Mars and you will kneel before me."

Chapter Twenty-Two
Lonely Planet

"**I KNOW YOU'VE** been through things we can't even imagine," said App. "But, please listen to us. We're just looking for answers. We aren't here to fight you."

"Speak for yourself," said Steam-Dragon. She glared at Rail Blade. "This bitch is crazy."

"The only crazy people here are those who fail to kneel," said Rail Blade.

"Y'all have to agree she's moved into full blown supervillain mode now, right?"

"Take her!" said Chimpion.

Before App could blink, Chimpion threw herself toward the statuesque woman, drawing a long blade from the scabbard on her hip. App threw his hands over his ears as a terrible, high-pitched whine threatened to liquefy his brains. Unfortunately, due to his helmet, he couldn't actually block any of the sound. A fraction of a second later, Rail Blade's head toppled from her shoulders in sudden silence. Steam-Dragon leapt forward and grabbed the severed head between her jaws and shook it violently.

"What the fuck?" App said, or thought he said, since he was completely deaf. "Reset!"

Suddenly, there was noise again.

"App! Shock her! Shock her!" Chimpion cried out. "My sonic blade has stunned her, but we can't let her form coherent thoughts." She plunged the blade into Rail Blade's heart, or at least where the heart would be on a human body, and twisted. The deafening shriek of the sonic blade disintegrating iron again burst App's eardrums.

App still didn't know why they had attacked, but also knew now that they were engaged, it was kill or be killed. Chimpion was right. If Rail Blade had even a second to focus, they'd all be dead.

Chimpion was also right about shocking her. If her mind was stored as magnetic bits, a good jolt of electricity was going to mess it up pretty badly. "Eel mode," shouted App. He lunged forward.

Either by chance or by the reflexes of an experience fighter, Rail Blade's body kicked out as he flew toward her, catching him in the sternum, shattering every bone in his chest with a pile drive kick. He was thrown backwards, good as dead, with only enough consciousness left to mumble "reset" before he hit the ground.

He rolled to his feet good as new, but was dismayed to see that Rail Blade's torso had grabbed Chimpion by the sword arm. Rail Blade flung her attacker away, throwing her far across the vegetable fields. The headless Rail Blade rose to her feet and punched Steam-Dragon in the jaw, a savage blow that knocked Steam-Dragon to her knees. Rail Blade's severed head, which Steam-Dragon had still had in her mouth, flew free and bounced into a nearby potato patch. The headless body walked toward the head as it rolled to a stop. App could see a fist sized hole through Rail Blade's torso, the work of the sonic sword.

Rail Blade knelt and picked up her head and set it back onto her shoulders. The hole in her torso closed as she turned around to face Steam-Dragon.

"I've decided against killing you swiftly," said Rail Blade, her dark eyes narrowed into steely hatred.

"Do your worst, bitch!" snarled Steam-Dragon, engulfing the iron woman in a jet of steam.

Rail Blade stepped forward from the cloud none the worse for wear, her fingers lengthening into razor-edged claws. She raked her blades across Steam-Dragon's face and looked a little surprised when the blow failed to cut through the carbon fiber scales.

Steam-Dragon leapt up, latching onto Rail Blade's shoulders with her fore claws, raking her belly with her hind claws. She dug into Rail Blade's iron skin to no avail. There was nothing soft beneath. Rail Blade had no blood to spill.

This wasn't the case with Steam-Dragon. Rail Blade calmly looked into the dragon's eyes. Inside the armor, Becky began to scream.

App ran forward, switching back into his eel mode. Rail Blade's back was to him, and she was focused on maximizing Steam-Dragon's pain. She didn't notice his approach at all until the last second, but by then it was too late. He placed his hands upon her and hit her with a full charge.

Rail Blade's body stiffened and she crumbled to her hands and knees. Steam-Dragon collapsed, utterly limp and lifeless.

"Reset!" App called out. His eel mode took forever to recharge naturally. But, after a reset, his body was brand new.

"Eel mode!" Again, he placed his hands on Rail Blade, putting his fingers on the sides of her temples. Again, he shocked her until his bioelectricity was exhausted, leaving him with spots dancing before his eyes. Rail Blade collapsed, limbs twitching.

"Get back!" Chimpion shouted. He jumped back. The chimp landed where he'd just stood. She held a pellet in her hand, crushing it against the back of Rail Blade's skull.

A cloud of greenish gas engulfed Rail Blade's form as Chimpion leapt away.

"Don't let the fumes hit you," she yelled. "Your suit won't save you."

"This seems like stuff you might have mentioned before now," App grumbled, backing away. "Ghost mode! How am I supposed to keep zapping her if I can't get near her?"

"You don't need to get near her," said Chimpion. "I did my research before coming. That capsule has all the acid we need to completely dissolve a human-sized mass of iron. The mineral residue left in the aftermath isn't capable of being magnetized, which means her magnetic mind is destroyed. She's dead."

"You're sure?" he asked.

"I'm certain," said Chimpion. "We've won."

App clenched his fists. "Won? Steam-Dragon's dead! Why the hell were we even fighting?"

"That was the whole reason for coming to Mars," said Chimpion.

"No it wasn't!" said App. "We came to Mars to ask questions, not kill Sarah's sister."

"Oh," said Chimpion. "I mean… didn't you see… you mean they didn't tell you?"

"Tell me what?" asked App.

"I mean, Mrs. Knowbokov? The full mission… you didn't know?"

"What the fuck are you talking about?"

"You… you should see this," said Chimpion, pulling her phone from her belt. "This video will explain everything."

She held the device toward App. He couldn't hold it in ghost mode, of course, so he said, "Reset."

He took the phone. There was a sudden whine behind him. Then there was nothing at all.

Chimpion pulled the sonic blade from App's skull. He dropped to the ground, his pulverized brains dripping across the damp soil beneath them. Chimpion dragged his body toward a nearby ditch and kicked him in. She took out a second acid capsule and smashed it onto his belt, stepping away from the billowing gas. If App had died on earth, he'd already have been remotely rebooted. But here on Mars, the computers didn't even know he was dead. Nor did they have any record of his final moments. She'd turned on the radio jammer hidden in her belt buckle the moment they'd come inside the dome.

She walked over to the red-gray bubbling mass that had been Rail Blade and took several photos. Steam-Dragon's head turned slowly toward her, her eyes looking dully in her direction.

"Still alive?" Chimpion asked.

"Wh—why?" asked Steam-Dragon, her voice gurgling. "Why did you kill... App?"

"Because there really was a secret mission," said Chimpion. "Though it didn't come from Mrs. Knowbokov. My only loyalty is to Pangea. My government earns essential revenue by selling my services to the highest bidder. Rail Blade destroyed a city holy to three religions. The price on her head was much too large for my nation to refuse the contract."

Chimpion knelt before Steam-Dragon. "You're a very tough woman. I can hear how injured you are. I can't believe you're even alive, let alone awake."

"I don't... don't feel anything..." said Steam-Dragon, softly.

"I'm sorry she didn't kill you," said Chimpion, searching for the latch that opened Steam-Dragon's chest cavity. She opened it, revealing Becky's sweaty, blood-stained face. "I liked you, for a human. But I can't take the chance you'll survive your injuries."

"You won't... won't get..."

"Get away with this?" asked Chimpion. "I already have. When I get back to earth, I'll kill Sarah and Mrs. Knowbokov. They may not be directly responsible for the destruction of Jerusalem, but the people writing checks to my nation aren't ones to parse degrees of guilt. Every Knowbokov must die to pay the blood debt."

"Fu—" Becky never finished the word, as Chimpion sliced across her windpipe with the razor sharp edge of a shuriken.

Chimpion watched silently as the light in Becky's eyes swiftly faded. A vague shadow moved at the furthest edges of her vision. She turned her head and found nobody there. She rose, taking more throwing stars from her belt, remembering the multiple footprints they'd found outside. Rail Blade wasn't alone in this dome.

She crept along the rows of plants, her eyes open for any motion. There were no more iron bees. The dome was hauntingly silent save for the whisper of wind across the outer glass.

She heard a murmur, distant, vague. She jerked her head toward the sound, then went still, ears straining to make sense of the noise. It was almost like a voice, a man's voice, far in the distance. But, the more she listened, the more she convinced herself it was only the wind vibrating some strut on the far side of the structure.

She briefly contemplated taking off her helmet. A few quick sniffs could probably determine once and for all how many people lived inside the dome. But, if there were other people here, or if Rail-Blade somehow reconstituted herself, many of Chimpion's most powerful remaining weapons were poison gas bombs. In such strange terrain, it was best not to take chances.

She quickly built a mental map of the pathways within the dome. Rail Blade hadn't laid the plants out in a strict grid, perhaps to enhance the illusion that life inside the dome was natural. Still, it soon became clear that the wider pathways led toward the center of the dome. She spotted a building and took cover behind a large barrel that collected the condensation inside the greenhouse. She peeked around and studied the structure she'd seen, a simple, modest cottage that would have looked perfectly at home in some mountain valley, save for the fact that it's walls were rusted iron rather than wood or shingles.

The cottage was completely quiet. She darted toward it, pressing flat against the side of the door. She listened intently. Not a peep came from within. Moving in silence, she tested the doorknob. It turned without resistance.

She pushed the door open. Hearing nothing, she rolled inside and came up with a throwing star in one hand and a gas grenade in the other. They weren't needed. The place was empty save for simple furniture. The interior was mostly a kitchen, with a few doors leading off into other parts of the house. Chimpion poked her head through the doors, looking around. In the bedroom, her heart doubled in speed when she spotted three small people sitting in chairs beside the bed. Her brow furrowed. The people weren't moving. Nor, it seemed, as she drew closer, were they people. They were dolls formed of iron, three naked little girls of varying ages, though none seemed larger than a child of five. Save for their cast iron hue, they were disturbingly lifelike in their detail. The hair wasn't a sculpted lump, but instead consisted of millions of fine wires flowing together. The dolls even had eyebrows, and up close the iron skin had pores and delicate wrinkles around the lips.

Chimpion shook her head. Rail Blade, in her loneliness, must have created these iron children to keep her company. With her powers, she could have made them walk, perhaps even talk. No doubt somewhere nearby she might find an iron husband, responsible for the larger, booted footprints in the dust. How pitiful.

She had no personal animosity toward Rail Blade. A contract to kill was merely business. No stranger to loneliness herself, she understood the madness Rail Blade must have slipped into on this lonely planet. Chimpion took some small comfort in the fact that her assassination had also been an act of mercy.

Chapter Twenty-Three
Wind-Tossed

SARAH WAS A MILE above the earth, beneath an endless blanket of crisp stars that made the clouds below her glow with a ghostly light. She threw a star map onto her heads up display and used it to locate Mars as she waited for Richard to call back.

Her mind was in turmoil. Since Carson had driven off, not even Richard's cryptic phone call had been able to focus her thoughts. Richard's call couldn't be trivial, but how could it matter as much as what she'd just done to her marriage? *I should have told him sooner,* she thought, only to instantly think, *I should never have told him.* The two possible choices seemed to battle for her to make a decision, as if unaware that the decision was already made. He knew. *He knew.* And he'd left her. What could she have expected? How could she ever have imagined he would love her after five years of lies?

She should have told him the truth when they'd first met. Only, how could that have been possible? If she'd been honest with Carson before they fell in love, he'd have reported her to the FBI, assuming he didn't just arrest her himself. What choice had she had but to lie? Didn't he see? Couldn't he understand? She hadn't possessed the luxury of being truthful. She'd never lied to hurt him. It was never her intention to seduce, fool, and trap him as part of some sinister scheme.

On the other hand, what did she think would happen? How could she have thought she could keep this secret? Right now, at this moment, floating above the world like a lonely, wind-tossed balloon, it seemed obvious. She could fly. She could fly because her father had broken physics. Ultimately, worst of all, he'd broken her. How could her father have ever hated her so much that he'd place the weight of the world on her shoulders? It was the sort of thing she would have liked to talk about, to process her turbulent emotions the way other, normal people were allowed to. With this emotional sword of Damocles hanging over her, it was inevitable that one day she'd finally reveal her true self.

"But this isn't my true self," she said out loud. She didn't choose to be Sarah Knowbokov. That person was a creation of her father, a reaction to her sister, a parody of the person they wanted her to be. Sarah Buchanan was who she chose to be. If she wasn't who she choose to be, who was she?

To define one's own identity was surely the most fundamental human right of all.

It was the word "human" in front of the word "right" that caused her problems.

Here she was, aloft in the heavens, an angel, a god of old, looking down upon the world. She might be an occasional visitor of the earth but at heart she was a spirit of the air. Sarah Knowbokov was no one she wished to be. Sarah Buchanan was someone she could no longer be. So who the hell was she?

She held her gloved hand before her. It glittered with frost. She always frosted up at this height. She was familiar with this because every day of her life had been spent riding the sky. For better or worse, Skyrider, the identity she wanted least, was the only one that truly fit her.

"Damn it," she said, with a sigh.

Her phone rang.

"Richard?" she said, transferring the call to her helmet. "How the hell are you—"

"Sarah, I'm hoping you've picked up your phone and this isn't going to voice mail."

"It's me, not voice mail. What the hell are—"

"Before you ask a lot of questions, you should know I'm still on Mars. There's going to be about a sixteen minute lag before I hear anything you say to me."

"Great," she said. "It's like a conversation with my mother."

"Forgive me for launching a monologue, but there's stuff you need to know. First, obviously, I'm alive, and so is Amelia. We're married. We'll, not married married, since, you know, there's not anything vaguely resembling either church or state on Mars. But we live together in this sweet dome with our daughters."

"Daughters?" said Sarah, not caring about the lag. *Daughters?* She couldn't imagine Amelia as a mother.

"Amelia is a terrific mom. Also, a pretty good architect and terraformer. And it turns out I'm not a bad farmer, and that my skills as a network tech from my pre-erasure life have come in handy. You know how satellites sent to Mars occasionally vanish?"

"Sure," she started to say, then realized it was a rhetorical question.

"We've borrowed one or two or four. The design and planning things on these missions is so long the hardware on board is stuff I was tinkering with in high school. I've hacked them to get us some internet. Slow, like way worse than AOL dialup, but it keeps us up to date on what's happening back on earth. Obviously, it's letting me make you a voice over IP call to the phone number we hacked from your mother's file on you."

Sarah grimaced. Should she start asking questions now, and presume he'd start answering them in a half hour? Or should she put up with his somewhat rambling storytelling and hope he'd answer her questions before she even asked them? Like, her big, number one question: Why call now? Did this have something to do with the Covenant going to Mars?

"Enough backstory," said Richard. "I mean, I know you want to know more, but right now you don't have a lot of time for conversation. Steam-Dragon, Chimpion, and App showed up here about two hours ago on some kind of assassination mission. Since we do get the news here, we knew these were your team members from the Covenant, and, yes, before you ask, I know you're Skyrider, even with the plastic surgery and the dark hair."

Sarah clenched her fists. Assassination mission? Amelia must have misinterpreted their intentions. Probably, all three of them were dead.

"I don't think App or the dragon were fully in the loop on the true mission," said Richard. "After Chimpion killed Amelia, she killed her companions to keep them from talking."

"Amelia's dead?" Sarah said, not believing the news.

"Wait," said Richard. "I probably just gave you a heart attack. The chimp didn't actually kill Amelia. Amelia's fine. What Chimpion killed was an iron manikin Amelia created that looked like her. Amelia fed your teammates some BS about how her real body had died years ago. Since superheroes put up with such weird shit on a daily basis, I think they bought it. Chimpion dissolved the doppelganger with some nasty acid, then turned on her companions and killed them both. Amelia had already hurt Steam-Dragon, but didn't intend for her to actually die. Right before Steam-Dragon died, Chimpion did the classic supervillain secret plan reveal. I was standing right beside her listening to the whole thing. She's being paid by some religious nuts to avenge the destruction of Jerusalem. Now that she thinks she's killed Rail Blade, she's coming back to kill you and your mother. I don't agree with the decision but

Amelia let her go. She says that once the chimp tells everyone we're dead, we won't have to worry about more assassination attempts. As far as the chimp killing you or your mother, Amelia says she's confident you can take care of this. I mean, you've fought Baby Gun. A chimp shouldn't be a problem now that she won't have the element of surprise."

"Why would Chimpion want to kill mother?" asked Sarah. "She had nothing to do with Jerusalem."

"You're probably just as confused as I am about why your mother's a target, since she had nothing to do with Jerusalem. I think they just want every Knowbokov dead. Which, of course, they've already blown, since Amelia's fine and they don't even know about our daughters."

"Shit," said Sarah, looking at the time. Chimpion would already be back at the island. Would she continue to play the double agent, or go straight for her mother?

"If I know you, you're already racing to your mother's side and you don't need me distracting you. Since the time lag makes phone calls sort of a chore, I'm going to drop you an email with more about our lives here on Mars. I'll expect back an email soon telling how you kicked a super-chimp's ass and saved the day. Deal?"

"Deal," she said, as the call went dead.

Richard was wrong about one thing. She sure as hell wasn't going to waste time flying to her mother's side when one phone call could take her there via space machine. She opened a channel and said, "Katya? Nathan? Whoever's on duty, I need a lift back to HQ, ASAP."

No one answered.

"Guys," she said. "Who's on duty tonight? I need to return to HQ. Copy?"

No answer.

"Hello?" she asked.

Nothing but silence. Could Chimpion have already killed everyone? Or, just as likely, with her demonstrated knowledge of the Knowobokov Foundation computers, could she have somehow rigged the coms to block any calls Sarah might try to make? Sarah clenched her fists and looked toward the east. Time to find out just how fast she could really go.

Chapter Twenty-Four
Heart of Wrath

CLINT WAS LOST in thought, barely paying attention to Sister Amy's words, when Brother Dunlap walked up to them and asked, "Sister, may I speak with you in private? I'll only need a few seconds."

"Of course," she said. "Clint, if you'll excuse me, I'll be right back."

Clint watched as they moved away, stepping into the next room. App had called him Christian Superman, but at this moment he really wished he had x-ray vision and superhearing. He hadn't brought up the question he had about her knowing that the team had gone to Mars.

He looked at his wrist. The smart fibers of his costume knew his intent and flashed the time. Maybe the team was back by now. "Call the base," he said.

He waited. He frowned when ten seconds had passed and he hadn't been patched through. He started to attempt the call again, but Sister Amy had walked back into the room. She always smiled, always looked happy, but at this moment she was positively glowing, beaming with unbridled joy.

"Brother Clint!" she exclaimed. "It's here! The calf is here!"

"Calf?"

"The red calf born without flaw or blemish. Leviticus tells us that this is the sacrifice that will sanctify the temple. We're ready to make our move! What a glorious moment to be alive!"

"I... I don't think I can help you," said Clint.

"I understand it's asking a lot," said Sister Amy. "And I know this seems sudden. I apologize for not including you in the full plan before now."

"Why didn't you?"

"Your work brings you into contact with super humans on a daily basis. What if you encountered a telepath? It was safer that you didn't know."

He frowned. Was this her real reason? Or was it because she knew of his past as a supervillain? Even if she would never say it, he knew his past was difficult to overlook. If he was in her shoes, would he trust himself with such a huge secret? As his thoughts traveled down a path of self-doubt, they suddenly collided with a more monstrous possibility. She hadn't told him because what she wanted to do was extremely dangerous. Moving the temple could only lead to war.

She placed her hand on his arm, smiling gently. "You've dedicated your life to this project. Certainly, you can see the need to proceed to the next step."

"I thought that building New Jerusalem was the next step," he said. He shook his head. "I can't help you. First, no one at the Knowbokov Foundation is going to use the space machine to move an entire city. If you were hoping I'd do it for you, sorry, but I have no idea how to operate the machine."

"We don't need your technological expertise," said Sister Amy. "You have many talents, Clint. You're a modern day Sampson. The lord gave you the heart and soul of a warrior."

"And it's warriors you'll need if you attempt to move this temple to Jerusalem," said Clint. "The wars in Syria, Jordan, and Egypt are being fought by radicalized armies equipped with deadly chemical weapons. Power players in the area, like Saudi Arabia and Iran, deny having nukes but everyone knows that they do. Move this temple and it won't be some tiny border conflict. You'll trigger—"

"Armageddon," said Sister Amy. "I know. It's part of God's grand plan."

"Nuclear holocaust is hardly what I'd think of as the plan of a loving and merciful savior," said Clint.

Sister Amy looked at him with sad eyes. "You've been neglecting your reading, Brother. The book I wrote on Revelation... did you study it?"

He shook his head. "I'm... not that great at reading. I'm not completely illiterate, but I've never made it through the end of a newspaper article, let alone a whole book."

"I suspected as much," said Sister Amy. "I wish you'd confided in me sooner. The book is available in audio format."

"I've listened," said Clint. "Honestly, it's hard to follow. All the talk about prophecy goes over my head."

"But you seem so fervent in your dedication to building New Jerusalem."

"I am," he said. "I've always been a man of action. I like to get my hands dirty. Building a city in the middle of a desert, it's a challenge. A mission. It catches my imagination."

"Then make use of that imagination," said Sister Amy. "We aren't just building a New Jerusalem. We're making a whole new world, a world of love and peace and obedience to God. For that world to be born, the old world must pass. There must be Armageddon. It's spelled out in full detail in Revelation. A quarter of the world's people must perish in the terrible war that proceeds the final trumpet."

"You're talking over a billion people."

"Oh, far more than that. According to prophecy, when the trumpet of the Lord sounds, the angels will sweep down from heaven and kill half of the people in the world. Of course, this is open to some interpretation."

"I would hope so," said Clint.

"It may not be angels that cleanse the world with flame. It is far more likely that ICBMs will do the job. If they're all fired at once, the prophecy will be fulfilled."

"There must be some mistake," said Clint.

"Perhaps," said Sister Amy. "The Bible says that no man may know the hour or the day. Perhaps we'll move the temple and the Lord will return at once. Perhaps we shall move it and war, famine, pestilence and death will reign upon the world for a thousand years. It's not for us to know the precise timeline. We must trust in the Lord that his plan is just and wise."

"You've always taught me that God was merciful," said Clint. "You've said he was loving, capable of grace. You've told me that even someone whose sins are as great as my own may be welcomed into the kingdom of Heaven. Now you ask me to believe he requires the slaughter of half the world's population?"

"Brother," said Sister Amy. "It's not half the word he slaughters if we fail to act. It's everyone living today. Everyone ever born faces death to atone for our original sin. There is forgiveness, yes, but that's to be part of our eternal life. In our mortal shells, until the Lord returns, we all must perish. Whether it be quietly in a bed or in a nuclear inferno, what does it matter? The price is the same. It's our blood. It must be paid."

Clint had no argument for this. Of course, everyone would die. Of course, the true reward would come in Heaven. But... but...

"I... I can't help you," he said, softly.

"Are you certain?"

"I am," he said. "I don't know. Perhaps... perhaps you're right. But you've always told me to listen to my heart. I can't take part in a plan that will cause the deaths of so many."

"Your heart?" she scoffed. "Now there's mercy in your heart? Now, when the Lord needs your wrath?"

"You're the one who showed me His mercy," said Clint.

"He's the one who placed the wrath within you," she said, her voice rising. "Think back, Brother. Think of the first emotion you ever felt. Was it happiness? Was it love? You told me that, before Rail Blade sealed you in that cube, you'd never known a single day of your life where you didn't wake up angry."

"Yes," he said. "For as long as I can remember, I've carried a burden of rage. It made me a murderer at an age when other children are still watching cartoons in their pajamas. It made me a monster. God's grace made me a man."

"You've always been a man," said Sister Amy. "The Bible is full of holy men who used wrath to do the Lord's work. Sampson slew the Philistines. The Israelites conquered their neighbors and salted the earth so that nothing could ever grow again. The Angel of the Lord slaughtered the first born of Egypt, killing children in their cradles. You're going to stand there and tell me that you'd turn your back on the Lord? He's given you a heart of wrath. Embrace this. Become his archangel, and lead the armies of the righteous into final battle."

Her face was alight with some inner fire. She believed. She believed every word she said. Her eyes were the eyes of God himself, judging him for his weakness. Clint turned away, trembling, the old demons clawing at the cage doors of the far corners of his mind where he'd imprisoned them. He'd said he'd never felt happiness, never felt love, before he found salvation. It wasn't true. When he was Ogre, he'd felt completely alive, perfectly joyous, whenever he'd been standing amid a circle of corpses, covered in the blood of men he'd just killed.

No. Not men. The gang wars were fought mostly by teens. Young teens. Children. He'd twisted the necks of children and tossed their limp bodies away like broken toys. Smiling. Laughing. Happy.

"No," he said.

"No," asked Sister Amy.

"I can't help you," he said. "I can't... I can't let those demons out again." He turned to her. "And I can't let you do this."

"I don't see how you can stop me."

"I'm a fully authorized officer of the law," he said.

"What law, exactly, have I broken?"

He furrowed his brow, uncertain how to answer. It didn't matter. "I'll leave that for others to judge. Once the courts have hold of you and all this hits the press, I don't think your New Jerusalem will remain standing for very long."

She laughed, rolling her eyes. "Brother, we didn't recruit you for your brains. I forgive you for being so dense. This will happen with or without you. Now that you know what you know, we can't let you tell anyone else."

"I can't even imagine how you think you're going to stop me."

"I have friends in high places," she said, with a sly grin. She snapped her fingers.

Clint saw a shadow on the dust behind her, a shadow that grew larger, as if something were dropping down from the heavens. He looked up and saw a man as large as himself, dressed completely in black. The man landed behind Sister Amy in a crouch. Sister Amy stepped aside, revealing the face of the man who'd dropped from the sky.

Clint gasped as the man rose to face him.

The man had his face. His old face. He was face to face with Ogre.

Chapter Twenty-Five
Between the Pillars

"**WHO ARE YOU?**" Servant asked, completely befuddled, as he studied the dark mirror before him.

"I'm you," said Ogre, his voice hard and bitter. "The monster you tried to deny."

"I'm losing my mind," mumbled Servant.

"You'll lose your head as well," said Ogre, his form blurring as he charged, delivering a two-fisted uppercut to Servant's chin.

The world went dark. Not because the blow had hurt Servant, but because his shields had responded to the explosive burst of kinetic energy the same way they would have reacted to a bomb. At maximum strength, his force fields blocked out even benign wavelengths of light as they strengthened to shield him from heat and radiation. When his shields calmed, he found himself high in the air, looking down on New Jerusalem.

As he reached the apex of his flight, he folded his arms to his side and dove, twisting his body to steer toward a crash landing on the temple. They couldn't transport the structure if he tore it to splinters first. He was still a quarter mile in the air when a black streak raced toward him. He spun toward his attacker as Ogre slammed into him, driving his shoulder into Servant's gut. Again, his shields darkened. Whoever this was, he seemed as strong as Servant. When his vision cleared again, the momentum of the blow had carried them far away from the temple, out past the ring of RVs surrounding New Jerusalem.

Servant slammed into the desert, dirt flying as he gouged out an impact crater. He had difficulty telling up from down for a few seconds amid the dust. He found his footing just in time to be kneed in the groin by the dark form that came out of the haze.

"Stop this!" Servant growled, reaching out blindly to grab his attacker by the throat. His attacker mirrored the move, and as the dust settled he found himself grappling with his demonic double, locked together like a pair of immovable sumo wrestlers. "Our fight is pointless," Servant growled. "You can't hurt me."

"Nor can you hurt me," Ogre said through clenched teeth. "We're destined to wrestle one another until Judgment Day."

"Why are you doing this?"

"I believe!" said Ogre. "I won't allow you to halt the blessed Armageddon."

"You're condemning billions to death!" said Servant.

"Not I," said Ogre. "This is the will of God. Who are you to say no?"

"I," Servant shouted, "am a member of the Covenant! I'm sworn to protect mankind. You are in my way."

He followed his words by changing tactics. Instead of pushing against Ogre, meeting force with force, he fell back, dropping to his butt, kicking his feet up to catch Ogre as he fell, launching him into a long arc across the sky.

In some ways, his speed was the opposite of Sarah's. On the ground, she was no faster than an ordinary person, but in the sky, she could move at supersonic speeds. Servant's strength let him race across the earth at nearly the speed of sound, but in the air he dropped at the same rate as any other body, a mere 32 feet per second per second. He had ten, maybe fifteen seconds before Ogre touched down. He raced from the crater, heading for the temple, determined to pull it apart in the seconds he had left. A hundred yards from the temple, while Ogre was still in the air, a second Ogre appeared in his path, then a third, then a fourth. He tried to evade them, but their speed was a perfect match of his own. They pounced upon him, knocking him backward. As he lost his footing, they were joined by the original Ogre who'd hit the ground a fraction of a second before. He struggled, but each of the four Ogres had grabbed him by a limb. Together they raced him back out into the desert, throwing him back into the crater carved by his original impact.

The world went dark as his shields strengthened to protect him from the hail storm of monstrous fists that came at him from every direction. Under assaults like this, his force field became a prison, so resistant to all forms of energy that he couldn't move them even from the inside. He might as well have been entombed once more in the iron cube.

Time passed. His mind swirled, then dulled, as his shields protected him from all stimulus. There were no sounds, no light, no smells, no sensation of pressure, or heat. He felt like a bodiless soul, trapped in eternity with only his own guilt for company. He didn't fully understand what had happened to him. Who was he fighting? Who was Ogre?

"I'm you," he'd said. "The real you."

So who am I, thought Servant.

Not Ogre.

Not that monster.

He no longer felt guilt for his old crimes. Now, his guilt was the burden of what he'd failed to do. Half the world might be moments away from annihilation. Worse, given how impossible it was to judge the passage of time within his shields, half the world might already be dead.

No, he thought. *Have faith.* Whatever God Sister Amy worshiped, it wasn't his God. His God would never allow such a terrible thing to happen. But... what if Servant was God's plan to stop the mass slaughter? What if God's faith in him had been misplaced?

After an immeasurable time, he felt a slight pressure on the back of his eyes. No, not pressure. Light. First deep reds, then purples, then dim shapes emerged. He blinked, and his sight was restored.

He didn't like what he saw.

He was stretched out, spread-eagle between two enormous silver pillars. He tried to move but couldn't. He seemed to be floating in midair. With great effort, he could turn his head from side to side but his limbs were utterly immobile.

"Everything's working exactly like the simulations," said a nearby voice. "Unlike the clones, his cells are regenerating as fast as we drain them."

"Good work, Brother Thomas," said Sister Amy, somewhere beyond Servant's field of vision.

"Sister Amy?" Servant asked, straining to move his jaw and tongue, trembling to exhale.

"You said he wouldn't be able to speak," said Sister Amy.

"His limbs are effectively paralyzed," said the unseen Brother Thomas. "But the power drain will be weakest at the exact center of the pillars. He may still have enough strength for a few words, but I doubt he'll retain this strength for long. According to the simulations, using the space machine to move the city is going to drain 93% of the energy stored in his cells. We can't promise he'll survive."

"Once we've moved the city, his survival won't truly matter, will it?"

Sister Amy walked around to face Servant. She was flanked to one side by one of the Ogres. At least, he thought it was one of the same doubles he'd fought. This one looked thin, emaciated.

To the other side of Sister Amy stood a gray haired man in a lab coat carrying a tablet. Sister Amy smiled gently. "Peace be with you, Brother

Clint. I'm glad you're awake. I'd hoped you might understand that you've been given a second chance. You'll be helping us move the temple after all."

"What… are you doing… to me," he whispered.

"The space machine requires a great deal of energy to move objects with significant mass," said Sister Amy. "Rex Monday, the inventor, had cut a deal with the Russians to draw power from one of their aging nuclear reactors. The Knowbokov Foundation has a fusion generator in their basement. But Brother Thomas tells me that moving New Jerusalem would take even more power than their reactor can produce. Your force fields tap into the vacuum energy of space itself. This energy siphon is draining that power. We literally cannot do this without you."

"Who… is he?" he said, eying the emaciated Ogre.

"A clone," said Sister Amy. "Even though you don't need to eat food, you still enjoy meals. Out of habit, I suppose. What goes in must come out. It was a simple, if somewhat disgusting, matter to recover your DNA from a toilet."

"He… doesn't… look healthy," said Servant.

"No," said Sister Amy, looking over the monster. "The clones we made were flawed. Their cells don't process energy as efficiently as yours. Stress them for more than a few minutes of sustained effort and they burn out, crumbling to dust. It makes them useless for powering the energy siphon. Fortunately, we can always make more as we need them. One of the brain trust happens to be an authority on cloning."

"Brain… trust?" he gasped.

She nodded. "I know that thinking isn't your strong suit, but I would have thought by now you've put together all the pieces. You know who Reverend Delilah McPherson was, don't you?"

"Your sister," he whispered. "The one… who killed… people."

"The one put to death in the gas chamber," said Sister Amy. "And the one pulled out of a tube of goo many years later, to learn she'd been used by a mad telepath named Dr. Knowbokov as an auxiliary brain. He'd used portions of my mind as a telepathic amplifier. When I woke from the goo, I found that I could hear the thoughts of everyone around me."

"You?" asked Servant. "I thought… this happened… to your sister."

She smiled. "You were probably told that Delilah McPherson died in a car wreck a few weeks after she was placed back into society under a new identity. They'd done their best to brainwash me, to imprint a new identity over my existing memories. All the other people pulled from the tubes were blank slates. It was simple to fool others into believing I, too, was an amnesiac. I never uttered a peep of resistance. I told them everything they wanted to hear. When I was released, it was a simple matter to kidnap my sister Amy, drug her, and turn her loose on a highway in a car with a stuck accelerator and the brake lines slowly bleeding out. I stepped into her life and no one suspected a thing. It wasn't difficult at all. Before she died, I'd stolen all of her memories."

"Stolen… her memories?"

She sighed. "I know that the energy syphon is draining you, but at least try to pay attention. It's tedious to have to repeat things. Niko Knowbokov was a powerful telepath but even he had difficulty coordinating the thoughts of his networked extra brains. While my brethren were tasked with solving exotic scientific challenges like cloning, time travel, energy harvesting, and unraveling the secrets of his daughters' powers, my mind was used as a sort of telepathic bridge, a hub through which the thoughts in all the various minds might meet and cooperate with one another. When I was pulled from the tube I still possessed this telepathic connection, not only with my fellow prisoners, but with anyone I focused on. Which such a gift, it's simple to deceive people. If anyone who met me had doubts or suspicions, I could address those doubts while seeing in their mind what they most wanted to believe. It became easier still once Brother Kelley was restored to the fold. His brain had been used to study the Thrill's vocal gifts. With my help, we liberated those memories, and learned how to mimic the effects of her voice telepathically. With her mind control, it's been easy to build my ministry into the world shaking force it's become."

"You… you can project Sarah's voice… into the minds of others? You're responsible for the—"

"Dervishes. Yes. Brother Ledo possessed Dr. Knowbokov's medical knowledge, and knew which glands I needed to mentally stimulate to give a man a quick, superhuman burst of strength and speed. With Brother Jacob unraveling the secrets of Rail Blade's iron creation, and Brother Smith perfecting his time duplicates, everything I needed for creating the dervishes was in place."

"Why?"

"Why the dervishes? The Middle East is a cauldron of war but most American's feel sheltered. I've brought the war to Main Street and the malls. The political pressure to send more troops to fight overseas is growing. The time is ripe. The nation is ready for war, and with a few telepathic whispers in the Thrill's voice, the president will be eager to reinstate the draft and send the youth of America off to put an end to this terrible, terrible threat."

"Why... do you... want war... so badly?"

"How can you ask why?" she said. "You've listened to my sermons for years. I have the ultimate marching orders. I'm tasked by the Lord to bring about the end of days. I have been given my gifts to see His prophecy fulfilled. Why else would a sham death sentence have given me telepathy? Why else would the Lord have given me a volunteer army of thirteen genius scientists, their talents hidden beneath the false programming of the mind butchers of the Knowbokov Foundation? These geniuses awaited the touch of my mind to waken and nurture them. These things cannot have happened by chance."

"The men... you use... were killers..." Servant whispered. "They... they can't... be eager to face... God."

Sister Amy shrugged. "They're eager because I'm eager. When the thirteen of us are together, we're of a single mind. A unified mind. I control that mind, or rather, the Lord does, as he speaks with me. Welcome to Doomsday, Servant. Please don't struggle. You can't break free. You may as well sleep, until you're awakened by the final trumpet of the angels."

Servant strained to move his limbs, strained all the harder, his heart racing, until he gave up, gasping for breath. Whatever held him, his fields couldn't protect him from the energy drain. If anything, he suspected that, the more he struggled, the more power they could pull from him.

As Sister Amy, or Delilah, whoever, turned away, Servant managed to find the strength to call out, "If... you can control minds... why pretend I had a choice?"

She shrugged. "Alas, Dr. Knowbokov's telepathy didn't work with his own children. As the son of Rex Monday, you're Knowbokov's genetic son. I'm also unable to control Katrina Knowbokov. I'm told that she was given some sort of technological aid created by Rex Monday that shields her from telepathy. If not for that, I'd command her to confess to her crimes, tell the world the full story of her complicity with the destruction of Old Jerusalem, then have her blow her brains out on live television. Since that's not an option, I've hired someone to take care of her confession and her death. Any more questions?"

He was too weak to move his jaw.

"Sleep well," she said, turning away.

Chapter Twenty-Six
Reboot

FOR DRAMATIC EFFECT, Chimpion slumped to her knees as the space machine placed her and Steam-Dragon's remains into the center of the room. Instantly, a swarm of technicians descended upon her, shouting out questions. Nathan reached her and she took his hand, rising on trembling legs.

"We were ambushed," she said. "The second we got inside, Rail Blade was waiting. She tore App apart, shredding his belt before he could reset. Steam-Dragon got in a few blows before Rail Blade did the same to her. It all happened so fast. I tried hitting her with poison gas, but she no longer needed to breathe. She'd become a creature of pure iron, but iron animated by a magnetic mind. I hit her with ultrasonics to disrupt her thoughts then destroyed her body with acid. She's gone for good."

"Why did she attack?"

"She'd been driven mad by isolation," said Chimpion. "Paranoid. Talking crazy. There was electrical interference once we entered the dome that glitched out my video recording, but I've got photos of the sick little fantasy world she'd made. Wait until you see the creepy dolls she thought were her children."

"Creepy dolls?" said a familiar voice from outside the room. "Man, it's bad enough I went to Mars and don't get to remember it. I missed out on creepy dolls, too?"

Chimpion's eyes doubled in size as App strolled into the room.

"App!" she gasped. "You're alive!"

"That's debatable," he said with a shrug. "But, yeah, they reset me once they got your call from Mars and learned I hadn't... oh my god." His eyes focused on Steam-Dragon's fallen form.

Chimpion didn't answer, still processing the fact he was alive. App dropped to one knee, placing his hand on Becky's pale face, visible in the open chest cavity of the armor. As he stared silently at her unmoving form, a team of medics approached. Nathan gently pulled App aside.

"I'm so sorry," said App. "Is there any chance...?"

Nathan shook his head. "She bled out long before we pulled them back. We have a lot of medical miracles available, but nothing that's going to fix this."

"I came in here making dumb jokes," App said, shaking his head. "I mean... I should have..."

"You couldn't have known," said Chimpion. "Could you?" Did he really not remember, or was this only a ruse?

"You know," said Nathan, "if you want to remember being on Mars, we did collect data from the time it took you to walk from the touchdown site to the dome. It was simpler to reboot you to a pre-jump state, but we can download those memories if you'd like them."

"I... sure," said App. "I mean, they're my memories, even if it sounds like they aren't going to be good ones."

"How is this possible? Your belt was destroyed," said Chimpion, furrowing her brow in confusion.

"No big deal," said Nathan. "We still have the data it transmitted, though it suffered some signal degradation due to the distance. We'll clean it up before we put it back into his brain."

"No," said Chimpion. "I mean... how can he have been reset without his belt?"

"I didn't reset. I was rebooted." App put his hand on his belt buckle. "Reset is the command I used to return to normal after using a power. A reboot is triggered remotely when the server realizes I've been mortally injured."

"But if your belt isn't intact to rebuild you...?"

App shrugged. "This thing gets destroyed all the time. Technically, it disintegrates every time I go into ghost mode. It gets recreated from data as easily as I can."

"Oh." She took a deep breath and managed her best imitation of a smile. "That's wonderful. I didn't know."

"In retrospect, maybe I should have gone alone," said App. "I wouldn't have been in real danger, and alone maybe Rail Blade wouldn't have felt threatened. Sarah told us not to go. She's not going to be happy with us when she finds out we killed her sister."

"I killed her sister," said Chimpion, letting her shoulders slump. "It was in self-defense, but, still, I'm responsible. I'd... I'd like to be the one who breaks the news to Sarah. Mrs. Knowbokov as well."

"Sarah still hasn't checked in," said Nathan. "As for Mrs. Knowbokov, she insisted on live updates. When you made your retrieval call and told us about Amelia's death, I gave her the news myself."

"How'd she take it?" asked App.

"Her usual stoicism," said Nathan. "Honestly, she seemed more concerned about losing Steam-Dragon. She's told us she personally wants to notify Becky's next of kin."

Chimpion nodded. "I should still talk to her."

"Understood," said Nathan. "But that can wait until you're checked out by the medical team."

"I'm fine," said Chimpion.

"No doubt you are," said Nathan. "But you're also the first pers—" He paused, reconsidering his word choice. "The first individual we've ever had travel to another planet and back via the space machine. In theory, it should be no different than traveling to any spot on Earth, but we still need to check for any physical effects."

"It can wait, can't it?" she said. "I'd really like to talk with Mrs. Knowbokov while the events are still fresh in my mind."

Nathan shook his head. "That's not a good idea. Since your recorder went dead, we've got a debrief team that will be interviewing you during the physical exam. It's important we get your story fresh, before you've told it to anyone else. It's been shown that the act of telling a memory actually alters the memory. You're also more likely to edit your memories if you're speaking to someone emotionally invested in your tale. We don't want to lose valuable information by having you filter your story based on Mrs. Knowbokov's reactions."

"My eidetic memory wouldn't allow that to happen," said Chimpion.

"I believe you," said Nathan. "Still, protocol is protocol. This will only take an hour, maybe two."

Chimpion nodded. She'd had to play the role of superhero for weeks in order to get close to Rail Blade. As tempting as it was to kill everyone in the room and make a straight line for Mrs. Knowbokov, patience was the best strategy. If she killed Mrs. Knowbokov before Sarah was located, it might put Sarah on guard. There was still hope that she could arrange a meeting with both at the same time. Certainly there would be a memorial service for Steam-Dragon. That might put both her targets in the same room at once.

She went to the debriefing room. For an hour she played along, calmly answering questions, moving between detached, emotionless reporting and voice-quavering remorse and shock as needed. Humans wore their emotions on their faces so well she was able to calibrate her answers to what they wanted to hear. Still, she gave her answers with only half her mind focused on the interview. App's presence at the base bothered her. How could she have missed out on the fact that he could reboot even if the belt was destroyed? He'd said several times the *belt* was the source of his powers, barely ever mentioning the servers that truly housed him. She saw now this was typical human verbal looseness. For a species that pointed to their gift of language as evidence of their superiority over other mammals, humans often mangled the most basic forms of communication. They said one thing and meant another, not because they were lying, but because they had no respect for precision in their vocabulary. What a waste of breath.

She hadn't activated her static field until they entered the dome. If she understood App's powers—a supposition now in doubt—his memories were going to be restored up to the moment he went inside the dome. This shouldn't be a problem. He hadn't acted as if he'd suspected anything during their walk. He wasn't an immediate danger to her mission.

On a more practical matter, while she wasn't being paid to kill App, she'd intended to kill him anyway. There was always the possibility he'd fight to defend Sarah and Mrs. Knowbokov, and an equally likely possibility that, once they were dead, he would lead the effort to avenge them. She had numerous strategies to neutralize him, but all had been built around the assumption that his belt was a source of vulnerability.

Obviously, the only way to truly kill him would be to destroy the computers that housed the code for the belt. A warm feeling spread through her belly as she thought about the high explosives she'd hidden around the base. It had been a while since she'd gotten to blow anything up.

Chapter Twenty-Seven
Dark Meteor

CHIMPION LEFT THE conference room where she'd met with the debriefing team and slipped into the nearest bathroom. Locking the door, she climbed to the ceiling and clung next to the air-conditioning vent. She removed the grate and stuck her hand far inside, pulling out a disk slightly larger than her palm. The plastic disk was made of two hemispheres swirled together like a yin yang symbol. She pressed a button and the two hemispheres popped apart and unfolded spidery black legs. She shoved them back into the vent and said, "Navigate to subbasement nine, server 12. Wait for my signal."

The twin robots silently skittered out of sight.

The robots were programmed with the latest Pangean A.I. It would take an hour or two for them to figure out a path through the vents to reach the correct server. They were smart enough to avoid any laser sensors in the vents and light and nimble enough not to trigger any motion sensors. They were mostly ceramic with no magnetic profile. Their only potential vulnerability would be to chemical sniffers, since they were each packing a small but potent load of plastic explosives. Fortunately, even if the search profiles in the sniffers were updated frequently, they probably weren't yet trained to detect the latest explosive combo designed by the Pangean laboratories. These explosives weren't on the market yet, not even the black market. Which meant, alas, she hadn't tested them, but she trusted the Pangean chemists to deliver good product.

She eyed the door. She hadn't been in the restroom long enough to raise suspicions. It was worth the risk of communicating with her employer. She pressed the pager on her belt and waited.

The skin between her shoulder blades started to crawl a moment later. She wrinkled her nose as a pungent, alien smell filled her nostrils, like a rotten fish soaked in kerosene blending into a vat of burning chocolate. The bathroom took on a sickly green hue as the florescent lights strobed with a nauseating flicker. The human telepath who'd hired her hadn't mastered the craft of activating the hearing centers of her brain without also bleeding into other senses.

"You have news?" a woman's voice asked, sounding as if someone were standing just behind her shoulder.

"Yes," she thought, mentally enunciating the word as clearly as she could without actually moving her lips or tongue. "Rail Blade is dead."

"You have proof?"

"I'm the only witness," thought Chimpion. "The body was utterly destroyed. You'll have to trust me."

"It would be foolish to lie to a telepath. You are no fool. I believe you. I'll see to it the funds are deposited into the Pangean account within the hour. What of the other targets?"

"Mrs. Knowbokov is still in the compound. I can kill her at my leisure. The Thrill, unfortunately, has left the base. Her current location is unknown."

"This *is* unfortunate," said the telepath. "Our time table has been accelerated."

"Things didn't go well with Servant?" thought Chimpion. "I warned you he'd prove uncooperative."

"His cooperation isn't voluntary. I'm told there's a small but real chance the energy siphons will kill him as they drain his power. If he dies, all our preparation is for naught. We must act today. I'll be taking telepathic control of mission personnel manning the space machine. I would prefer that Mrs. Knowbokov not see the blessed Promised Land. You must kill her within the hour."

Chimpion frowned. With such an accelerated timeframe, her robots probably wouldn't have time to reach the server that housed App's data.

"I sense unease," said the telepath.

"App survived the Mars mission. I know he's not a target, but he's irritatingly difficult to kill and could attempt to thwart us. I've a plan to eliminate him, but I can't execute it within your timeframe. Mrs. Knowbokov should be no problem, however. As for the Thrill, I don't think I'll be able to locate her with such short notice."

"That won't be necessary. The Thrill has revealed herself. One member of my team specialized in protecting the Earth from destructive asteroid strikes. His particular skills didn't seem to be of much use to my larger plans at first. Fortunately, he monitors the NORAD system that tracks atmospheric disturbances corresponding with incoming meteors. He's spotted the shockwaves of an anomalous atmospheric object moving at twice the speed of sound aimed directly toward your coordinates."

"Sarah," thought Chimpion.

"He's attempting satellite confirmation but I don't wish to wait. I've already launched an intercept."

"Why intercept?" asked Chimpion. "Let her come. I can kill her when she gets here."

"No doubt," said the telepath. "But the time of triumph has arrived. There is no need to hold resources in reserve. Go. Kill Katrina Knowbokov. Avenge Jerusalem. An archangel will deal with the Thrill."

"There's still App to deal with," said Chimpion.

"As you say, he's not our primary target," said the telepath. "Have no fear. In about ten seconds, he'll be too distracted to stand in the way of your mission."

SARAH PAUSED FOR only a moment after finishing her call with Richard, allowing the computer in her helmet to determine a flight path. If she remained two miles above the earth, she faced very little danger of collisions with birds or bugs. Her helmet was mapping out the current flight paths of all commercial aircraft and hacking military systems to determine the locations of any military flights. The helmet also checked weather systems. Flying into raindrops at the speed she'd be travelling would be like flying into bullets.

It took seven minutes for her helmet to gather the data it needed, the longest seven minutes of her life. Her mind jumped in a thousand directions at once. Chimpion, a traitor? Her mother, a target. And Steam-Dragon was dead. Was she to blame? The decent thing to do would be to feel guilt, but her mind couldn't hold onto the emotion. Amelia and Richard had children? What were their names? Would she ever meet them?

And where was Carson right now? Should she call him? Try one more time to explain? Explain what? That she'd like to tell him more, but at the moment she was about to run off to fight an evil chimpanzee? Her world had no place for a grounded, decent, sane person like Carson. Would she ever see him again? Should she? She'd stolen five years of his life, tricking him into loving a woman who didn't truly exist. This wasn't something that could ever be forgiven. It wasn't something she even wanted to be forgiven for. She deserved his contempt.

Her helmet gave a cheerful chime as a bright green path suddenly glowed before her on her heads up display, a straight line of laser light to guide her back to the island. She clenched her fists and jaw, leaned forward, then *BOOM!* Zero to Mach 2 in sixty seconds. The sky exploded before her in a glowing shockwave. The turbulence rattled her teeth. While her body was immune to the inertia of her acceleration, for some reason she felt lightheaded. She hoped it would pass but the faintness grew worse, and darkness began to nibble at the edges of her vision.

Through sheer force of will, she pushed back the darkness. She'd covered fifty miles in a little over two minutes, a new record for her. A bright red warning light flashed in the corner of her heads up display. At this speed, the air vents in her helmet that let her breathe were developing vortexes, sapping her airflow. Did she dare go slower? She was moving roughly 1500 miles an hour. She'd still need an hour and a half to get back home.

Home. The word was like a cold blade in her mind. Home. She loved Carson. She wanted to be with him. But that wasn't her home. It had never been her home. It had been the home of a woman who had imagined herself into being but who'd never really existed. Her only true home was Knowbokov Island. She accepted this now. Home was the place she'd fight to defend until the last drop of blood spilled from her.

Still, it would be dumb to suffocate before she arrived and sheer willpower couldn't beat out oxygen deprivation for more than a minute or two. She slowed, dropping to 1200 miles per hour, the turbulence pummeling her like mattresses stuffed with sledgehammers as the shockwave twisted and reformed. She gasped, taking a deep breath as the vortexes in her vents collapsed and ice cold air flooded her helmet. She breathed deeply to fill her lungs. The green line she followed shifted to yellow.

"Great," she sighed. She'd plotted her flight path for Mach 2 and been in the clear. At her reduced speed, the yellow indicated she'd pass close to an obstacle. She looked ahead on the flight plan and saw that in twenty minutes she'd be near an American Airlines flight. Near, in this case, was within two miles. Not exactly a dangerous distance, though since she was covering two miles in under five seconds, there wasn't a safety margin if her flight computer had made a bad calculation. She decided to risk it rather than wasting time plotting a new path.

The sky was clear now. Cities and towns twinkled beneath her, brighter and more tightly clustered than the stars above but she had no time to appreciate the view. She focused intently on the yellow pathway displayed before her, counting down miles and minutes. She'd never flown this fast but it felt as if she was crawling. What if Chimpion had already attacked her mother?

She took a long, deep breath and let it out in a stuttering groan as her fear and frustration grew heavier.

"It's okay," she whispered to herself. "It's okay."

Very likely, it was okay. Her rational mind kicked in, weighing Chimpion's next move. As far as Chimpion knew, Sarah knew nothing about what had happened on Mars. If App and Steam-Dragon were dead, Chimpion could weave any story she wished. She'd have no urgent need to kill Sarah's mother and strategic reasons to leave her alive. After all, only her mother knew Sarah's secret identity. Chimpion would need that information. It seemed more Chimpion's style to try to get that information through trickery than through something as messy as torture.

If Chimpion was biding her time, what should Sarah do when they met again? Attacking her immediately had a certain gut level appeal. On the other hand, someone had to have hired Chimpion to act as an assassin. Finding out who had to be a priority. There were plenty of people who wanted Rail Blade dead, but whoever had planned this was a mastermind equal to Rex Monday. The dervishes had been so perfectly crafted to place Amelia under suspicion that it now seemed obvious that Chimpion must have had some connection to the attackers.

Before Sarah could decide on a plan an alarm sounded. The path before her switched from yellow to red. She slowed to subsonic speed and waited for her path to clear again. Had she wandered into a plane's airspace, or had it wandered into hers? Halving her speed should cause their vectors to diverge dramatically.

She frowned. The alarm kept sounding and the path stayed red. In fact, several red circles appeared on her screen. Just how many planes was she near? Her eyes flickered across the display. Not planes... the radar pings were too small.

She slowed further, until she hung in the air. It now became obvious that she hadn't been unintentionally approaching airborne objects. The objects, instead, were approaching her. Her display helpfully informed her that she was getting pinged by multiple lasers, the types used by missiles to lock on their targets. Had she triggered some defense system at a military base? But she'd dodged missiles before, and these didn't fit the profile. They were too small and had no heat signature, no exhaust.

"Magnify," she said, focusing her gaze on one of the red circles. Her display zoomed to reveal what looked like a bottle rocket lacking a flame. It wasn't much bigger than a tube of lipstick. She doubted it could be packing much in the way of explosives, but she didn't plan to stick around and test that theory.

She dove, accelerating toward the ground. Whatever was coming toward her, the targeting lasers would need a clear line of sight. It wouldn't be difficult to baffle them with cover and the land beneath her was thickly forested hills. She spread her arms just above the tree tops, slowing to a safe speed, then slipped down through the limbs into the shadows. Instantly, the targeting lasers lost her location, and just in time, since the nearest mini-missile was barely a quarter mile away.

She sank lower, hovering mere inches over the leafy floor of the forest. She searched the sky through the branches, realizing a flaw in her plan. Whatever was targeting her couldn't see her, but she also couldn't see them.

Then, *BANG! Bang bang bang BANG!* Bright lights exploded all around her as trees burst into flames. Shockwaves slammed her against a tree trunk. Her armor absorbed most of the impact, but she was still disoriented by the noise and flashes. She lost focus and dropped to her hands and knees, shaking her head to clear it. She took a deep breath, steadying her thoughts. Was that all? Was the attack over? Her helmet had tracked six bogies. How many had gone off?

She looked up, wondering if she should rise above the trees just enough to get a clear radar scan. Before she could move, she saw a shadow above her, coming closer.

"Magnify," she whispered. "Illuminate." Her jaw went slack as her helmet magnified the approaching form and digitally enhanced its brightness.

An angel, wings and all, with glowing red eyes looked directly at her as it dropped from the heavens like some dark meteor.

Chapter Twenty-Eight
Judgment

AS THE ANGEL drew closer, tiny objects flew from its wings, smaller, bullet-sized copies of the rockets that had targeted her. There had to be hundreds of them, if not thousands. Instead of targeting her, they swarmed above her like an explosive net, blocking her from zooming back into the sky.

The angel came to a halt above the treetops.

"Sarah Knowbokov," he announced. "My name is Judgment. I am the reaver. I am the waster. I am the inescapable will of God. Your hour is at hand."

"Bullshit," she shouted back, as the sensory array in her helmet deciphered the details of the form before her. Judging from the infrared data, this was a man in a fancy suit of mechanized armor. Fancy and familiar—it plainly shared a lot of design elements with Steam-Dragon's armor, and seemed to be made of the same carbon composite. His wings were huge, but wings required motion to work and he was standing motionless in mid-air. The big power pack between his shoulder blades had a strange energy signal. Some sort of reactionless drive? Her father had built one a few months before he died but the prototype had gone missing following his death. A reactionless drive would explain the lack of any sort of exhaust on the tiny missiles that had chased her from the sky.

"You're one of the thirteen," said Sarah. "That's some fancy armor you've got there. I'm guessing it's not terribly maneuverable among the trees with those wings, though."

"You cannot hide from me, sinner," said Judgment, a large iron sword suddenly appearing his hands. "I shall burn the earth to cinders to bring justice to your wicked soul."

As he spoke, his sword glowed brightly. Sarah knew this trick. Rail Blade had been able to agitate the outer molecules of iron to make it white hot while keeping the inner molecules stable to retain strength.

"You've stolen my sister's secrets," she said. "It think there's a commandment telling you not to do that."

"These weren't your sister's secrets," said Judgment. "Your sister stole the secrets of the Lord. His is the power to create something from nothing. His is the power to slay all who displease him. Your sister has paid a terrible price for her blasphemy."

Sarah started to tell him he was mistaken but held her tongue. No point in tipping off this idiot that Amelia was still alive.

"I don't get it," said Sarah. "You're obviously one of the thirteen prisoners my father accidentally turned into geniuses. I know that all of you were murderers, so, sure, I get that you'd like to kill me. But why the theatrics? Why pretend that Jerusalem meant anything to you?"

"The hour is nigh, sinner. It is the dawn of New Jerusalem. Come forth, and face your death with dignity, should you possess any."

Sarah furrowed her brow. The New Jerusalem. *Servant*. That crazy female preacher Servant worked for. What was her name again?

"You wouldn't be a friend of Amy McPherson, would you?" she asked.

"You're not worthy to speak her sacred name!" Judgment cried, rocketing toward her, swinging his sword to clear the branches in his path. She decided it was time to test her suspicion that he couldn't maneuver well among the trees by darting backward. Her helmet had been building a radar map of her immediate surroundings since she'd touched down. She couldn't build up much speed among the trees, but she could easily stay a tree or two away as he touched down and started marching toward her, crying in incoherent rage as his sword chopped into trees in this path. His blade was hotter than lightning and the trees exploded into splinters as sap flashed into superheated steam.

Unfortunately, with her attention focused on staying out of the grasp of Judgment, she'd forgotten the swarm of mini missiles he'd unleashed above the canopy. On some hidden signal, they rained down around her, *POP POP POP POP,* dozens of explosions per second, hitting her from every side. Her armor proved capable of dealing with the shockwaves and shrapnel, but the flashes blinded her and the noise masked the sound of Judgment racing across the leaves until, with a terrible blow, he drove the tip of his blade hard into her belly.

She was thrown backward by the impact. The sword hadn't penetrated her armor, but it still felt like getting kicked in the stomach. She bounced on the leaves, rolling down a slope, landing on her back. She stared up the slope and saw Judgment's dark form illuminated against the red flames behind him.

The cacophony of tiny explosions faded. She rose on trembling legs, her skull vibrating from the dozen alarms going off in her helmet all at once, warning her of the smoke, the flame, the dangerous proximity of trees overhead if she took flight, and, extra-helpfully, putting a bright red warning circle around the armored angel who loomed over her, since this apparently wasn't something it trusted she'd notice on her own.

"Fuck this," she said, tired of the distraction. "Power off."

A small command box appeared in the middle her helmet display asking if she was sure she wanted her armor to power off.

"Yes," she said.

All the reality augmentations in her display vanished, leaving her with only her own eyes to track her opponent. The last echoes of the alarms faded from her ears, leaving the roar of flames the only sound she heard.

She placed her gauntleted fist against her palm and cracked her knuckles.

"I've got bad news," she said. "You've been worshipping a false God."

"I'll... I'll tear your blasphemous... tongue from... your mouth," Judgment said. Winded. He was panting. But of course he was panting. Even with his armor supplying all the real muscle work of chopping through a forest, if this was one of the thirteen prisoners, she wasn't facing a young man. Most had gone into death row in their twenties, but due to appeals, had faced execution in their thirties. Then, some had spent over a decade in a goo tube, and another six years had passed since they'd been freed. Whoever was inside the armor was probably at least fifty, and maybe close to sixty. With any luck, Judgment might keel over from a heart attack.

She hoped not. That wouldn't be very satisfying.

"You sound a little winded, Judgment," she said. "The servant of a real God would probably be feeling pretty mighty right about now. Maybe you'd have better luck switching sides."

"Shut up!" he yelled, sounding more like a frustrated child than an avenging angel. If this was one of the thirteen, in addition to being old, he probably wasn't terribly emotionally stable. You didn't wind up on death row by being a calm-natured soul with healthy mental tools for dealing with people who displeased you.

She held up her left hand, her forefinger and pinky extended, her middle fingers folded beneath her thumb, and said, in a cheerful voice, "Hail Satan!"

Judgment howled, raising his sword overhead, leaping into the air to fly down the slope toward her. She charged to meet him, aiming low, driving her shoulders into his knees, flipping him heels over head, so that he hit the forest floor blade first and drove his sword into the ground all the way to the hilt. The damp soil exploded in a blast of steam, spattering Judgment's faceplate with boiling mud. She suspected his armor would protect him from the blast, but it still had to make his heart race a little.

Time to make it race a lot. She grabbed him by the boot, set her jaw, turned her face to the sky, and WHOOSH! She accelerated to the speed of sound, climbing straight for the stars. Again, her powers protected her from the ill effects of sudden acceleration. As long as she held Judgment, he wouldn't feel the effects of his sudden speed either. Three miles up, she let go as she came to a stop. His wings caught the wind, whipping him chaotically from side to side, with what had to be several g-forces tugging his internal organs in different directions. His black armor quickly vanished into the darkness above.

She was about to turn her helmet back on to use its radar when at last she spotted a large black form tumbling to her left. It turned out to be one of the wings from the armor. Folding her arms to her side, she moved toward at, drawing closer until she was suddenly stopped by a second shadow at the corner of her vision. She turned and saw Judgment tumbling toward earth, utterly limp. An athlete in peak condition might have survived the g-forces. Odds were good that the old man inside the armor had died the second she'd let him go.

Not that she was feeling so hot herself. The acceleration hadn't hurt her, but since she'd been dumb enough to turn her helmet off, the atmospheric control system built into her suit hadn't kicked in to compensate for the sudden change of air pressure between sea level and three miles up. With each heartbeat, she felt like tiny knives were slicing through her muscles as tiny bubble of nitrogen formed in her tissues. Worse, during the heat of battle, adrenaline had kept her from feeling more than a dull pain from the blow she'd taken to the gut. Now, she felt certain that once again she'd broken ribs. If she survived this, it was back to the drawing board on her armor. She liked the flexibility and comfort of her flight suit, but if she had to wear a plate steel vest to keep from taking another gut punch she'd do it.

"Oh god," she moaned, pulling her helmet back off to let the night air cool her. She wiped her lips. She stared at the dark streak on the back of her gauntlet. Even in the darkness, she could see the red tint.

"Passing out is always an option," she reminded herself. She shook her head. Not yet. She had to get back to the island and save her mother. First, she had to be certain that Judgment was finished. She steeled herself against a wave of nausea and pulled her helmet back on, powering it up.

"Silence all alarms," she said, before it had a chance to tell her she was racing toward a collision course with the ground. "Magnify."

She slowed, letting the distance grow between her and Judgment. She was a half mile above the ground now, he a matter of yards. She blinked. When she opened her eyes, there was a crater in the forest beneath her and trees falling away from the center of the shockwave. She pulled up, searching for any sign of her attacker. Her helmet locked onto the angel's head. Then on his torso. Then on his arms. None were within ten yards of each other.

She dropped to the edge of the crater, falling to her hands and knees. Her legs had gone well past rubbery, far into wet noodle territory.

Just how hurt was she? She put her helmet back on and pulled up the biometrics display. She studied her vital signs and found them to be not completely terrible. Her blood pressure, while low, looked to be stabilizing. Her heartrate was still in the zone she aimed for in her morning runs. Her oxygen levels were low but climbing.

"I might survive this win after all," she whispered. "Okay, suit. Hit me with pain killers and something to keep me awake." She felt the prick of needles pressing into her forearms as the suit's first aid mode sprang to life. She had no time to wait until she felt better, though. Without bothering to stand or even look up, she rose into the night, slowly at first, like a child's balloon, until the drugs took hold and she zoomed toward the horizon.

Chapter Twenty-Nine
Do Your Worst

THE SOUND OF DISTANT shouting told Chimpion that the telepath had already put in place the promised distraction. She pinpointed the commotion as coming from the command room for the space machine. The telepath had obviously seized control of one or more techs. The remaining techs sounded like they were trying to wrest their possessed team members away from the controls.

Finally, the cry she'd been waiting for: "App! Hurry!"

Now that she knew that App was going to be distracted by events elsewhere in the compound, it was time to make her move. Mrs. Knowbokov had her private suites on the penthouse floor of the Knowbokov Foundation Tower. Chimpion ran on all fours at top speed to reach the elevator banks in the main lobby. Mrs. Knowbokov had a private car there, under the watch of two armed guards. Even without the guards, the elevator bank required a biometric scan to activate and had a dozen different defense mechanisms should someone attempt to breach the elevator shaft by force.

Luckily, the shouts from the command room had carried all the way to the lobby. The two guards had their guns drawn, looking in the direction of the commotion as Chimpion ran toward them.

"What's going on?" one of the guards shouted.

"Another dervish attack!" Chimpion answered. "We've intel that one's in the penthouse. I've got to get up there!"

One of the guards pressed the com button next to the elevator. "Omega station, situation red. Repeat, situation red!"

"What's happening?"

"Chimpion says a dervish is in the penthouse with Mrs. Knowbokov."

"Hold on..." said the voice on the com. "Motion sensors are clear. Nothing on infrared. No one's up here but the boss and her guards."

"The dervish is cloaked by some sort of temporal device," said Chimpion, breathlessly. "He's hiding between the ticks of a clock, out of phase with ordinary time. You won't see him until it's too late! I'm going up."

"There's a confirmed incursion in the jump room," said the guard before her. "As of now, the elevator's on lockdown."

"I'm the only one who stands a chance against these dervishes," Chimpion. "Let me up or she'll die!"

The guard looked indecisive. Chimpion felt precious seconds draining away due to his inability to take charge.

Fortunately, the voice on the com proved more willing to take a risk. "I'm overriding the lockdown. Get her up here. You saw how she took apart those dervishes in New Jersey."

"It's your ass on the line," the guard said, placing his palm on a pad next to the door. The mirror-finished door slid open and Chimpion leapt inside. The doors slid shut and she felt the shift in momentum as the car whizzed up the shaft. She rolled her eyes, feeling almost embarrassed by how easily humans could be fooled. How, exactly, had they become the most ecologically successful primates?

The doors slid open. She bolted out, looking toward the nearest guard. "Where is she?"

"In her office," he said, pointing toward impressive double doors at the end of a long hall.

"Hold your position," said Chimpion. "Watch the lights! They'll flicker if the temporal cloak passes near. Open fire if that happens, even if you don't see anything. By the time you see them, you'll be dead!"

She raced down the hall without turning back, so that the guards couldn't see the amusement in her eyes. Honestly, she'd dealt with lemurs who were less gullible.

"The doors are locked!" the guards shouted after her.

"I figured as much!" she called back, dropping into a roll as she neared the door, springing up feet first to kick at the seam where the heavy oak doors met. The wood splintered and the doors flew open. She rolled into the room, rising up on her legs, her sonic sword drawn.

Mrs. Knowbokov sat behind her desk. She had a gun in her hand, a pearl-handled revolver that looked quite old. She had it aimed directly at Chimpion, perhaps anticipating the dervish attack Chimpion had warned against.

Mrs. Knowbokov pulled the trigger. Chimpion dodged from the bullet's path with lightning reflexes. Mr. Knowbokov fired again and Chimpion deflected the bullet with her sonic blade. Before the gun could be fired a third time, she flicked a throwing knife into her hand from her wrist holster. When Mrs. Knowbokov pulled the trigger, the bullet was blocked in its chamber by the expertly thrown blade. Fire shot from every seam on the handgun. The pistol fell as Mrs. Knowbokov cried out, clasping her burnt fingers to her chest.

"You've come to kill me," Mrs. Knowbokov said, her voice trembling, though not with fear. The exploding gun had left her in a good deal of pain.

"I have," said Chimpion. "I'm curious how you knew."

"I received a call from an old friend," said Mrs. Knowbokov. "He said you killed your teammates on Mars. He said you tried to kill my daughter."

"Now you and Sarah shall die as well," said Chimpion. "The destruction of Jerusalem will be avenged."

"What can such a thing matter to you?" Mrs. Knowbokov asked.

"I can't pretend that it does," said Chimpion. "All that matters to me is that Pangea's budget woes will be wiped away by my work. As an added bonus, if all goes according to plan, there will soon be a war that significantly thins the human herd. My kind will be grateful for the additional breathing room. The whole planet, for that matter, will be better off. Humans are the world's worst invasive species."

"I hardly think that's a logical argument from a Pangean," Mrs. Knowbokov said. "Elevated chimpanzees are a sort of pollutant, a mutation loosed upon the world by Rex Monday's mad tinkering."

"Really?" asked Chimpion. "You're about to die and you want to debate ecology?"

"You brought it up," said Mrs. Knowbokov, her eyes flickering away from Chimpion's face.

Chimpion spun around, unleashing a pair of throwing knives in the direction of the running feet she heard behind her. The two armed guards coming to Mrs. Knowbokov's rescue dropped in mid-stride, the knives buried deep in their necks. She turned back. "If you want to discuss something before I kill you, let's talk about Rail Blade. You said I tried to kill her."

"Didn't you?"

"I didn't try," said Chimpion. "I... ah."

Mrs. Knowbokov grew stone-faced.

"I should have known. The iron figure I killed... it was a decoy?" asked Chimpion.

Mrs. Knowbokov's face seemed paralyzed. Chimpion could read every human tell, but Mrs. Knowbokov had no reaction at all to her words.

"Stay quiet if you wish," said Chimpion. "It doesn't matter. My telepathic ally has stolen the answer from your thoughts already."

"I think not," said Mrs. Knowbokov. "If a telepath could have entered my mind, controlled me as the dervishes were controlled, why bother sending you? I could have been commanded to jump to my death. I lived with a telepath for years. I know more about hiding my thoughts than anyone in the world. My secrets are safe."

"Don't be foolish," said Chimpion. "I don't need a telepath to make you talk. Wouldn't you rather die a quick, clean death than endure the agony and humiliation of torture?"

"Do your worst," said Mrs. Knowbokov.

"Such pointless bravado," said Chimpion.

"I wasn't talking to you," said Mrs. Knowbokov.

"Acid mode!" said App's voice behind her.

Chimpion whirled around, knives at the ready, as the first splats of App's acidic vomit landed on her left foot. She jumped away with a back flip, landing on Mrs. Knowbokov's huge desk. She hurled a knife directly into App's heart. The young man fell backwards, with his dying breath whispering, "Reset." She hurled a second knife, but he cried out, "Ghost mode!" as the weapon left her fingers.

She heard a scuffle behind her and summersaulted from the desk as Katrina Knowbokov swung a big, heavy vase through the space where Chimpion's head had just been. She still needed to find out what the woman might know about Rail Blade's survival. She landed on the table by the window with her blowgun in hand. Half a second later, the old woman raised her hands to her collarbone, clawing at the dart stuck deep into the junction of her neck and shoulder. She pulled the dart out too late to keep her next heartbeat from flooding her brain with the sedative payload. She dropped to one knee, grabbing the edge of the desk, before slumping to the floor.

Chimpion eyed App, who looked worried. She couldn't touch him in ghost mode, but he had no way of knowing Mrs. Knowbokov wasn't in imminent danger of death.

"My poison has stilled her heart," Chimpion said in a casual tone. "It's possible CPR could save her long enough for an antidote. In ghost mode, all you can do is watch her die."

"Clone mode!" he shouted. Suddenly, there were two of him. "Clone mode!" they both shouted. And now there were four. "Clone mode!" and suddenly, eight. "Clone mode!" Now, sixteen.

Chimpion furrowed her brow. "This is a new trick."

"The guy with the time doubles inspired me," said all sixteen Apps at once. "I mean, the computers can build me a new body anytime I die. I asked Nathan if there was any practical reason they had to wait for my death. They finished programming this new command less than an hour ago. Luckily, I'd already tested it out. Right now, my first double is down in the jump room dealing with that situation. I came up here immediately at Mrs. Knowbokov's request, once she got the phone call revealing your treachery."

"Ah," she said, as a light on the back of her wrist started to blink. "What perfect timing."

"Couldn't agree more," said the Apps, as a pair of them split off from the pack to run to Mrs. Knowbokov. "Since now two of us can focus on keeping Mrs. K alive while the rest of us kick your ass, traitor."

"I meant this perfect timing," she said, raising her wrist. "My spiderbots have reached the server that stores your backups." She pressed the flashing button. A distant, muffled boom made the floor tremble. "No more reboots, I'm afraid."

"Fuck," all the App's said in unison.

Which was, for many of them, the last word they'd ever utter, as Chimpion jumped off the couch and into the crowd of Apps, swinging her sword with abandon. There was chaos as seven of the Apps were gutted before they even had time to react. Seconds later, the survivors started calling out, "Acid mode!" "Eel mode!" "Glue mode!"

She'd known that some of his most frequently used body modification programs were stored in the memory of the belt itself. With any luck, the new clone mode wasn't one of them, since it would prove tedious if she wound up having to kill a hundred different copies of him. As she killed three more of the Apps without any one using the clone mode, she assumed that ability had been kept in the server.

"She's breathing on her own!" one of the App's near Mrs. Knowbokov shouted.

"She has a heartbeat!" the second cried out.

Chimpion leapt up and grabbed the ceiling to avoid a spray of acid vomit, then dropped behind that App and thrust her sword behind her without even looking. As acid App fell, she charged forward and drove her shoulder into glue App's torso with enough force to shatter his rib cage and drive the bone shards into his heart. As he fell away, eel App charged her, sparks leaping from his fingertips. Her wooden nunchakus bashed in his skull while insulating her from shock. Only three of the sixteen were left, by her count. Two stood next to Katrina Knowbokov. She threw knives at them. Both opened their mouths to cry out, "Ghost mode!" but her knife caught one in the throat before he finished the command.

She heard a scrape above her. She looked up to find the App she'd lost track of clinging to the ceiling directly overhead. He let go of the ceiling and said, "Ghost mode!" as she jabbed her sonic sword into the light fixture he'd been covering. His ghostly form fell, so that her arm up to the elbow was buried in his chest.

"Reset," the falling ghost whispered.

She screamed and stumbled backward, dragging the corpse of the solidified App with her. Her digital nerves had overrides to protect her from the pain, but nothing could save her from the wave of revulsion that ran through her as she realized that her right arm from the bicep down was molecularly woven into the body of the sacrificial App.

Her disgust changed suddenly to confusion. She could no longer move her right foot. She looked down and found she'd stepped into a wad of glue that had been flung from the fingers of the glue mode App whose chest she'd caved in. She was trapped.

She felt dizzy. The blending of her body with App's was forcing human blood into her veins. Her body's cellular defenses kicked in to fight the foreign cells. She shivered as her fever spiked. Her legs weakening, she sat down and used a knife to start sawing her arm off at the shoulder.

At the last second, she remembered the final App. Under any other circumstance, he would have been no threat, no threat at all. Unfortunately, since she was feverish, mutilated, and half immobilized, the knife she threw at him went wide of its mark.

App was standing a safe distance from her, holding the rifle of one of the guards she'd killed.

"What?" she asked. "No acid mode? No eel mode? You're just going to shoot me?"

"Yeah," he said, raising the gun. "I'm going to fucking shoot you."

Chapter Thirty
Closer to the Ledge

APP WAS A CHILD of California, a hardline lefty who couldn't understand why any ordinary citizen would ever need to own a gun. He'd been forbidden to play with toy guns as a kid. He'd had to hide video games with guns from his mother. He'd never fired a real gun before, never even held one except for those he'd taken from suspects. All he knew about firing one was to point it and pull the trigger.

He stared down the barrel of the assault rifle. Chimpion glared at him defiantly. If he let her live, she would find a way to kill him.

He pulled the trigger, releasing a spray of bullets. The recoil pushed him back with far more force than he'd expected. He staggered, regaining his balance.

Chimpion fell over. She'd already been covered in blood from her rampage through his clones. Had he even hit her? Was she faking? He stepped closer. She looked dead. He built up his courage and knelt at her side, feeling for a pulse.

He felt nothing. She wasn't breathing. He could see the trio of bullet wounds in the center of her chest.

App dropped the rifle, feeling weary. Chimpion was a murderer. She'd killed his friends and colleagues. But he hadn't acted in self-defense. He'd appointed himself executioner. He let out a long, slow, shuddering breath. This was going to take him a while to process.

The streams of social media information that forever flowed through the background of his mind had gone silent. With the servers that normally communicated with his belt offline, at least no one had witnessed his kill. But he would remember it, right? It was part of him now, wasn't it? Or, once the servers came back online, would he just be rebooted to forget all this?

Assuming the servers would come back online. Had she really blown them up? In addition to his social media feeds being down, he couldn't access any apps beyond the half dozen cached in his belt. Did that mean he could really die now? He felt a tension he hadn't fully been aware of go slack throughout his body. It felt as if an invisible weight had been removed from his shoulders. His mind had squirmed away from any attempt to grapple with the ramifications of his potential immortality. Knowing that his current life might be his last made him feel as if it had some value.

He shook off his reverie. He had work to do, starting with Mrs. Knowbokov. He ran to her side and again checked to see if she was breathing. Still alive. Peacefully asleep, actually. He guessed that Mrs. K had yanked out the poison dart before it could deliver a lethal dose. Or maybe Chimpion had only used a tranquilizer? Why drug her instead of killing her? App rubbed her cheeks, attempting to rouse her, but she didn't move at all. His first aid skills were somewhat limited without being able to google answers on how to wake someone who'd been tranquilized.

"We need a med team to the penthouse, fast," he said.

His request was met with only static in his head. Right. His coms had been routed through the server as well. He rose and picked up the phone on Mrs. Knowbokov's desk. There was a row of buttons along the side marked Security, Jump Team, Finance, etc. He pressed the one for security. He waited for a moment as the phone kept ringing.

Either he didn't know how to use a phone or the whole security team was tied up. The timing of Chimpion's attack couldn't be a coincidence. It had to correspond with the techs in the jump room acting possessed. Whoever was behind all these dervish attacks had made their move. Why now? What was their goal?

Whatever the situation, he wanted Skyrider and Servant by his side before he went back downstairs. He tried the line for the jump room. Again, no answer.

He glanced back at his internal phone controls in his mind's eye. He never actually needed to call anyone by dialing a number, so it took him a few seconds of fumbling through mental screens to find the numbers for Skyrider and Servant's phones.

He tried Skyrider first. It went to voicemail, then gave him the helpful message, "the mailbox is full."

He dialed Servant. It rang three times. He prepared for another voicemail.

"H-hello?" Servant answered. At least, he thought it was Servant. His voice sounded weak, like he had a cold or something. Could Servant even catch a cold?

"Servant!" said App. "Where are you? Our headquarters is under attack. Chimpion's a traitor!"

"I'm... captive..." said Servant. "Being... d-drained..."

"Wait, someone captured you?"

"Y-yes."

"Why the hell did they let you keep your phone?"

"It's b-built... into... my costume... controlled... b-by voice."

"Who the hell could capture you?"

"Sister Amy," Servant gasped. "I'm... in... the t-temple."

"What temple?" App asked, wondering if this was some stupid joke. Servant being held captive was the most implausible thing he could imagine, and this was on a day when he'd personally been murdered by a chimpanzee over a dozen times.

"New... Jerusalem," Servant whispered. "Use... the s-space machine... to... free...."

"That's a swell idea, except the jump room has been taken over by dervishes. Why didn't you call and tell us you needed help?"

"P-passed... out. Your call... woke me."

"Right," said App. "Hang tight, buddy. I'll save you."

"Hurry," said Servant. "They... plan to use... my energy... to move... to move..."

"Servant?" asked App, as his teammate's voice trailed off. "Servant?" No answer. "Fuck." No scolding followed. Servant must have passed out again.

As he hung up the phone, a loud rumble outside made him turn toward the window. The night sky was clear but the windows rattled like they'd been shaken by thunder. He moved to the window, looking out over the starlit ocean. A small dark form was moving fast over the water, raising a wake. His brow knitted as he studied the object. A missile?

No. Skyrider, coming in fast. He blinked and she was no more the fifty yards away, pulling up into a sudden stop.

"Ghost mode!" he shouted, just in time. The reason Skyrider had slowed was to allow the full force of the sonic boom to race in front of her to shatter the window. Instinctively, App curled up and covered his head with his hands, even though the shards of glass went right through his wraith form.

He straightened up as Sarah floated into the room.

"App!" she said. "My mother?"

"Alive!" he said. "But she needs medical attention. Chimpion poisoned her."

Sarah looked around the room, which was littered with App's corpses. "What the hell happened here?" she asked.

"Chimpion killed me," said App. "More than a few times. Then I shot her."

"You have a gun mode now?"

"Just a gun."

Sarah pulled off her helmet. Her face was pale and the corners of her lips were crusted with blood. She wiped her mouth with her sleeve. "I was attacked by someone wearing a knock-off of Steam-Dragon's battle suit. My mother's not the only person in need of medical attention. I'm only still awake because of drugs. Lots and lots of drugs, actually. A gal could have quite a party with the first aid kit in my costume."

"Maybe you have something in your suit that can help her," said App, switching back to his normal form and moving to Mrs. Knowbokov's side. He knelt and checked her pulse once more as Sarah drifted over. "Though, I don't know. She's breathing okay. Pulse is steady. Maybe she's just sedated?"

"Chimpion might have wanted to keep her alive as a bargaining chip against me," said Sarah. "Have you heard from Servant? He's tied up in this whole mess. If he's also turned traitor—"

"He hasn't," said App. "I spoke to him. He's literally tied up in this whole mess. They've taken him captive."

"How the hell do you hold Servant captive?"

"He said something about an energy siphon, but he wasn't super clear. He sounded pretty out of it."

"Get the jump team on the line," said Sarah. "They can pluck Clint from wherever he's being held—"

"Can't raise the jump team," said App. "Or security. Just before I got into my fight with Chimpion, a second me had to deal with an incursion of dervishes in the jump room."

"Second you?"

"I'll fill you in later," said App. "Right now, here's the short version of everything I know. One, Chimpion destroyed the server that housed my backup. It's cut off all but the powers I store locally in the belt. Also, if I die, I can't be rebooted. Two, we have to assume that everything from this floor down is under the control of religious fanatics who work for Sister Amy. They have control of the jump room. Servant said they were planning to move New Jerusalem using the energy they were draining from him."

"Move it? Move it where?"

"He didn't say, but I assume—" his voice trailed off as light flooded the room. The cool night breeze of the ocean suddenly gave way to a blast of dry, scorching air, hot as a furnace that rushed through the shattered window.

"Did this whole building just get jumped?" App asked, confused.

"More than just the building," said Skyrider, raising her hand to shield her eyes as she turned to the window and stared into the face of a blazing afternoon sun.

Neither said a word as they moved closer to the ledge to look out on the landscape below. The tower now sat in the middle of a desert of fine white dust, surrounded by wooden buildings located around a central hub of an imposing, palace-like structure.

"Is this New Jerusalem?" App asked. "Have we been taken to Texas?"

"It would still be dark in Texas," said Sarah.

"Servant said they had him in a temple," said App, taking a closer look at the big building in the center of the city. "That looks like a temple to me. But if we're not in Texas, where are we?"

"Israel," said Skyrider. "She's moved New Jerusalem to the site of the old one." She spat a gob of blood out the window, then wiped her lips. "This is the last place on Earth I ever wanted to see again."

Chapter Thirty-One
Let's Go Save the World

"YOU DIDN'T DESERVE to see Jerusalem again," said a woman's voice behind Skyrider and App. They spun around to find a tall woman in a flowing white dress who said, "Take comfort that your stay will be short."

The woman in white pushed her hands forward. App shouted, "Ghost mode!" Skyrider vanished.

The woman frowned when she saw that App remained.

"Interesting," she said. "Why can't the space machine move you?"

"The space machine?" said App. "What the hell did you do to Skyrider?"

"I had my team in the jump room cut and paste her into orbit. No doubt it will be a painful death but at least she'll have a lovely view in her final seconds. But why are you still here?"

App knew, but certainly wasn't going to tell her. In ghost mode, his atoms were in a state of quantum uncertainty that made it impossible for the space machine to isolate him if he hadn't initiated a jump before dematerializing.

"No matter," she said. "Whatever the genetic quirk that protects Skyrider and Servant from my telepathy, you plainly don't have it. You'll solidify and slit your wrists for me now."

"Why, exactly, would I do that?" he asked.

Again she frowned. "Hmm. Your mind is too faint for me to latch onto in your phantom state. No matter. As long as you're intangible, you're helpless. The second you solidify, I'll take control of your mind. I don't believe I'll have you kill yourself once you're mine. With your powers, you'd make a formidable dervish."

"So you admit to being behind the dervishes, Sister Amy?" asked App.

"You know who I am?" she asked.

"Servant's dropped your name more than once. I warned him about getting mixed up with a nut job like you."

Sister Amy smiled gently. "You should address me with more respect, brother. I'm the will of God given flesh. I command an army of angels. I can travel to any point in space with but a thought. The thoughts of the vast majority of mankind are open to me. Anyone I focus upon, present company excepted, dances like a puppet when I pull their strings. It's unwise to show such contempt for the Lord's chosen messenger."

"Wow," said App. "I kind of meant it as a generic insult, but you really are nuts."

She stepped closer, her eyes locked with his. "If I am crazy, I'm on the verge of causing unspeakable harm to the world. The heroic thing to do would be to try to stop me."

"Yeah," he said. "But since you boasted you can control my mind if I solidify, that would also be the stupid thing to do."

She shrugged and turned away. "I didn't arrive at this moment by treating my time as a trivial asset. You may not be free to move about, but I have much to do. Blood must be spilled. There is a third of the world to sacrifice."

"A third of the world? What are you going to do?"

"I don't see why you need to know," she said. She snapped her fingers. Two guards in fatigues and face masks with machine guns appeared beside her. "Gentlemen, the man before you is named App. He is currently intangible. He will have to speak in order to become solid again. When he does so, shoot him."

"Yes, Ma'am," the two guards said.

"Now, if you'll excuse me, I have a firestorm to unleash." She suddenly disappeared.

"Hi," said App to the two guards. "I don't suppose either of you happens to be sane?"

Neither responded.

"You're working for someone who is going to destroy the world."

"She's going to cleanse it," said the first guard.

"She will fulfill the prophecy," said the second guard.

"Okay," said App. "Crazy it is then. Guess I'll just have to see if my reflexes are faster than yours." He lowered himself into a crouch, then sprang up, crying, "Target mode!" This was an utterly meaningless command for his belt.

Both guards opened fire. The bullets passed straight through him. He'd fought a lot of people with automatic weapons in his short career as a superhero. Unless it was belt fed, a machine gun would empty its clip in about ten seconds. The guards both fired until their guns clicked, then reached for fresh clips.

"Eel mode!" he shouted, dropping to the ground and leaping forward. The guards slid their clips in as he moved. They raised their guns, turning toward him. He reached out and grabbed the metal barrels. Both guns fired, burning his hands, but he held on despite feeling like his palms were being struck with hammers, pushing the barrels wide so the bullets flew past him. Both men shuddered and jerked as he hit them with all the current his cells could crank out. Finally, both guards dropped. "Ghost mode!" he called out, worried that Sister Amy might be watching her guards' thoughts and might try to take control of him.

Maybe she did try. How would he know? He certainly felt as if his thoughts remained his own. Presumably, if she'd known her guards were down, she could have used the space machine to send in more guards. Since no fresh guards appeared, maybe he was in the clear. Sister Amy was getting ready for the end of the world. Despite her powers, she was only human. No doubt she had a lot of things on her mind. With any luck, he wasn't at the top of her to-do list.

Behind him, he heard thunder. He looked over his shoulder in time to see Sarah flash back into the room. She came to a halt, trailing smoke.

"How was space?" he asked.

"That bitch sent me into space!" said Sarah. "Wait, you knew?"

"We had a little chat after you left," said App. "Your pressure suit saved your life?"

"It did its job this time since I hadn't been dumb enough to turn it off," she said. "Still only had the air in my lungs and a tiny bubble caught in my helmet. Fortunately, I only needed a second to get my bearings. You know how in movies spaceships are engulfed in flames on reentry? Turns out that's a thing. I had to slow down to keep from baking myself."

"You might have a second chance at getting burned to death," said App. "Sister Amy said she was about to cleanse the world in a firestorm. I don't believe she was speaking metaphorically."

"Okay," said Sarah. "Then... nukes? She somehow has control of the nuclear arsenal?"

"Why not?" asked App. "She can take over anyone's mind. Why not take control of the president and make him give the command?"

Sarah pulled out her phone and pressed a button. "This is Skyrider," she said to whoever picked up the line. "This is a priority call for the

President. Security code gamma nine beta nine whiskey seven. Initiate full bunker protocol against psionic incursion. Please acknowledge." She paused, waiting for a response, then said, "Thank you."

"You have a hotline to the president?" App asked.

Sarah shrugged. "Mother has a lot of powerful friends. Luckily, the White House wasn't happy about dealing with my father when he used his telepathy to get his way, so they built a bunker beneath the White House with psionic baffles that's supposedly shielded from all telepathic access. Dad used to get a chuckle out of it. The shields worked, apparently, and the president and his team used to meet in the bunker to figure out how to deal with my Dad. But the second anyone left the room, he'd know what they'd discussed. He said the only way it would have really worked would be if they never left the room."

"Great. But the president isn't the only one with nukes."

"No," she said. "But Mother says that the Russian military was so corrupt that she's been able to cripple their nuclear capabilities just by throwing money around. They have a lot of missiles sitting in silos that won't go anywhere because the rocket fuel has been sold on the black market. Lots of other missiles are essentially empty shells because terrorists have paid top dollar for the fissionable material."

"So we have to worry about her taking control of those terrorists?"

"Only if the terrorists were real and not a CIA black op funded by my mother." Sarah knelt over her mother once more. "I'm guessing Sister Amy didn't notice mom was here, or she would have finished the job Chimpion started. She may be telepathic but she's not omniscient. She obviously didn't know my suit was pressurized, and she apparently didn't know you'd be immune to her telepathy in ghost mode."

"Hoping that her plan has big holes isn't exactly a strategy," said App. "We've got to find Servant. Clint said they were draining his power. We free him, and we cut off their power supply."

"Finding him might take forever," said Sarah. "We need to assume it's just you and me."

"Which effectively means it's just you," said App. "I'll be controlled by her the second she realizes I'm free. Servant is the only good option we have. Give me your phone." He reset himself, weighing the risk versus the reward and deciding to take the chance.

"Who are you going to call?" she asked, passing it to him.

"If I needed to make a call I'd use your mother's phone. When my server went down, I lost my internet connection. But my belt has wifi so I want to use your phone as a hotspot. There are people online who might help us."

"Gotcha. Password is InvisibleMan, capital I, capital M."

"Excellent," he said, typing on the onscreen keyboard. The seconds dragged, but after half a minute he had data streaming again. He logged into the App Room. "My spectrum vision was stored on the server but I'm hoping one of my developers will have a backup copy. If they're using Servant to generate power, there's no way they can be 100% efficient in the power transfer. If I had infrared vision, I could probably spot where they're venting any waste heat, which would get us pretty close."

"You think they brought him here?"

"They brought the whole damned city."

"Right," she said. "We don't need your powers to look for a heat vent. I have infrared in my helmet." She flitted out the busted window. "Hold on." She drifted slowly in the desert wind as she scanned the surroundings. "Holy cow!"

"What?"

"I either found Servant or a nuclear reactor about a minute away from meltdown. There's a ceramic chimney in the rear of what I'm guessing is the temple. It's white hot."

App moved to the window. "Awesome. I need to keep your phone though. CodeDog has a back-up of my spectrum vision and airbag mode. He's downloading them into the belt, but it's going to take at least ten minutes."

"I don't think we have ten minutes," said Sarah. "Can we hunt for Servant while you update?"

"I'm game," he said. "What should we do about your mom?"

"There's a safe room behind that painting. We'll lay her on the cot in there then seal the door."

"Sounds like a plan. Let's go save the world."

Chapter Thirty-Two
Go to Hell

"**D**O YOU STILL have your foam mode?" Sarah shouted above the roar of the wind as she veered toward the brick chimney.

"As luck would have it, yes," App said.

"Foam up. We're heading right into the heart of the furnace."

App foamed up as they reached the heat plume of the chimney. The heat distorted the air around them. They dropped until they touched down on a red hot iron grate. There was an access door in the center. Sarah knelt and tried to move it but it was locked.

"Can't stay here long," she said. "The heat is overloading the cooling systems in my suit. Wish I hadn't got rid of the energy absorbing mesh after our fight with Sundancer."

"I can switch to acid mode," said App.

"You'll fry before this grate gives," she said. "Let's get out of here."

They flashed back up the chimney.

"We're going to find another way in?" asked App.

"Nope," she said, setting him down on the lip of the chimney. "We're going to use brute force. Give me a second. There's construction gear all around. It won't take me long to find what I need."

She swooshed down into the alleys surrounding the temple, aiming for a tower that was under construction about a quarter mile away. She flew back seconds later carrying a pair of cinder blocks.

"Keep back," she called out as she zoomed past him and shot into the sky until she was just a speck. He looked around. The rim of the chimney was maybe a foot thick. Where the hell was he supposed to go?

He looked up and leaned back as far as he could, giving Sarah a clear path as she rocketed back toward the chimney, holding the cinder blocks before her. Fifty feet up, she dropped the blocks and veered away. App waved his arms to balance himself as the rush of wind from the passing blocks caught him. The whole chimney shuddered and he toppled backward. He was about to switch to ghost mode when Sarah circled back and plucked him from mid-fall.

"Maybe warn a guy next time," he said.

"I said keep back," she answered.

They whipped around and dove back into the chimney. The cinder blocks had shredded the iron grate. They slipped through with ease. They reached some of the scaffolding they had seen further down and found an iron access door.

"I'll ghost through then hit the door hinges with acid," said App.

"Do it," she said.

He did it. Thirty seconds later, the door dropped from its hinges. Sarah came through. "Did I hear gunshots?"

"Yeah," said App, nodding toward a fallen guard at the end of the hall. "Your cinderblock trick wasn't exactly stealthy. There's probably more on the way."

"Fine," she said. "Maybe I can convince one of them to lead us to Servant."

"That isn't going to be a problem," said App, moving toward the iron door at the end of the corridor. "Look at this."

On the back of the door was a safety map showing the routes to the nearest exits.

"Nice of them to comply with OSHA regulations," said Sarah as she studied the map. Though it couldn't have been the intent of the designer, the mapped out evacuation routes did a surprisingly effective job of showing the part of the building that most people would want to run from.

"That's got to be where the energy siphon is located," said App, tapping the map. "I've transmitted the map to CodeDog. He's got a program that will turn it into a 3-d map for us to follow. You ready to do this?"

"I'm ready for heavy drinking but I'll do this instead," said Skyrider, as the sound of men running in heavy boots came from the other side of the door.

"I got this," said App. "Dense mode!" With his enhanced strength, he kicked the door open. There were three men running toward them. They skidded to a halt and raised their rifles but in the half second it took for them to act App was already on the move, summersaulting to the midpoint between them and kicking into the chest of the first guard. All three men went sprawling. One squeezed the trigger of his rifle and sparks flashed around the concrete walls as the bullets bounced wildly. Two seconds later, all the guards were out cold as App landed powerful punches to their heads.

"Man," he said. "I needed that. There's some days when hitting people is the only thing that makes you feel like there's hope in the world."

"Savor your testosterone rush later," said Sarah, grabbing him by the forearm and lifting him into the air. "Which way?"

"Left," he said, as the 3-D map overlay appeared in his vision. "We're heading for a locked doorway."

"You strong enough to bash through?"

"Sure but I'm also smart enough to have grabbed this keyring off the lead guard," he said, jingling the keys.

They landed in front of the door. He tried four keys of what had to be at least thirty, then gave up and kicked the door in.

They flew down the stairs, all the way to the lowest level.

"It's going to be through this door," he said.

"Kick it in," she said.

Inside, they found two large angels, their armor and wings polished black and glinting in the glow of what seemed to be a captive sun floating between two pillars at the rear of the room.

A woman in white robes stepped from behind the angels.

"Kill her," said Sister Amy, but she wasn't speaking to the angels.

Fortunately, Skyrider wasn't touching the floor. She spun just as App opened his mouth to speak. She didn't know what mode he was going to use to attack her and didn't plan to find out. She drove her elbow into his mouth with all her strength, knocking him backward. As he fell, she grabbed his arm and flung him around, slamming him into nearest wall hard enough to knock gravel loose, praying that, in his dense mode, she'd knock him out without killing him.

She turned back toward Sister Amy, preparing to accelerate to supersonic speed. It was a large room, but in an enclosed space the sonic boom would likely incapacitate all of her foes. She froze as she found herself staring at her mother, whose limp body was now held by one of the angels, a sword against her neck.

"Placing your mother in a safe room meant nothing to me now that I have control of the space machine," said Sister Amy. "When App took out his guards, he didn't bother to check to make sure they were dead. One regained consciousness as you were moving your mother. I knew where she was and I knew where you were going. Make one move and she dies."

"You intend to kill her anyway," said Sarah.

"She wasn't present when Jerusalem was destroyed," said Sister Amy. "I'm prepared to accept she had no part in that desecration. You, on the other hand, were at ground zero."

"Watching someone else destroy the city."

"Someone you could have stopped."

"You don't know what you're talking about. Amelia was—"

"Out of control? Dangerous?" Sister Amy shook her head. "You called yourself a hero. You could have stopped her in any of a thousand ways, given your powers. You stood by and did nothing. The blame rests squarely on your shoulders. For that you must pay a price."

Sarah nodded slowly. "You don't think there's a day of my life when I don't second guess what I could have done? What I should have done? If you were gunning for me, there's some small part of me that would probably be willing to surrender."

"But you will surrender," said Sister Amy. "Take off your helmet. Strip off your armor and kneel. When my angels remove your head, your mother will go free."

"You still plan to trigger Armageddon."

"That," said Sister Amy, "is the Lord's plan, not mine. Who are you to deny His will?"

"I'm Sarah Knowbokov." Then she moved. Her strategy was still a good one. She hit the speed of sound on her way to the angel that held her mother. The shock would probably rupture her mother's eardrums, maybe cause internal bleeding, but she had to count on the possibility that she'd survive this and be able to get her mother to medical care once Sister Amy was down for the count.

The shockwave sent Sister Amy flying. The angels' armor kept them grounded, at least until she got her hands on the one who held her mother and accelerated him straight up into the roof. Her mother fell and she swooped down to catch her, racing her toward a far corner of the room. She had no time to check her vitals or even to be gentle as she placed her on the floor and swung back around. Assuming that the angels had the same sensory arrays in their helmets that Steam-Dragon had possessed, they were likely tracking her with radar. This was confirmed as a swarm of tiny missiles launched from their spiked shoulder pads. She smiled, slowing to give the missiles time to lock on, then yelled out, "Didn't any of you watch cartoons growing up?" She swooped around the edges of the room, the missiles close on her heels as she paced herself to keep them bunched up behind her. Then, *whoosh,* right back around, straight toward the angels, who spun to face her. They may as well been moving in slow motion. She dove, passing between their legs, feeling the heat as the missiles crashed into the crotches of the angels and exploded.

She spun around to find both angels bent over, dropping to their knees groaning, victims of the most painful kick to the nuts in the history of mankind.

She frowned as she saw Sister Amy rising on one knee. She really had expected her to stay down. The priestess raised her head and locked her eyes on Sarah. "You survived outer space. Let's see how you fare the molten core of the Earth!" She thrust her hand forward, shouting, "Go to hell!"

Sarah tensed, expecting to be instantly dead. She didn't go anywhere. Sister Amy's eyes grew wide.

"Skyrider!" a voice crackled in her helmet. "You there?"

"App?" she said, recognizing the familiar voice. She glanced near the door and saw his still crumpled body lying there. "Where are you?"

"The jump room," he said. "Sorry, things have been crazy here. Sister Amy took control of the techs. I got stuck in ghost mode to keep her from taking control of me. My pals in the App Room just downloaded a patch to the belt that lets it transmit the same psionic shields they use at the White House. It took me, like, ninety seconds once I had that power to capture Sister Amy's goons and get them locked up. I'm in control of the space machine now."

"Excellent," said Sarah. "You have a lock on Sister Amy?"

"Where do you want her to go?"

"I just received an excellent suggestion."

"You haven't won," said Sister Amy, rising on trembling legs. From the folds of her gown, she pulled a pistol, raising it toward Sarah.

Sarah put her hands on her hips. "I'm bulletproof, remember?"

"She isn't," said Sister Amy, swinging her gun toward the corner where Sarah's mother lay.

"No!" Sarah shouted, though she didn't hear the word as it left her lips. She was already moving faster than the speed of sound. Her helmet locked onto the bullet's trajectory. She whipped to a stop in front of her mother's limp body. The shockwave of her sudden movement was so strong it tossed her mother like a rag doll, slamming her into the wall. Sarah felt the bullet hit the small of her back. She'd already turned before the bullet fell to the floor. She spotted the fallen sword the angel had used to menace her mother. She snatched it up.

Sister Amy stumbled backward, fighting the effects of being hit with yet another sonic boom. The fact that she was still on her feet at all hinted that either she really was protected by the Lord, or that one of her brain trust had whipped up some sort of biological enhancement.

The only thing that mattered to Sarah was that Sister Amy was alert enough to realize what was about to happen. The prophetess turned her face toward Sarah, who flew with sword outstretched. Sister Amy's face went pale.

With a swift, well-aimed thrust, Sarah finished the fight.

Chapter Thirty-Three
Something Like a Man

WITH SISTER AMY'S head no longer completely attached to her body, Sarah's next priority was to make sure her angels didn't recover their wits enough to give her problems. Fortunately, it took only a few seconds to slam them around sufficiently that she was confident the humans inside the armor were thoroughly broken.

She zoomed back to her mother's side. Her heart sank when she saw how still and gray her mother's face looked. She dropped to her knees and pulled off her helmet, pressing her ear to her mother's chest.

"No," she whispered.

"Sarah, what's happening?" said App over the coms. "Where do you want me to send Sister Amy?"

"She's dead," said Sarah. "So's my mother if she doesn't get immediate medical attention. Cut and paste her to the medical unit, now."

"Can do," said App.

Her mother's body vanished. Sarah flew to where the local App had fallen. He hadn't moved an inch and she wondered if she'd killed him too. To her relief, as she landed she could see his chest rise and fall. "We have a second target for the medical unit. It's, uh, you."

"Me? Oh, wait, you mean the double I created with that new clone app?"

"Yeah, he's here. He fell under Sister's Amy control. Maybe. Anyway, I had to take him out."

"Hmm," said App. "My clones should vanish when I reboot, but I can't reboot with the servers down."

"How do you know he's the clone and you're the original?" she asked.

App didn't answer. After a few seconds of silence, the App before her vanished and the App on the coms said, "He's in the medical ward."

"Excellent," said Sarah, raising her hand to shield her eyes as she turned toward the glowing sun dangling between the two pillars. "Now let's cut and paste Servant out of that energy siphon."

"No!" the sun said, in a voice that sounded like Clint, only full of static.

"Hold off on the cut and paste," said Sarah, floating toward the ball of energy. With the faceplate of her helmet set to maximum darkness, she could just barely make out the human outline at the center of the light.

"Clint?" she asked. "You okay?"

"No," he answered.

"Then let's get you out of this."

"No!" the outburst was followed by heavy, ragged breathing. Then, in a barely audible whisper, "Texas."

"Texas?"

"The space machine is locked onto his position," said App.

"Wait," she said. "If we free him, New Jerusalem stays in old Jerusalem. He's the only power source that can move the city back into place."

"I'm reading his vitals," said App. "That machine is killing him. He won't survive if we try to move the whole city back."

"Move... the city," said Clint, his voice trembling. "Or... it's... war."

"He's right," said Sarah. "We can't leave the city here. Sister Amy didn't need to control any nuclear weapons to trigger a global firestorm. You think the players over here are going to stand by passively and let a city built by Americans sit on sacred ground? We know there are nations in the mix that have nukes. We also know they have a history of spreading the pain around. This city has to go back. Every last nail."

"I'm telling you, we'll kill Clint," said App.

"Do... it," Clint begged.

"Do it," said Sarah, clenching her fists.

"I'm not going to—"

"Do it! That's a fucking order!"

App said nothing.

"Acknowledge!" said Sarah.

"Acknowledged," said App. "The specs are still programed into the space machine, but its thirty petabytes of data. It's going to take a minute for the command to process."

"Then let's hope there are no nukes already in the air." She turned to Clint. "We're doing it. We're moving the city back."

"I'm... sorry," said Clint. "All... my fault."

"Save your strength," said Sarah. "Don't try to talk. No one blames you. A terrible person did a terrible thing today. A good person is going to do a good thing. You have nothing to apologize for."

Clint didn't respond. As the silence lingered, she wondered if he was even still conscious. Suddenly, she went blind. The humming of the machinery all around her fell silent.

"It's done," said App. "You're back in Texas."

Sarah pulled off her helmet, blinking as her eyesight came back. Clint was no longer a glowing sun but a man, or something like a man. His body was human in shape, but distorted into cartoonish proportions by his massive musculature. His face was similarly distorted into a monstrous mask of oversized features. This was Clint's true form, the shape of the man who'd been known as Ogre.

Clint's eyes were open. He fell to his knees, staring at his misshapen hands. He whispered, in a deep, gravelly voice, "It's gone."

"You're alive!" she cried, flying forward to wrap her arms around him. "Oh my god, I've never been so happy to hear someone speak."

"It's gone," he said again.

"What's gone," she asked, pulling back to look into his face.

He met her gaze. "My force field. I can… I can feel your touch. I've never really been touched before."

He dropped backward to sit, looking dazed.

"We need to get you to the med unit," said Sarah.

"I'm… I'm okay," he said.

"I think that's for the doctor's to decide," she said.

"I'm okay," he said, looking up at her. "It's gone. My power… the machine tore it free. I… I could feel it come loose, like a thing that had been living inside my body, like a demon. It's gone. I'm… I'm free."

"Yeah, let's get a second opinion on that," said Sarah. "App, med unit for both of us, please."

The dark basement that smelled of blood and ozone gave way to a brightly lit medical ward smelling faintly of bleach. App ran up to her. "I thought you were in the jump room?"

"That's my clone," said App. "I'm the original App, the one you slammed into a wall. Once I woke up I shifted to ghost mode then back again to fix myself. That was fast thinking on your part. You were right. Sister Amy had taken control of me."

"How's my mother?" Sarah asked.

App's face went slack. He took a deep breath.

Sarah already knew what he would say.

Chapter Thirty-Four
Good-Bye

THE FUNERAL WAS OVER. The last guest had gone back into the house, leaving Sarah alone beside her mother's grave in the family plot that held the body of her father and brother. She waited a long time, watching her shadow creep across the grave. At long last, with the sun nearly gone, a second shadow joined hers. Sarah turned around to find Amelia standing behind her, dressed in a simple black suit with a long skirt and black leggings, an outfit similar to Sarah's own funeral attire, if you overlooked the fact that it wasn't made of fabric, but of coal-black iron. On the lawn in the distance was a rather retro looking rocket ship gleaming red in the sunset, resting on three swooping tail fins.

"I knew you'd come," said Sarah.

"Why were you so certain?" Amelia asked. "I didn't come to father's funeral. Why should today be any different?"

"Well, dad did try to kill you," said Sarah. "I imagine that creates some conflicted feelings. Mother never did anything to earn our contempt."

"That's not precisely true," said Amelia, crossing her arms. "As we grew older and more powerful, all I ever saw in her eyes was fear. The only thing I heard in her voice was despair. One can only feel pity so long before it changes to contempt."

"Mother didn't ask to be married to a telepath," said Sarah. "She certainly never expected to give birth to children who weren't bound by the ordinary laws of physics. I think she bore her lot with dignity. While you've been gone, I think she rose to being great in her own right."

"I try to avoid the news from Earth," said Amelia. "But Richard has told me about the Covenant. It sounds like Mother tried to carry on our father's legacy, even knowing how much damage he'd done."

"Dad wasn't God," said Sarah. "He was just a man with strange powers. You can't be bitter that he had flaws. He really did want to make the world a better place. He did some damage along the way. I get how that happens now. I… I'm the one who killed Mother. I was trying to save her from people who would have killed her anyway and I subjected her to multiple sonic booms in a confined space."

"You did what you had to do," said Amelia. "Mother had to know she'd make enemies carrying on our father's legacy. Tragedy is the inevitable outcome of trying to make the world a better place."

"After Jerusalem, I would have agreed. But I see things differently now. What would you have wanted Mother to do? Make it a worse place? Turn her back on the world's problems, even though she had the power to at least try to make a difference?"

"I've come to appreciate the Hippocratic Oath. First do no harm."

"If that was the only rule that doctors followed there'd never be surgery or chemotherapy. Sometimes you have to inflict harm for the chance to save someone from a greater harm. Dad tried. Mother tried. I finally see the necessity of their choices. If they sometimes messed up, well, they were only human."

"I don't agree that father was only human," said Amelia. "He was something more. Like you are. Like I am. We're…" she paused, looking for a word, "apart from humanity."

"You started to say above," said Sarah.

"Perhaps," said Amelia. "Is this inaccurate?"

"Yes," said Sarah. "So we were born different. Guess what? Everyone is born different. Some people are smarter, some are taller, some can jump high, and some have the kind of courage that lets them run into burning buildings. You think we're something special because we could fly or toss tanks around? I've known people who were braver than us. I've known people who were kinder. We're part of the great spectrum of mankind. Thinking we're either cursed or blessed is pure vanity."

"Vanity of vanities, all is vanity," said Amelia with a smirk.

"Is that… the Bible?" asked Sarah, pretty certain it was. "Since when did you start quoting the Bible?"

Amelia shrugged. "After I moved to Mars I had a lot of time to kill. I decided to read the book that had caused so much grief. Ecclesiastes stuck with me. The rest, meh. I don't get what the fuss is about. The book is so big and vague that a person can find anything they want to find inside it."

"You should have a little chat with Servant," said Sarah. "He seemed to find something useful in it."

"Useful enough to throw himself into prison for the rest of his life," said Amelia.

"Another thing he has in common with you," said Sarah.

"Excuse me?"

"Isn't that what Mars is? Your prison?"

"No," she said. "Mars is... work. It's the one place where I can make full use of my powers and not worry about hurting anyone."

"I'd like to offer you another place," said Sarah. "I want you to come back to earth. I want you to be part of the Covenant."

"No."

"Hear me out. What you did in Jerusalem... there are so many myths and conspiracies surrounding that day, no one really knows what's true anymore. There are a thousand cover stories we could come out with that would let you operate in the open as a hero again. You loved being a superhero in a way I never did. It was in your blood. The world still needs you, Amelia."

"It doesn't," she said. "Fanatics sent a ninja chimp all the way to Mars to kill me. You think I'd ever get any peace here on Earth?"

"So there are lunatics who'd try to kill you a couple of times a week. It would be just like old times!"

"No," said Amelia. "I'll be returning to Mars after paying my respects. I also... I wanted to say good-bye to you. I know I left without... without..." She took a deep breath. "I wanted to tell you personally that my leaving had nothing at all to do with you. I know we fought all the time. But, I love you, Sarah. The hardest part of life on Mars is not having you near."

"I could stop in and visit," said Sarah.

"I don't think that would be wise," said Amelia. "My children have been ill ever since your teammates visited my home. When I let them inside, I neglected to consider that they'd be carrying microbes my children had never been exposed to. I'm confident they haven't picked up anything fatal, but still hope to spare them further misery."

"If you don't toughen up their immune systems, they'll never be able to come to Earth."

"They couldn't come to Earth even if I wished it. Having been born on Mars, they'd be too weak to stand on Earth, or even to crawl. Their internal organs would fail from the strain even if I provided them with exoskeletons. Richard, too, has adapted to Martian gravity, and can never return."

"You seem pretty healthy," said Sarah.

"I work out every day," said Amelia. "Even so, I'd be flat on my back if my limbs weren't supported by iron."

"So, that's it?" said Sarah. "You show up, say good-bye, and fly off never to be seen again?"

"It's best this way," said Amelia, walking to her mother's grave. She knelt and placed her hand upon the sod. "Good-bye," she whispered.

She rose, opening her arms as she turned to Sarah. "One last hug?"

"Did we ever hug?" asked Sarah. "I don't remember us being big huggers."

"One first hug?"

Sarah smiled and walked forward, spreading her arms. The two sisters embraced. Amelia whispered in Sarah's ear, "The world is in good hands."

Sarah whispered back, "It feels like it's on my shoulders."

Amelia pulled away. "I should go."

"You only just got here."

"I've done all I came to do," she said. "Take care." She stepped into the air onto a rail that formed from nothing. The black rail arced and grew into a solid path to the hatch of the rocket. Amelia's black boots sprouted wheels and she kicked off, gliding back toward her ship.

"Take care," Sarah called after her.

Amelia entered the ship, looked back from the door and gave one final wave. Sarah crossed her arms, feeling like she didn't want to acknowledge her sister's efforts to never see her again.

The hatch to the rocket closed, the rail disintegrated into dust, which swirled as the rocket rose, slowly at first, then vanished as it streaked over the horizon, leaving thunder in its wake.

"TEN MINUTES," SAID the guard, as he motioned for Clint to take a seat in the cubicle in front of the glass.

"Thanks," said Clint.

On the other side of the glass in the visiting room sat App. Two Apps, in fact. Though, since they were in civilian clothes, he guessed they were actually two Johnnies.

"Hey," said the left Johnny.

"Good to see you," said the right Johnny. The right Johnny looked like he hadn't shaved in weeks. His beard was thin and spotty, downright ugly, actually, which didn't bother Clint but he was surprised since Johnny was normally more groomed.

"I, uh, heard about your, um, problem," said Clint.

"It's not a problem," said the bearded Johnny.

"We've given up on trying to figure out which one of us is the original," said the beardless Johnny.

"With the server that housed our original data destroyed, we'll never know the truth," said bearded Johnny. "A lot of that hardware was Rex Monday's own design. Some of the code was hardwired into the system."

"Does that mean…"

"The next time I die, I die for good," said bearded Johnny.

"That's not the Lord's plan for you," said Clint.

"Nailed it," said beardless Johnny. "Forty-five seconds. You're buying dinner."

Bearded Johnny rolled his eyes. Then he said, "You know, man, I've been thinking a lot about souls."

"You talking to me, or him?" asked Clint.

Bearded Johnny shrugged. "It's just, what was my backup if not a soul? A digital soul, the real part of me, the thing that turned the meat and bones and guts of me into a man."

"If so, it's gone now," said beardless Johnny. "Meat and bones and guts is all we have left. And brains. Which means we're just like everyone else."

"Everyone else doesn't get to talk to themselves and have to listen as they talk back," said bearded Johnny. Then, he grinned. "And I'm okay with that. I mean, for my day job, I dress in a red jumpsuit and fight crime. This isn't the career choice of someone who wants to be like everyone else."

"So you're sticking with it?" said Clint. "Even though you might get killed for real now?"

"Sarah could be killed just as easily and she's sticking with it."

"She is? I thought she'd go back to her other life."

"We've talked about that," said Beardless Johnny. "Apparently she and her husband have split up. And, hey, she told me her real name."

"I was there. Sarah Knowbokov."

"No, I mean her married name. Get this. It's Sarah Lee."

Bearded Johnny sighed. "I don't know why he still thinks that's funny. Just how many snack cake jokes does the world need?"

"I hope she can work things out with her husband," said Clint.

"She's pretty busy running the Knowbokov Foundation. She's got a plan to relaunch the Covenant. She was wondering if—"

"No," said Clint.

"She says she could have you a full pardon inside a day if you give the word," said bearded Johnny. "You were just a kid when you had your crime spree as Ogre. The public likes a good redemption story. You could come back and be a hero."

"Or I could stay here and do what I was meant to do," said Clint.

"Rotting in a cell is a waste of your talents," said bearded Johnny. "Even without your powers, you're still a big tough guy who can handle himself in a fight."

"I'm not rotting in a cell," said Clint. "I'm serving my time. I'm talking every day to men who need to hear what I have to say. Servant was an example of how to escape justice, proof that a lie could bring rewards and fame that truth could never purchase. But truth has a value of its own. Repentance means something. By owning up to who I was, I'm finally free to show the world who I am. Maybe, in the long term, I'll do more good for the world behind bars than I ever could as a free man."

"Damn," said beardless Johnny. "That's a much better argument than I came here with."

"What argument did you come here with?"

"The whole Spider-Man 'with great power comes great responsibility' thing."

"I'm doing the responsible thing for the first time in my life," said Clint. "That, my friend, is the only power I'll ever need."

Epilogue
Your House Too

SARAH DROPPED FROM the sky over Park Station a little before midnight, descending slowly into the backyard of the house she'd once called home. The lights were on in the living room. She landed at the back door, her fingers hovering inches from the doorknob. Should she knock? Just go inside? One might look too cautious, the other too confident.

As she decided the safest way forward would be to knock, she heard Carson's ringtone go off. She listened closely, but except for "Hello," she couldn't make out what he was saying.

She waiting patiently, wondering if his call was done, not wanting to interrupt. "Bullshit," she mumbled. She wasn't waiting to knock because she was worried about being rude. She was afraid to knock because, after tonight, everything would be over. He would listen to what she had to say, she would listen to what he had to say and then… then she'd probably fly off and never see him again.

Sarah Buchanan Lee would be done. She might as well erect a tombstone in the family plot.

She took a deep breath, steeled herself, lifted her hand and froze as the porch light switched on. A second later, the door opened.

Carson looked out at her. He didn't say hello.

"Can I come in?" she asked.

"Why not," he said, stepping back to give her room. "It's your house too."

"Is it?" she said, moving inside.

"I mean, not legally. You signed the mortgage using a fake name and a fake ID. I guess, realistically, the house might not even be mine any more, if the documents were fraudulent. I kind of need to see a lawyer about that."

"I'm truly, truly sorry," she said. "I promise you won't lose the house. I, um, kind of own the bank that holds our mortgage."

"Yeah," he said. "I've been hearing your name come up in the news. So. You're a billionaire now." He moved toward the fridge without looking back at her. "I need a beer. You want a beer? Or is it safe to drink and fly?"

"Do I need to fly?" she asked. "I was hoping... you know. Maybe I'd stay here tonight."

He chuckled as he reached into the fridge. "You know it's fucked up that you think that, right?"

"Yeah," she said. "But I thought... you know."

He opened two beers and offered her one. "You know?" he asked before taking a drink. He swallowed, then shook his head. "No. I don't know. I don't know anything anymore."

"It's... it's a lot to take in," she said.

"Why?" he asked. "Why did you come here? Why did you pick my life to ruin?"

"I didn't pick your life to ruin," she said. "I came here because I was running. It was just chance, or luck, or fate, that you're who I ran into."

"Running from the law. That whole Jerusalem thing."

"No," she said. "Running from myself. Jerusalem wasn't... I don't want to sound shallow, but Jerusalem really wasn't something I thought about much by the time I met you. I never blamed myself. Amelia did what she did and there was nothing I could have done to stop her. When I came here, I wanted to be done with the craziness. I wanted to forget I could fly. I no longer wanted to be who I had been. I wanted to be normal."

"Well you fucked that up royally," he said.

"Yeah," she said. "How the hell did you know I was standing on the porch by the way?"

He smiled. "Bud called from the airport. Once I learned who you were, I told him about it."

"So, the whole town knows now."

"Probably," said Carson. "Funny thing is, no one has asked me a single question. No one. I don't know if they're scared or what. Anyway, since Bud works in the tower, once he learned you'd been flying in and out of town for the last year playing Skyrider, he was able to start finding radar traces. He knew what it looks like when you're zooming in and out of town. He called to let me know he thought you'd come back."

"That's some good detective work," said Sarah. "Maybe he should have been the cop in the family."

"He gets sick even thinking about blood," said Carson. "My first night on the job, I was called to the scene of a three car accident involving a pedestrian who got dragged under the fender for a good thirty yards. I think Bud might have followed me into the business if I'd never told him about seeing that."

"But you went back to work the day after seeing that," said Sarah.

Carson shrugged. "I never thought the job would be easy, or clean. I don't think I'd quite prepared myself for some of the stuff I smelled that first night but, you know."

She nodded.

"No regrets. I love being a cop. Which is why, you might imagine, I'm not completely thrilled about finding out I married a fugitive."

"Well, it's like the mortgage," said Sarah. "Technically, I don't think we're legally married. I'm sure any court in the land would annul your marriage to someone who didn't actually exist."

"That's still going to be a hassle," he said. "All the fucking paperwork. I can't escape it."

"Let's just skip the paperwork," she said. "Let's keep pretending we're married."

"I think we're past the point of pretending," he said.

"You're right," she said. "That was dumb of me to put it like that. Because, honestly, I came here to tell you we shouldn't pretend. We can make this work if we're honest with each other."

"When have I ever lied to you?" he asked.

"Fair enough. We can make this work if I'm honest. I promise I'll tell you everything you want to know about me."

"To make this work."

"Yes."

He took a long drink, finishing his beer. He looked down at the bottle, lost in thought. Finally, he looked her in the face. "Why would you think I'd want this to work?"

"Because you love me," she said. "And I love you. More than anything in the world, I love you."

"Well, I am lovable," he said with a grin. A look of pain crossed his features. "And so was Sarah Buchanan." He shook his head. "Who never really existed."

"But she did," said Sarah. "I did. Everything we did together—"

"Was a lie!"

"No!" she said. "I mean, it started with a lie. But, Carson, everything we've been through together… everything was real. Think about everything we've done. I mean… I drained your goddamned wound when you were shot. And you brought me the worst chicken soup anyone's ever tried to make back when I was flat on my back that winter with the flu. We both sweated side by side fixing this house up. Once a man and a woman have installed a toilet together, it forms a certain bond."

He didn't say anything, just stared down at the floor his arms across his chest.

"And, look, I didn't mean to play this card, but let's just get it on the table. You and I are great in the sack. If anyone, anywhere, at anytime has better sex than we do, wow, I want to meet these people, because they must fucking sparkle."

The ghost of a grin crossed his lips, but he still wouldn't look at her.

"We've lived the better and worse parts of marriage. We've done the sickness and health. Why not be in this till death do we part?"

He finally looked up at her. "How is that even possible?"

"How is any marriage even possible?"

"What? You just move back in here? We pretend nothing happened? We pretend, what, that you aren't a goddamned billionaire superhero?"

"Does the money bother you?"

"Yes," he said. "I mean, no! Fuck no. If you'd won the lottery you think I'd complain? But... Christ. You can't live here. I mean... the town would just fall apart. It's too much for people to take."

"You're right," she said. "I can't live here. So you could come live with me."

"Great," he said. "I come, what? Be your pet? A kept man on a tropical island?"

"No," she said.

"No?" he asked, looking at her sideways. "Because, seriously, I might consider that if you made the offer."

"No you wouldn't," she said.

"No," he sighed, "I wouldn't."

"You're a cop," she said. "You're not in it for the money."

"Is anyone in it for the money?" he asked.

"I'm just saying it's more than a job to you. It's who you are. You protect and serve."

"Yeah," he said. "You know those stories about people who show up for work after they win the lottery? I've always known I was one of those people. I'm sorry, Sarah. I wouldn't be happy on some island. My job is who I am."

"Which is why I'm offering you a better version of that job."

He looked confused.

"You probably saw Steam-Dragon on the news," said Sarah.

"Sure."

"We have the designs for her armor, as well as armor we captured from terrorists built with a similar design. We also have a team of geniuses who know how to improve upon it. I'm going to be busy running my family's business empire. App needs new teammates. A squadron of armored cops are what I have in mind. You'd be perfect for the team."

"You have to be joking."

"No," she said. "You'd be bulletproof. You could fly. And you'd be legal, not a vigilante, a fully authorized law enforcement officer with the tools to do some real good. I know it would be a change in scope for you. You'd spend a lot less time filling out reports on traffic accidents and lot more time battling mad scientists with death rays."

"You aren't joking?"

"No," she said. "This is a serious offer. It's a serious offer whether or not we're still married, or even if you never want to speak to me again after tonight. You're a good man, Carson. I can't think of a better person to handle the job."

"You know I've already got a job," he said. "I told you the night we met I wanted to make a difference in my own backyard."

"Yeah," she said. "But our backyard happens to be part of a larger world, grand, and scary and sometimes out of control. You'll still be making a difference, and you'll be there to remind your teammates why what they do matters. Sometimes, you have to save the world in order to protect your backyard."

He rubbed his chin, weighing her words. At last, he said, "I'm going to need another beer."

"Take mine," she said, offering him her bottle. "I haven't touched it at all. I thought I'd need to fortify my courage, but, you know what? This wasn't so hard. Talking to you has never been hard. Talking to you makes the world safe and sane. Besides, you're right. It's really not a great idea for me to drink and fly."

"Did we come down on a firm position on whether you needed to fly back tonight?" He gave her a grin as he lifted the bottle.

For the first time that evening, Sarah smiled.

ABOUT THE AUTHOR

James Maxey lives in Hillsborough, North Carolina, with his wife Cheryl and too many cats. He's read 1,302,017 comic books, give or take a few. His mother warned that reading all those funny books would warp his mind—and she was right! Now unfit for ordinary society, James is reduced to typing out his depraved daydreams and asking strangers to pay money for them. It beats real work.

For more information about James and his writing, visit his jamesmaxey.net. If you'd like to sign up for his mailing list to be alerted when new novels are released and receive sneak peaks at works in progress, email James at nobodynovelwriter@yahoo.com.

Made in the USA
Columbia, SC
23 September 2024